The Day After Never

Retribution

D1522391

Russell Blake

Books@RussellBlake.com

ISBN: 978-1539183068

Published by

Reprobatio Limited

Chapter 1

Houston, Texas

A pall of inky smoke obscured the glimmer of stars in the night sky, the air toxic from oil fires that dotted the huge abandoned refinery across the ship channel from Houston. Armed guards manned outposts along a walled section that ringed the plant, a sprawling complex easily as large as a medium-sized town – a collection of buildings and tanks that occupied a two-and-a-half-mile square section of the promontory. Spotlights roved across the area outside the wall, fueled by the output from a crude oil-heated steam turbine.

It had been barely a week since Snake had announced Magnus's untimely demise to the Crew, as well as the astounding defeat in New Mexico. He'd assured the regional chiefs that the change in leadership would result in no disruption to the Crew's ongoing operations and domination of the surrounding states, and had vowed to proceed more prudently than Magnus to eradicate the threat posed by Shangri-La.

The loss of almost a thousand men with nothing to show for it had stunned the Crew's upper echelon, and Snake had been quick to exploit their shock by enacting draconian new rules to crush dissent to his domination of the group: anyone questioning Snake as its head would be summarily executed, which quickly chilled any disgruntled murmurs and cemented his leadership.

The majority had gone along with Snake's plan, but almost a third of the Houston branch had splintered off and refused to recognize Snake's authority, believing him too unstable and weak to lead effectively. They'd seized the refinery as their territory, the strait between it and the city a natural barrier, and had recruited a growing membership of Crew fighters who were unhappy about the recent turn of events.

The faction was led by the Salazars, a trio of cousins who'd been incarcerated with Magnus and had despised Snake as he'd risen through the ranks to become one of their leader's inner circle. The idea of a meth-addled madman running things was unacceptable, and they'd split from the main group on the second day, taken over the refinery, and raided adjacent Baytown to reinforce their stake.

The Salazars had no long-term plan, but as the number of their followers grew, they began formulating a scheme to spread east and claim nearby Louisiana – it wasn't as though the Crew membership that operated in that area was particularly loyal to Snake, and if the cousins offered them a better deal, it was likely they would jump at it. They'd sent a few riders to feel out the New Orleans leadership and were waiting to hear back. A positive response would spread through the Crew ranks like wildfire, further weakening Snake's support in Houston and swelling the cousins' gang with disgruntled fighters. Their hope was that at some point they would become too big to challenge and could work out a cooperative deal where they existed autonomously from the Crew, operating as an ally.

But for now they were Snake's enemy, on alert against an attack that grew less likely with each day. Their spies had told them morale was at an all-time low as Snake settled old scores with enemies and bolstered his power through cunning and treachery.

The Salazar cousins' faction now boasted over seven hundred gunmen, a powerful force growing stronger with each hour. The fighters had set up a tent city in the center of the massive refinery, whose main buildings housed the cousins and their lieutenants. A quarter of the force was on guard at any given time, armed and ready for whatever Snake ultimately managed to throw at them – assuming the weasel didn't leave the Baytown area to them.

Night had fallen three hours earlier, and the evening shift was halfway through its watch. The warm air was sticky with humidity, and bright trees of lightning over the Gulf pulsed in a cloudbank on the horizon. The sentries manning the guard posts were equipped with handheld radios, and roving patrols along the perimeter checked in with clocklike regularity. One of the details near the southern approach had failed to call in five minutes earlier, and the boredom of long hours of monotonous inactivity was replaced by anxiety as the shift leader attempted to raise them.

"Repeat. Scorpion, this is Ruger. Do you read? Over."

Ruger, a seasoned killer with a face hardened from a lifetime spent behind bars, listened intently to the soft hiss of static from his handheld, his eyes darting along the area outside the wall. After ten more seconds of silence, he shook his head at his subordinate.

"Could be their battery's dead," he said. Two days ago the same thing had happened – one of the patrols had gone dark, sending a chill through the guard detail until the patrol appeared out of the gloom ten minutes later, unharmed, their radio out of juice. "Damned things are getting worse every week."

"Could be," his lieutenant agreed, his voice doubtful.

"They still have fifteen minutes before they're due back, so let's not freak out until they don't show."

The subordinate nodded, and then his head jerked back like he'd been swatted by an invisible hand, and the back of his skull erupted in blood. Ruger gasped at the sight, and then another muffled pop sounded from beyond the range of the spotlight, and the guard to Ruger's right grunted, the thwack of a high-velocity round through the base of his throat barely louder than a slap. Ruger fumbled with his radio and ducked down. He was almost below the wall when a slug sheared the top of his head off, sending him tumbling backward, the radio and his Kalashnikov assault rifle clattering beside him.

The fourth guard raised his weapon, searching for a target. He saw nothing, but when he squinted into the shadows to better make out any movement, his left eye was replaced by a neat hole, and he slumped to the side, dead before he hit the ground.

The suppressed sniper rifles had been nearly silent, and when six gunmen appeared from the perimeter, walking unhurriedly, they were indistinguishable from a genuine patrol. They made their way to the access gate, and one of the snipers drew a bead on the nearest spotlight and fired.

The light exploded in a shower of glass and blinked out, triggering a rush of men who swarmed toward the gate from across the field. The intruders moved in silence, the night quiet other than the dull pounding of their footsteps on the grass. When the first reached the opening, he led the rest through, signaling to his companions with curt gestures. Within a minute several hundred men had breached the refinery's defenses and were spreading out, gliding like wraiths in the gloom as more gunmen crossed the field and entered behind them.

Shots rang out from north of their entry point, where another mass of gunmen had used the same ruse to breach the refinery, and then the staccato chatter of assault rifles filled the air as the defenders engaged the attacking force. A tall Crew gunman motioned to his fellows and pointed to the occupants' tent city off in the distance, and the men advanced at a trot toward the heart of the compound.

They'd made it no more than two hundred yards when a grenade detonated in their midst, followed instantly by a hail of bullets as a half dozen defenders fired at them from atop one of the storage tanks. The attackers took what cover they could as they returned fire. One of the attack force shouldered an RPG and launched it at the top of the tank, where it exploded near the rim, sending a shower of metal and flesh skyward in a shower of destruction. What oil remained in the tank ignited and added to the clouds of toxicity as the gunmen pushed forward, the defenders above no longer raining death down upon them.

The intensity of the shooting increased as they neared the cousins' headquarters, and the attack force suffered heavy casualties as it fought for every inch against a determined group of cornered rats who could expect no mercy if captured. Both sides lost hundreds of men as they brought their heavy machine guns to bear, the .50-caliber rounds shredding through everything in their path.

Eventually the attack force overwhelmed the defenders, and the headquarters exploded in a fiery blaze. Anyone trying to escape the inferno was gunned down, and a half hour after the assault began, the last shots died away, leaving only the moans of the wounded and a cloud of black smoke from the blaze.

Snake's radio operator turned from the shortwave console, removed his headset, and fiddled with it nervously.

"Well?" Snake barked from the corner of the room.

"It's over. We won."

A harsh smile creased Snake's hatchet face, twisting the tattoos that covered it so they resembled squirming insects. He nodded in satisfaction and rubbed a hand over his shaved head.

"Of course we did. Any survivors?"

The operator shook his head. "No. As you ordered, everyone we found was executed."

"How bad are our casualties?"

"They're still searching, but it looks like almost two hundred."

Snake's smirk transformed into a frown. "Christ."

The operator had nothing to add. Snake spun toward the door and dismissed the man with a wave of his hand. "I'll be upstairs if anything else comes in."

"Yes, sir."

Snake pushed the metal door open and appraised the six fighters waiting for him outside – his security detail of the bodyguards he trusted with his life. He'd known each man for years, and they'd proved their loyalty – a commodity he'd learned to prize since taking over Magnus's throne, when he had become a target for every malcontent in the Crew.

He'd been insulated from resentment-driven reprisals when Magnus had been alive, his rivals' enmity blunted by their leader's ferocity. But Magnus was dead, and when Snake had assumed permanent command, many had refused to play along, culminating in the Baytown refinery faction presenting him with an open challenge that couldn't go unanswered.

Victory there had been essential to maintaining control, but he knew his problems were far from over. The Crew had far too much influence and wealth for his underlings to give up on their schemes. Snake had known when he announced Magnus's death that he would face numerous obstacles, but he was ready for them. Inside of a week he'd managed to eliminate the immediate threats, starting with his murder of his rivals among Magnus's inner circle. The Salazars had been a surprise he hadn't foreseen, but his swift and absolute elimination of them would send a clear message to anyone else thinking of challenging him.

Framed by his guards, Snake mounted the steps from the basement, lost in thought. He leaned toward his security chief and spoke in a low voice.

"I want my guard detail tripled. Can you find enough loyal men?"

"Of course."

"I'll hold you responsible if any prove…unreliable."

"I understand."

Snake bypassed the ground level and proceeded to his quarters – a lavish suite of rooms cooled by air conditioning on the upper level of the cavernous hall. His men could hold off a battalion from that vantage point, but he still had difficulty sleeping for more than a few hours at a time, his mind revving into the redline even in slumber. Part of the problem was the meth he consumed in prodigious amounts, but the constant stress of being in the crosshairs wasn't helping, and he'd taken to softening the buzz with downers, which only partially worked.

The guards took up their station outside his main chamber door and he triple-locked it behind him. The idea of taking over the Crew had seemed like genius, but now, barely a week in, the pressure was wearing at him. The tic in his left eye had started three days ago, and the surge of blinding rage that threatened to drown him when he received bad news had become the norm rather than an occasional aberration. He shook his head as he removed the Desert Eagle he wore at his hip, set it beside the bed, and then lowered himself onto the mattress, fully clothed. His breathing was ragged; he hadn't slept in thirty-six hours, his time consumed with planning the elimination of the Baytown threat, and now even the meth wasn't keeping him alert enough to function.

Snake's eyes drifted to the bag of white crystals on a round table by a floor-to-ceiling bookcase, and he forced himself up, the lure of the drug stronger than his body's demand for rest. A little hit would enable him to keep functioning for a few more hours as reports from the refinery came in. He would sleep after the situation was completely resolved, not before.

That was how Magnus would have handled it.

The snap of the lighter and the crackle of the meth as he sucked in as much of the pungent vapor as he could manage were replaced by the thud of his pulse in his temples, and then he was soaring, his heartbeat spiking, stamina flooding his system as he closed his eyes, the rush almost impossibly euphoric.

Snake coughed twice and sat motionless for a long, silent beat before leaping to his feet. A manic smile revealed yellowed teeth, and he paced the room with jerky movements, muttering to himself, scratching his bare arms, glaring at the furnishings as though they'd insulted him. After several minutes he froze in the center of the room, eyes closed, and then exploded into motion and retraced his steps to the entry door.

When it swung open, his guards maintained neutral expressions at the sight of their leader obviously amped, the corners of his mouth spasming in an unconscious grimace.

"Bring me a girl. Now," he ordered.

The chief of the guards nodded. "Anything special?"

"Young. I want her young. And scared. A new one."

The chief took in Snake's leer and smirked.

"I'll be back shortly."

Chapter 2

"They should have called in by now. Something's wrong."

Elliot Barnes was standing with his hands on his hips, transfixed by the radio. The riders he'd sent north from Shangri-La to Colorado to scout the most promising location for a new settlement had been gone for five days. The prospective site, Pagosa Springs, was a little over a hundred miles from their valley, in the mountains and sufficiently remote to avoid attention, with water and power from an experimental geothermal plant – assuming that hadn't fallen into complete disrepair or been destroyed by looters.

The only negative to the location was the harsh Colorado winter, which Elliot was confident they could withstand as well as they had the snow and freezing conditions in their former mountaintop sanctuary. But they had little time to prepare the new location, assuming it was livable – which brought him back to waiting for a report from the scouting party, which had failed to check in.

He'd last heard from them three days earlier, and they hadn't responded to any of the transmissions Elliot had broadcast over the last twenty-four hours. The coil of anxiety in his gut blossomed as the time had raced by, and he'd spent most of the day in the radio room, fidgeting as the operator sat nearby.

Michael frowned in his seat near the window. "They might have gotten delayed."

"Or hit a snag. Lame horse. Bridge collapsed. Robbers. We don't really have any idea what it's like up there these days," Arnold said from the corner of the room where he sat with his arms crossed, his face drawn after the hardest week of his life.

After taking stock of the survivors, it had been immediately apparent that the group's most capable fighters had fallen, leaving women, children, and about sixty able-bodied males – a far cry from the nearly two hundred and fifty militiamen they'd had before the confrontation with the Crew. Many wounded during the battle had succumbed to their injuries over the last six days, and there were now fewer than twenty still hanging on, tended to by Sarah, the sanctuary's physician, using what slim supplies had survived the shelling.

"What do we do if we don't hear from them by tomorrow?" Elliot asked, his voice soft. "We have to get moving. One way or another, we need to put some distance between us and this valley – the surviving Crew members may have reached their headquarters by now, and an army could be rolling our way."

Arnold scowled. They didn't have the resources to hold off another attack and couldn't spare anyone to mount guerilla forays against an approaching force, so they were sitting ducks should the Crew decide to finish them – which was highly likely in everyone's opinion, even with Magnus dead.

And then there was the matter of Santa Fe, with plenty of opportunistic miscreants who would be more than willing to complete the Crew's job if they thought they could get their hands on Shangri-La's wealth of antibiotics, gold, and arms. It wasn't whether anyone would make a play, it was when, and the clock was working against them with each passing hour.

"I still think we should have gone after the survivors," Arnold griped. "If nobody had gotten away, there would be nobody to report back on what happened, and we'd have bought ourselves more time."

Michael shook his head. "It would have been impossible to catch everyone. They had too much of a head start. For all we know, they could have radioed from the river, and there's already a column rolling toward us from Houston or Dallas or Lubbock."

"Probably not. There's little chance their mobile transmitters would have reached Houston," Arnold countered.

"They might not have had to. They could have left some men in Albuquerque to relay messages," Elliot said. "We've gone over this a dozen times. Let's not bicker over what's done. We need to focus on the challenges ahead."

Michael nodded agreement. "Like how we're going to transport the wounded and all our supplies – not to mention the lab gear."

Elliot sighed. "I can't see any way for the equipment other than by horseback over the dam trail. We'd never be able to get it down the canyon with all the rockslides, not to mention the mines."

"Lucas suggested using the Crew's vehicles for as long as they last. I think it's a good idea," Arnold said. "Even after being shot up, some of them are serviceable – the horse transports and a few of the buses. And a couple of the Humvees."

"A fine idea, but impractical until we have a destination," said Michael.

Arnold shifted from foot to foot. "We can't just sit here forever, hoping to hear from the scouts. We all agreed we had to move within a week. Tomorrow will be the seventh day."

"Thanks for the reminder," Michael grumbled. "We can all read a calendar."

"My point is that we're jeopardizing our survival if we stay any longer. My vote was to leave earlier, if you remember."

Elliot interrupted the exchange. "We'll leave tomorrow. One way or another."

"But go where, if we don't hear back?"

"There were some other locations we considered. Pagosa Springs was only one."

"It was the most promising, as I recall," Michael countered.

"No argument. Worst case, we can discuss it on the road. But I agree we can't stay." Elliot paused. "Arnold, how's the inventory going?"

Arnold ran down a list of their weapons and ammunition, as well as their portable food stocks, medical stores, and necessary equipment – lathes and tools from the machine shop, the lab essentials, hospital gear. The report was disheartening. Much of their equipment had been damaged by the bombardment in spite of its underground location, the incessant vibration from the shelling having caused some minor cave-ins. When Arnold finished, he glanced out the window at the lunar landscape surrounding the few buildings still standing. The trees that had shaded the river were now bare, their branches transformed into skeletal fingers clawing at the sky.

"Well, that's more than we had when we started Shangri-La," Elliot said. "We should consider ourselves lucky. That we survived a full-scale attack by the most powerful group in the region is a testament to the bravery of our people and the preparation that went into creating our defenses." He hesitated. "I'm sure that wherever we land, we can apply that same determination and make ourselves a home worth taking pride in."

"The hurdle being the wherever part," Arnold said.

"We have enough problems without all the negativity," Michael snapped.

"I'm not being negative. I'm being realistic," Arnold said coldly. "Without a destination in mind, it's just a matter of time before we're picked off on the road. We need to choose somewhere and make tracks, not pat ourselves on the back for surviving." He frowned slightly at Michael and then looked away. "We have a lot of logistical issues no matter where we go, and they aren't being solved by standing around and waiting for a call that may never come."

Elliot nodded slowly, his cherubic face hanging slack with fatigue. He was preparing to speak when the radio crackled and a voice drifted from the speakers, distorted and faint, fading in and out as it spoke the code words everyone had been waiting to hear.

"Papa Bear, this is Baby Bear. Do you read? Over."

Chapter 3

Elliot rushed to the radio and snatched the microphone from the startled operator.

"This is Papa Bear. What kept you?" he demanded.

"Ran into some trouble. Unfriendlies on the road."

"Are you all right?"

"Sam took a bullet, but he'll make it."

Elliot and Arnold exchanged a troubled look. "What kind of hostiles?"

"Scavengers. About ten of them. Thankfully they didn't know what they were doing. But they kept us pinned down for half a day, and when it was over, we had to patch up Sam and tread lightly."

"You make it to the objective?"

"Affirmative. Appears the plant's on standby. There's nobody here but us. I'd say it's perfect."

"Can you give us more of a rundown?" Arnold demanded from beside Elliot.

The lead scout spoke in oblique terms, assuring them that there were sufficient buildings intact to house them, and that after a half day of exploration, they'd detected no signs of life. He avoided mentioning the area so any eavesdroppers would learn nothing more than they'd known when he started to speak.

When the scout was done, Elliot nodded to Michael and Arnold and told the man to stay put and radio if there were any developments.

"When do you expect to be here?" the scout asked.

"A few days. Over and out."

Elliot straightened and eyed Arnold. "That's one problem taken care of. So now we have to shift into travel mode."

Arnold cocked his head. "I'll go with you and the lab equipment. Lucas and Colt can supervise the main group getting to the vehicles. They're both more than capable."

Everyone had been issued responsibilities during the meetings that had occupied much of the prior week, and Lucas had reluctantly agreed to ride herd on the caravan in Arnold's absence. Duke, Colt, and Luis would assist. Colt had spent the last several days clearing and marking a safe route through the mines that lined the canyon, while the trader and the former cartel head had spent much of the time with Lucas at the vehicles.

The gathering broke up, and they emerged from the building into the bright light of the afternoon. The sky overhead was as blue as painted porcelain, with only a few clouds drifting lazily in the distance. The valley stood in stark contrast to the ethereal tranquility: the buildings were largely ruins, and the ground was scarred with shell holes.

Arnold waved to Lucas, who was speaking with Duke and Sierra near the stream while Eve chased her piglet along its banks. Lucas returned the gesture and said something to Sierra before making his way to them.

"Well?" Lucas said, by way of greeting.

"We heard from them. Time to mount up," Arnold said.

Lucas squinted at the security chief. "Going to take the rest of the day to load the gear and get everyone down the canyon. Probably want to spend the night at the bridge and hit it at first light."

"I figured. Do the best you can. We're going over the mountain to the dam. We'll rendezvous tomorrow and stay in touch on the two-ways," Arnold said.

"Going to be touch and go with the wounded. No guarantees," Lucas warned.

Elliot nodded gravely. "I know, but it can't be helped. Sarah offered to stay here with them and join us later, but we can't risk discovery if she's captured. It was a difficult decision, but the right one." He paused. "Let me know if you need anything."

"We should be fine. We're ready. Everyone's been preparing, so I don't anticipate any problems," Lucas said.

"That's good to hear. We're going over the trail sometime in the next few hours," Michael said.

"Then we better get moving," Lucas agreed, and strode back to where Duke and Sierra were waiting.

It took longer than Lucas had hoped to organize everyone into a ragged column. The wounded were strapped to travois slung behind the strongest horses, while the other animals bore smaller equipment from the machine shop and the medical clinic. Lucas surveyed the line of survivors with Sierra by his side – Duke, Aaron, and Luis heading the column with Colt waiting at the top of the ridge on his horse – and nodded to them.

The trip down the canyon was grim, even after crews from the valley had transferred the visible remains of attackers and their fellow defenders to funeral pyres for cremation. The rocks were still stained with dried blood, every step of the trail a reminder of how close they'd all come to the abyss. Colt led the procession, sticking to a trail that Lucas, Duke, and Luis had been up and down half a dozen times in their search for Magnus's gold, which had turned out to be a fraction of what he'd been rumored to be transporting – fifty kilos, still a vast fortune, but nothing compared to the hoard Luis had heard about.

They'd divided it up as agreed, but Lucas still had substantial misgivings about his portion of the loot. A superstitious part of him nagged that no good could come from blood money in any shape. Sierra and Duke had done their best to convince him that he'd earned it, but he remained doubtful that he'd done the right thing and reserved the right to parcel it out if he still felt on edge when they reached their final destination.

The column picked its way along the rockslide that had buried so many, the cliff walls sheer and ominously shadowed. A soft wind whistled past and a chill ran up Lucas's spine, as though the ghosts of the departed were lingering in the ravine, reluctant to let go of their crushed bodies, their turn in any afterlife sure to be as unpleasant as their deaths.

The sun brooded in the western sky like an angry red eye as they finally crossed the rickety wooden bridge over the Rio Grande. The procession stopped at the vehicles gathered along the road, and Lucas dismounted before calling out to the survivors.

"Tend to the wounded and make camp. We'll load the horses before dawn and be on the road by sunup."

Sierra joined him with Eve in tow. The little girl's nose wrinkled at the stink of death that permeated the area even after the bodies had been disposed of, tossed into the river with a prayer. Sierra stared at the long line of vehicles, most pocked with bullet holes or ruined by grenade blasts, and frowned.

"This place gives me the creeps."

Lucas nodded. "Same here. But it's only for one night, and then we're rid of it for good."

"Which one was Magnus's?" she asked softly, eyeing the Humvees.

"The one over by the tent. But the engine took a hit from some shrapnel, so it's staying put. The only two that run are that one and that one," he said, indicating a pair of vehicles parked on the shoulder. Lucas and Colt had already inventoried the vehicles and selected for the trek four horse trailers with intact tires, two buses that looked to be on their last legs, and the pair of Humvees equipped with .50-caliber Brownings.

Sierra glanced at the horses. "At least we don't have to ride all the way there."

"Small mercies." Lucas looked down at Eve for a moment, who didn't seem to be listening, and then shifted his attention back to Sierra. "Problem's the fuel situation. They ran the damn trucks near dry, so we're not going to make it all the way."

"I thought it was only a hundred miles or so?"

"More like a hundred and fifty following the road." Lucas

15

shrugged. "I'm going to help Duke and Aaron siphon what's left from the buses that are out of commission. Mind pitching a tent for me?"

Eve had wandered out of earshot, and Sierra gave Lucas a knowing smile. "Only if I get a tour later."

Lucas answered with a smile of his own and then removed the saddlebags and tack from Tango and left the stallion to forage. He made his way to where Duke was standing with Aaron and Luis with a pair of red plastic jerry cans in his hands.

"Going to be like getting blood from turnips," Lucas advised. "We already checked most of them – they're close to empty."

Duke nodded. "But between 'em all, there might be enough to get the trailers and the two buses all the way there."

"I wouldn't bank on it."

The sun was sinking into the mountains as they moved from bus to bus, draining a gallon here, two there. Once both cans were full, Lucas emptied them into the Humvees. "Those are the most important. They'll eat the least fuel, and they've got the big guns," he explained. "We'll load them with the more delicate gear and the heaviest of the weapons – when we run out of diesel, no point in working the horses any harder than we have to."

Bats flitted along the river, giving chase to mosquitoes as the crew worked through dusk. Two hours later they had exhausted what the convoy had to offer. When they finished pouring the last of the cans into the second bus, Duke appraised the fleet in the darkness.

"How far you think we'll get?" the trader asked.

"Depends on how much these things use. But if we make it more than halfway there, we'll be lucky."

"About what I figured. Oh well. Better than nothing." Duke frowned at Aaron. "Think there are any fish in the river?"

Aaron rolled his eyes. "That's his not so subtle way of asking me to try to catch dinner."

"Luis and I will be right beside you. No point digging into our rations if we don't have to."

Luis smirked. "I'm a city boy, but I'm willing to give it a go. Not like we have much else to do."

"That's the spirit. A rich man who's willing to do a little work for his supper. The needle's eye might have just gotten just a little bigger," Duke joked.

"Better hope so, moneybags," Luis fired back.

Lucas yawned. "You boys enjoy yourselves. I'm going to get some shut-eye after I check in with the sentries." Colt had assigned six of the best fighters, all equipped with night vision goggles and on high alert, to take the first watch, to be relieved in five hours. There had been no evidence of looting, but everyone knew it was a matter of time before scavengers materialized to pick the bones clean. The post-collapse world was an efficient place, and nothing went to waste – one man's loss was another's gain, everything zero sum in the barren wasteland.

After checking in with the guards, Lucas strode to where Sierra's tent stood beside his. He unslung the M4 from his shoulder and slid it through his tent opening, and then twisted to where giggling drifted from Sierra's.

Moments later, the flap lifted and Sierra's head appeared, a smile in place. Lucas gave an answering grin. "You girls behaving yourselves?" he asked.

She winked. "I can't speak for Eve, but I'm looking for trouble."

Lucas sighed. "Best we get some rest. We're going to be up with the chickens."

Sierra gave a small pout, but it was clear she understood. "You eat anything?" she asked.

"I'll gnaw on some jerky. You?"

"We dug into our provisions. Might as well while they're still fresh. Could be a long time until we taste fruit and vegetables again, especially where we're heading."

"Look at the bright side. At least it'll be freezing."

"Always silver linings with you."

Eve's head poked out next to Sierra's, and Lucas tipped the brim of his hat. "Good night, ladies. Sleep well."

"Already?" Eve complained.

"Stay up as long as you want. I'm hitting it," Lucas said.

Sierra made a face and Eve mimicked it. "Party pooper."

"Let's see what tune you're singing when you're up before dawn."

Sierra gave the little girl a quick hug. "He's got a point."

Eve nodded with a wisdom beyond her years. They watched as he disappeared into his tent. The rustle and chirping of night creatures around them seemed suddenly louder for his absence, and the thin tent fabric inadequate to shield them from the menacing shadows. Eve scooted closer to Sierra and blinked her big eyes.

"My ears are still ringing from the shells," she said.

Sierra nodded resignedly. "I know, sweetie. It'll get better with time."

"How long?"

Sierra looked up at the heavens, where a thousand stars pulsed like living things, and then back to the little girl, and said with what hope she could muster, "Not much longer now."

Chapter 4

Green and blue streaked the sky and a neon orange glow spread from the eastern ridge as Elliot forced himself to his feet with a groan. His bones ached from a night spent on the rocky slope beside the trail to the dam, and his sacroiliac felt like a spike had been driven through his back. He drew several deep breaths to steady himself before making his way to where Michael, Arnold, Ruby, and Terry were munching on dry rations while they huddled around a small fire, the night's chill lingering in the morning air.

Michael looked up as Elliot approached and rose with the ease of the young, his wounded arm giving him only slight difficulty.

"Morning," Elliot said.

"Morning," Michael responded. The rest of the group mumbled greetings as Elliot took in the panoramic view of the valley below. The lake and Abiquiu Dam looked like he could reach out and touch them, but he knew it would be another six to seven hours of treacherous trail before they made it there. "We got a broadcast from Lucas. They're still loading the horses, but they'll be on their way shortly."

"Excellent. We should do the same."

Arnold nodded. "That's the plan. I told everyone we'd get moving in fifteen minutes." He checked his mechanical wristwatch. "That was ten minutes ago."

Terry held up a canteen. "Welcome to some water, if you like."

Elliot shook his head. "No, thanks. I'll just find the gents and compose myself."

The group was smaller than the one with Lucas, only twenty strong, and all capable fighters except Ruby, who had elected to accompany Terry. They'd grown closer over the week since Terry's near miss with his beloved plane and were now nearly inseparable, easy in each other's company in a way only those comfortable in their own skins could be.

The party mounted up and resumed the slog down the mountain. The forest road they followed at first quickly degraded to little more than a goat track along the side of a deep gulley, the original trail long before fallen victim to the effects of snow and rain. A line of animals drawing carts loaded with lab equipment and larger gear followed Arnold and Craig, the engineer who'd worked at the dam and who knew the route better than anyone due to his regular trips. They gingerly picked their way along the most perilous stretches as the sun rose and warmed them, the three thousand feet of grade to the lake making the trip easier than the one they'd made yesterday to cross the northern summit pass.

Terry cried out behind Ruby when his horse misstepped. By the time she twisted around to see, one of his heavy burlap sacks had dropped down the side of the ravine and his horse was regaining its footing. Terry's face was pale and tight at the near miss – it could just as easily have been him falling a hundred feet onto rocks as sharp as knives.

"Are you okay?" she asked.

"I…I think so. But my bag…"

"What was in it?"

He looked sheepish. "A bunch of spare odds and ends from my hangar. Parts, mostly."

She studied him as Craig retraced his steps to where they were stopped. "Look at the bright side. No more plane, so you won't need them."

He nodded glumly. "I suppose you're right. Still. A lot of time and work went into sourcing them."

"How's your horse?" Craig called to him.

Terry swung down from the saddle and inspected the animal's leg. He looked up and nodded. "Seems fine. He just got one wrong. Happens to the best of us."

"You're lucky you didn't follow your sack down," Craig said. "Mount up. Time's a-wasting."

"But I need to get my bag…"

Craig glanced down the steep slope and shook his head. "Not unless it's absolutely life-threatening to leave it. We're on a schedule, and we're running badly behind."

"Just give me a minute."

"Terry, that's going to take more than a minute. More like fifteen, at least, by the time you make it down and hoist it back up, and more like thirty if anything goes wrong. We can't spare it. Sorry."

Craig spurred his horse forward, the discussion at an end. They resumed their plodding along the edge of the ravine, moving more cautiously after the near miss, the prospect of a disastrous plunge fresh in everyone's minds.

~ ~ ~

As dawn broke across the alluvial valley, Lucas and Arnold watched the last of the horses loading into the trailers. Sierra sat with Eve nearby, who kept careful watch over Ellie the pig; she'd insisted the animal travel with her instead of with the rest of the livestock, promising to keep an eye on her, and Sierra had reluctantly agreed. It kept her occupied, at any rate. When Duke and Luis returned from the truck at the end of the short column, Luis addressed them.

"That's it. We can get rolling," he announced.

Lucas had been reassured at the ex-cartel boss's willingness to lend a hand, but even more by Duke's gradually warming to him. The trader was a keen judge of character, and he seemed to think that Luis was, if not reformed, at least uninterested in resuming his wicked ways now that he was a man of means. It probably didn't hurt that he'd also seen how precarious his perch as the head of the Locos had been, the gang's longevity seriously in question once the Crew recovered and moved back into Pecos in earnest.

"Let's start them up. We'll lead the way," Lucas said. They'd agreed that he, Colt, Sierra, and Eve would ride in the first Humvee, and Duke, Aaron, and Luis in the second, with the cargo areas packed with gear. All the chosen vehicles had been started the night before to verify their batteries would turn over, and the drivers were awaiting the word from Lucas to roll.

The roar of truck exhausts filled the air as the four horse trailers started their motors, followed closely by the pair of buses carrying the wounded and the rest of the survivors. Lucas twisted the ignition and the Humvee's engine ground to life. He waved out the window and eased the vehicle in a slow circle, the truck's oversized tires crunching on the gravel shoulder as the trailers maneuvered to turn around. Five minutes later, the column was traversing the highway back toward the junction that led north as Lucas and Colt watched for threats, the unimaginable luxury of air conditioning drying the sweat on their faces as Sierra and Eve contented themselves in the rear seat.

They reached the deserted hamlet of Pojoaque and pushed past several abandoned cars, and then picked up speed along the ribbon of asphalt that stretched into the distance, the sky a vibrant turquoise streaked with high wisps of white. The trucks crossed the Rio Grande at Española and proceeded through a landscape of bluffs eroded over eons, red clay faces stark against the backdrop of unending beige and muted green scrub. Heat waves rose from the pavement and distorted the two-lane highway, lending it an otherworldly quality under the relentless sun.

Two hours into the trip one of the trailers lost a tire, and they were forced to wait while the men changed it. They'd loaded as many good spares as they could fit and still have room for the animals and equipment, but the first tire they tried, its sidewalls brittle as parchment, popped like a balloon when the truck's weight settled on it. The second proved sturdier, and the vehicles lurched forward once again, keeping their speed to a minimum in order to conserve fuel and minimize the damage to the rubber from the scorching road.

They reached the dam at midday, where they found Elliot waiting in the shade of a grove of trees fifty yards off the road. When the horses and gear were loaded, they resumed winding along the highway through canyons striated with russet and beige, the temperature now in the triple digits.

"The poor horses," Sierra said, her hair stirred by the air conditioning. "It must be brutal in those trailers."

Lucas nodded, eyes on the road. "Probably. But still better than having to walk."

"I don't know about that. At least they'd be in the open. I'd get claustrophobic in a carrier."

"Can't be helped," Colt said gruffly.

"How's the snakebite?" Sierra asked him.

"Almost healed. Although I won't be offering dancing lessons anytime soon." He twisted to look at Lucas. "I can spell you whenever you get tired of driving."

"Appreciate it. I'll let you know when that happens," Lucas said.

"We going to keep driving after dark?" Sierra asked.

"Probably not. The scouts were attacked between here and Pagosa Springs. If we find an area we can easily defend, that would be better than trying to fight it out on the road in a location they pick."

"And if we don't find one?"

Lucas scowled at the windshield. "Then we'll circle the wagons and keep the big guns trained on either side of the road. Anyone stupid enough to take us on won't last long."

Colt eyed the Humvee behind them in the side mirror, its .50-caliber machine gun pointed at the sky, and nodded. "Let's hope so. They'll definitely hear us coming, no matter what."

"They'd have to be suicidal to try to ambush a motorized column, wouldn't they?" Sierra asked, her eyes fearful.

Lucas's lips formed a thin line. "Or desperate. Lot of that going around these days."

Chapter 5

Houston, Texas

Snake listened intently as Dale, the scout he'd dispatched from Lubbock to Albuquerque following the debacle in Los Alamos, reported in via shortwave radio. It had taken Dale nearly a week to cross the state and arrive in New Mexico, where he'd rendezvoused with the shell-shocked survivors of the battle.

"We're leaving tomorrow to see if we can pick up the scent, but we're not hopeful. There's no way they're still there."

"We don't know that. Don't jump to conclusions. It's possible they believe they're safe now," Snake said.

Dale didn't sound convinced, but didn't argue the point. "I'll proceed as agreed."

Their communications had been brief and largely coded. There was no question in Snake's mind that someone from Shangri-La might be monitoring transmissions, but issuing orders was a risk he had to take.

Dale was a bulldog of a man who was unstoppable once given a task. He'd served several of Snake's pet causes and had yet to meet with failure, his tenacity one of his favorable traits, coupled with his willingness to do anything required to achieve an objective. Under Snake's direction, he'd dismembered rivals, incinerated whole families, pursued rebellious subordinates and terminated them, never questioning his orders or the legitimacy of his methods.

When Snake had made the decision to send Dale alone rather than a score of fighters, it had been a risk, given that Snake might be perceived as showing too little interest in evening the score for the defeat of the Crew, not to mention the death of its leader. Snake had entertained debate on it among his circle, but ultimately determined that one competent man would stand as good a chance as a dozen – Magnus's rout had more than adequately demonstrated that large numbers didn't necessarily guarantee successful outcomes.

Snake stepped away from the radio with a frown. His enthusiasm for continuing Magnus's crusade was close to zero; the toll of a thousand men was incredible to him personally and a threat to the Crew's influence, and also left him shorthanded in Houston and having to pull men from Dallas and other Crew hubs. Word had spread of the defeat, and he was already hearing rumors of isolated outbreaks of revolt in some of the outlying areas, which he'd instructed his lieutenants to put down with extreme prejudice. There could be only one way of dealing with rebellion, and that was with shock and awe.

But there was also the matter of saving face. If he didn't at least attempt to follow up on Magnus's mission, which had been largely supported by the Crew rank and file, it would further weaken his claim to the throne in their eyes. So he was stuck devoting resources to a cause he didn't believe in, although the chances of Dale finding the Shangri-La survivors were exceedingly slim. Only an idiot would remain in the valley now that the Crew knew the location, and nothing about the group that had wiped the floor with Magnus's best fighters struck Snake as foolish. On the contrary, the Shangri-La defenders had proved more than a match for a far larger force and had shown remarkable innovation in their guerilla tactics, based on the accounts of the Crew survivors.

Snake's strategy was to go through the motions to placate Magnus's loyalists while he consolidated power. Even if by some miracle they located the Shangri-La survivors, he had little interest in mobilizing another army if he didn't have to – his hands were already full dealing with the realities of his regime change.

He'd organized an advisory council and after some turmoil had ten strong hands whose opinions he trusted. All had agreed that it would be foolhardy to go on the attack right now; it would be better to focus on developing the vaccine Lubbock was working on, and contend with the Shangri-La variant if and when it surfaced. Given the level of difficulty his big brains were having developing an effective solution to the virus, Snake doubted that a group on the run in the wilds could do better.

Then again, Magnus had been sure that destroying Shangri-La would be shooting fish in a barrel, and it had been that hubris that had cost him everything.

Snake wouldn't make the same mistake.

Chapter 6

The next morning, Lucas emerged from his tent to find Elliot and Michael standing with Arnold, their grim expressions just visible in the dim predawn. They'd made it more than halfway to Pagosa Springs with only one pause for another blown tire before stopping for the night, but the fuel gauges were ominously low, and even at crawling speed it was obvious they wouldn't be able to stretch the diesel all the way.

Lucas nodded to them and fit his hat into place.

"What's up?" he asked.

"Two more of the wounded didn't make it," Elliot replied, his tone dispirited.

"Always a risk."

"Yes. But it's one thing to risk, another to lose." Elliot sighed. "We were just discussing where to bury them."

Lucas checked his watch. "Have to be by the side of the road. We don't have a lot of time if we're going to make it to Pagosa by nightfall."

Arnold grunted. "I'll get some shovels."

"And I'll rouse the gang so we can get under way when we're done," Michael said.

The soil was hard as brick, and the burial took forty-five minutes even with three men working hard. When the remains of the pair were interred, the survivors stood in a ragged semicircle around the freshly turned earth mounds, and Elliot said a heartfelt prayer. The gathering murmured an *amen*, and then Elliot raised his head and addressed the crowd.

"Even as we head to a new home, a new beginning, the hardships follow us. It was my decision to transport the wounded. I take full responsibility. Believe me when I say that a part of me was just buried as well."

Sarah, the doctor, laid a hand on his shoulder. "There was nothing you could have done, Elliot. They wouldn't have lasted the week no matter what you'd done. They were both very badly wounded."

Elliot nodded, too choked up to speak, and Arnold cleared his throat. "Let's load up. We need to get some miles under our belt before the heat rises."

The group dispersed and made its way to the buses. Sierra took Lucas's hand and gave it a gentle squeeze. "I hope this was the right decision. Seems like death follows us wherever we go."

Lucas looked into her eyes. "That's the world we live in. We didn't ask for it, but we'll damn sure deal it out when it comes looking."

"I just wish we could catch a break."

Lucas shook his head ruefully. "Afraid this *is* the break."

The engines started again and the procession rolled forward through the inch of sand that covered the road, only a few rusting vehicles impeding their progress as the sun ascended overhead. The grade steepened when they entered the mountains, and the landscape grew green and lush, with pine trees appearing along the route, fronted by tall grass billowing in the wind.

When the first horse trailer motor coughed several times and then stalled, Lucas was unsurprised. He glanced down at the odometer and braked.

"How are you boys doing?" he called to the drivers from his window.

"On fumes," the first said. The others echoed the news. Lucas stepped from the Humvee and strode to the nearest bus. He climbed aboard to look at the fuel gauge and then shook his head.

"We knew this would happen. The good news is we're only twenty or so miles away, tops. The bad news is we can't run the trucks dry –

they'd leave a trail even a blind man could find, and it would be only a matter of time before we attracted the wrong kind of attention," he said to Elliot, whose bulk filled the doorway as the passengers looked on. Lucas turned back to the faces staring at him. "So this is it. Everybody out. We'll off-load the horses and find somewhere we can ditch the trucks where they won't be obvious."

Lucas pushed past Elliot to where Arnold was waiting at the roadside, one hand shielding his eyes from the glare. "Arnold, help me siphon a gallon for the stopped trailer so we can get it off the road." He paused. "You see anywhere promising we can leave these rigs?"

Arnold nodded and pointed to his right. "Looks like there's a drop there. Might want to ride over and see how far down. Best would be if the trucks wound up where nobody would find them for a long time. Weather should take care of the rest."

"Got to get the horses off the trucks anyway. Probably itching to stretch their legs," Lucas agreed.

"This is their chance."

They made their way to where six men, including Duke and Aaron, were unloading the animals, and claimed their mounts. A short ride south yielded no love – the gulley there was too shallow to conceal the remains of the column. It was to the west of the highway that they hit pay dirt – a steep gorge with the remains of a fire access road running along its crest.

Lucas and Arnold exchanged a satisfied look and rode back to the trucks. When everything had been off-loaded, they directed the drivers to the area they'd found and instructed them to use heavy stones to hold down the throttles in first gear and then jump clear of the vehicles at the edge of the drop.

The process took fifteen minutes, and the only evidence left when they were through was a curl of black smoke from one of the buses. Lucas checked the time as Tango ambled alongside the drivers trudging back to the road – it would be tough, but they could make it to Pagosa Springs by night if they pushed.

The wounded were loaded onto carts along with the precious

equipment from the lab and machine shop, and they continued up the paved grade after the two Humvees, the horses trailing the vehicles in a line. Colt studied Lucas's profile while he negotiated the twisting route and frowned. "Think we'll make it without running out of gas?"

Lucas tapped the fuel gauge and nodded. "We should. That's one of the things we've called right so far."

"Let's hope we're also right about Pagosa. With the wounded and all the gear, we don't have a lot of good options."

"True. And there's going to be logistical issues once we arrive. I've never been there, but if there's a road running through it, we won't be able to hide out like you did in the valley. Eventually someone will stumble across it, and we'll need a coherent response."

Colt smiled. "That's what Arnold's for."

Lucas wiped a bead of sweat from his cheek and sat back in the driver's seat, the landscape crawling by at a snail's pace. "Better him than me."

"What do you make of the ex-Crew guy? Luis?"

Lucas considered his next words, which were guarded. "So far, so good."

"I don't like him. There's a jailhouse stink to him."

Lucas nodded. "He's no saint. But he seems to be pulling on the oars with us. That's what counts, right?"

Colt stared through the side window, lost in thought. When he turned toward Lucas, his voice was low. "For now."

Chapter 7

Elliot called a halt to the trip as it got dark. Their destination was still several hours away, but the ride was more arduous than they'd expected, due to the elevation and the amount of weight the horses were hauling. The survivors once again pitched camp by the side of the road with an armed Humvee facing in each direction and a sentry on guard, spelled every three hours, to enable them to sleep.

They'd lost one more injured fighter that afternoon, and the group offered a brief prayer while the sun dropped behind the mountains, heads bowed as the air cooled in the gloaming. When they were done, the mood was somber, and they ate and spoke in hushed tones, extinguishing their small fires quickly once their rations had been warmed.

Lucas spent a restless night tossing and turning, his dreams filled with nightmarish visions of those he'd killed. When he finally dragged himself from his tent at dawn, his eyes were red and the shadows beneath them pronounced. He glanced around at the dense ground fog that gave the impression they were floating in a cloud and inhaled the crisp mountain air to clear his head. After a brief meal washed down with water, his melancholy cleared and he was ready to go. He spent a few minutes with Tango, smoothing his mane and whispering to him, and then waited by the Humvee with his kit packed while the rest of the party prepared to mount up.

Sierra approached, gave him an appraising look, and shook her head. "Tough night?" she asked.

"I've had better."

"Well, it's almost over. We'll be there soon, right?"

"Should be there in a couple hours."

His guess proved optimistic; the final leg took closer to three. When they turned off the highway at a faded stone sign welcoming them to Pagosa Springs, he exhaled in silent relief and managed a small smile for Eve, who was peering through her window with an expression of wonder at the San Juan River. The column crossed the river over a bridge, and Lucas spotted a pair of riders awaiting their arrival at the far end of the main street. One of the men waved his rifle overhead, and Lucas increased his speed slightly, mindful of the animals in tow.

He stopped when he reached the scouts and leaned his head through the open window.

"Morning."

The older of the two nodded. "It's a nice one."

"You find a good area to off-load our gear?"

"Couple."

"Lead the way."

He followed the scouts to a pair of resorts near the river and shut the engine off to conserve what little fuel remained. A sign on the closest announced a hot springs spa and restaurant. Lucas stepped down from the Humvee with Sierra and Eve in tow as Elliot approached from the other vehicle, eyes on Colt. The scouts dismounted, and one of them approached Lucas.

"We set up in that one," the man said, pointing at the resort on the riverbank. "Water's unbelievable. And the place is really nice, even after all these years."

Elliot nodded. "Lovely. But we can't all fit in those two buildings."

"True. But we searched some of the houses – most of them are in decent shape. With a little work, we should be able to rehab them and they'll be fine."

"And the lab and hospital?" Elliot asked.

The scout pointed at a nearby building. "The post office will work

32

for the hospital, I think. For the lab…there are a number of places that will do the trick. Probably the community center just over yonder would be the best, but it's up to you. There are plenty of places to choose from."

Michael neared with Arnold, who was surveying the approaches to the area with a seasoned eye.

Elliot turned to them. "Well? What do you think?"

"I'll have to look it over some, but it's promising," Arnold admitted. "We can block the entry road with the vehicles and some barricades, and set up defense points."

"That was my instinct as we rolled through town," Elliot said. "And you, Michael? What say you?"

"Not as secluded as the valley, but it'll do."

Elliot returned his attention to the scout. "And the geothermal plant? Where is that?"

"Outside of town, on the way to the airport."

Terry called out from beside the second Humvee. "Airport! Are there planes?"

The scout shrugged. "Didn't look, tell you the truth."

"What? Sacrilege!" Terry turned to Ruby. "You know the first order of business for me."

She smiled. "I can guess."

Elliot clapped his hands, suddenly animated, the slumped shoulders and defeated air from earlier gone. "Everybody! Gather 'round."

When the survivors were all within earshot, he studied them with approval and spoke in his orator's voice. "It is a big day for us — we've found our new home, delivered safe and sound, and with a little elbow grease we can make it into something magnificent. All of you have sacrificed so much for this cause, and it's heartening that we've been rewarded with an oasis of plenty in this barren world. Join me in giving thanks to the Lord for leading us here, and let's ask for His blessing in our new life in our own private Eden."

Elliot led the prayer, and when he was done, he snapped into business mode, handing out assignments, delegating duties, and dividing the survivors into groups. Once he'd issued instructions, he left with Craig to inspect the community center and, after that, the geothermal plant.

Lucas watched him trundle off with a bemused smile. Sierra took his hand.

"Feel like going house shopping? We should try to pick a good one before they're all gone," she suggested.

"Sure. Not much on this side of the river. But I saw some promising places across the water."

"Let's see what we can find."

Lucas asked Duke to feed and water Tango and Nugget while they went in search of suitable lodging, and he, Sierra, and Eve walked together, their shadows preceding them across the overpass that bridged the river. They passed a commercial area and several churches and made for a cluster of homes.

Sierra nixed the first two based on their appearance, but smiled when she appraised the third — a ranch house that, in her words, looked "cozy."

Lucas led her to the front door and tried the knob. "Open," he said, unslinging his M4. "Wait here."

"I thought the scouts said there's nobody here."

"Just in case."

He pushed open the door and stepped over the threshold. A film of dust blanketed the furniture, but there were no broken windows or evidence of water damage, telling him that the roof was probably sound. Lucas checked each of two smaller guest bedrooms, the closets still full of clothes, and paused outside what was clearly the master at the end of the hall. The hair on his arms stood up and a chill ran along his spine.

He eased the door open. The room was gloomy, the curtains drawn, and it took a moment for his eyes to adjust. The bed was made, the room as neat as though a housekeeper had recently been through it, except for the skeleton sitting in an easy chair by the window, its sightless eye sockets fixed on the curtains.

Lucas took cautious steps across the hardwood floor and stopped by the chair. A Smith & Wesson revolver on the planks beside the skeleton told the story, not that the gunshot holes in the skull left any doubt. Whoever this was – male, by the looks of the clothes – had called it quits by taking his life, either because he was sick or just couldn't stand living any longer.

Lucas leaned over, scooped up the weapon, slid it into his belt, and retraced his steps through the house to the entrance.

"Well?" Sierra asked.

"It'll do. But I need to clean up the prior occupant in the master. Probably want to keep Eve out of there while I do, unless you want a lot of sleepless nights."

Sierra grimaced. "Bad?"

Lucas shook his head and looked over to where Eve was playing in the yard. "Won't take long. Go on in and have a look around, but stay out of the room at the end of the hall."

Sierra brushed past him to get Eve, planting a peck on his cheek as she did, and he went to check the closets for a suitable tarp or blanket with which he could dispose of the bones. Not finding anything, he made his way into the garage and spotted a metal trunk near the front bumper of an ancient Buick sedan resting on flat tires. He opened the trunk and dumped out the collection of automotive waxes and fluids before carrying it back into the house.

It took several minutes to fit the skeleton into the trunk. When he was done, Lucas scowled at the black stain on the back of the chair and hoisted the container, barely heavier than when it was empty, and headed to the front porch, secure that Sierra and Eve were exploring the kitchen, judging by their giggles.

He would bury the body later. For now, he wanted to agree with Sierra that this would be their place and stake a claim so there was no confusion with any of the others, and fetch Tango and Nugget so they could munch on the vegetation that was threatening to overtake the huge backyard.

The thought stopped him. *Their place.*

Lucas hadn't questioned that they would get one together. After a week in each other's company following the battle, they'd relaxed into an easy companionship, the only friction between them being the matter of her son. He'd forgiven her for sneaking away – he understood her reasoning, even if he didn't agree with it, and believed that she was being genuine with him. Her affection for him was more than obvious, and their time together had planted a seed of hope for a future he now believed was more than an impossibility.

"Sierra?" he called.

"Yes?"

"So what do you think?"

"Are you done?"

"Mostly."

She poked her head from the kitchen doorway. "So it's safe to look at the rest of the house?"

"Have at it."

Sierra returned a few minutes later, her face serious. "Going to need to clean the master some."

"I was thinking of tossing that chair."

"Probably a good idea. I'm not going to ask."

"That's best," he agreed.

"Which room is mine?" Eve chimed in.

"Either of the smaller ones you want," Sierra said.

"The one facing the backyard!"

Lucas nodded solemnly. "Good choice."

"So this is really home?" Eve's face glowed.

Sierra smiled. "For now."

The little girl's ebullience faded, but only a little. "Let's get Tango!"

Lucas adjusted his hat. "You read my mind."

She gave him one of her oddly penetrating looks and grinned. "I know."

Eve skipped away before he could say anything, making for the entrance. Sierra took his hand again and pulled him closer. "It's perfect. Except for the chair."

He looked into her eyes, and he felt dizzy for a moment – probably the fatigue finally hitting.

"I was hoping you'd say that."

Her expression grew serious. "How long are we going to stay?"

They'd discussed Sierra's desire to search for her son, and Lucas had reluctantly agreed to help – but only once they'd gotten Eve settled and fulfilled their commitments to participate in creating a new sanctuary to ultimately call home. Obviously, any hope that Lucas had that she'd cut him some slack had been misguided.

"At least until they have the vaccine. Elliot made me promise that."

She stepped away from him, her face rigid. "What? We don't know how long that's going to take. You already promised me you would find my boy."

"Sierra, they need us here for now. Once they begin distributing the vaccine, we can take some south with us, to Texas or wherever, and kill two birds with one stone."

"I never agreed to that."

"Because you want to just take off. But it's better to plan things," he cautioned. "That way we'll have safety in numbers, and we'll have helped Elliot, which means we can come back and be welcomed with open arms."

"I don't care about helping him."

"Right. Because you're thinking short term. But let's say we find your son. Then what? Where do you take him? Where do you live? And what about Eve? Do you try your luck on the road? How's that worked for you so far?"

Sierra didn't have an answer but was clearly upset. "It just feels like time's slipping away, Lucas. My boy's out there somewhere, and every day here is one more with him I'll never get back. I...we need to do something. I have this terrible feeling we're going to be too late."

Lucas took her in his arms. "Please. Let's do this my way. I'll help, but only once we aren't needed here."

"You have a ton of gold. You're rich now. You could make a home anywhere. We don't need them."

"Gold has nothing to do with it. I don't want to have to look over my shoulder every day, waiting for the next band of scavengers to come over the hill. There's safety in numbers, Sierra, and Elliot has a good thing going. Power. Water. Meds. Where else are we going to find that?"

She shook her head and asked the question again. "How long are we going to stay?"

"As long as it takes."

She looked away. "Fine. But don't expect me to be happy about it."

Lucas sighed and released her. "I don't. But I'll keep my promise. Which means you need to keep yours. No going off half-cocked on your own, remember?"

She walked toward the door. "I do. Make sure you remember yours, too. I won't wait forever, Lucas. Not for you, or anyone."

And then she was gone, leaving tension and anxiety in her wake. Lucas chewed his lower lip and followed her out, silently reminding himself that Sierra believed her son to be alive, whereas he doubted it, so their priorities were different. He wasn't eager to risk it all going into the heart of enemy territory on a wild-goose chase, but she would do anything to find her son, even if it meant her own destruction.

He understood.

He also wasn't looking forward to the next few weeks as she turned the pressure up on him. Which she would, he was sure. He knew her that well by now and could expect to be reminded of his commitment on a daily basis.

"Well, nobody's holding a gun to your head," he muttered under his breath, and then stepped onto the front porch, from where he could see Sierra already walking with Eve back toward the vehicles, leaving him to hurry to catch up.

Chapter 8

Dale stood with his hands on his hips and surveyed the scene at the bridge over the Rio Grande. The Crew's abandoned vehicles, already stripped by scavengers, clogged the road, and Los Alamos shimmered in the distance halfway up the side of the mountains to the west. The surviving Crew fighters were grouped around him, and Manuel, one of the ranking lieutenants, pointed with his bandaged arm at a spot near the bridge.

"There were two more Humvees. They're gone now. As are at least a couple of the buses and horse trailers," he said.

Dale nodded wordlessly, taking in the destroyed vehicles. Manuel had told him about the retreat from the canyon and the pitched battle with the remainder of Magnus's guard detail against dozens of fighters who'd appeared out of nowhere. One of the guards had heard the grenade blast that had killed their leader, and had slipped away to confirm that the worst had happened before rejoining the fight. Dale had questioned Manuel several times, but his story never varied.

"Where did the guard say Magnus died?"

"Back along the river, near a ravine. He said there wasn't a lot left of him."

"Let's take a look. The rest of you, stay here," Dale ordered, and the dozen men nodded agreement.

Dale and Manuel made their way south along the bank, stopping

39

periodically to study the terrain. When they reached a gulley, Manuel gestured at the hill beyond it. "This looks right."

"Come on."

Dale traversed the ridge at the top of the gulch, eyes searching the ground. He stopped several hundred yards up the rise – part of a scapula lay in the dirt, picked clean by insects and carrion birds. He knelt by the bone and stared at it for a long moment, and then continued more cautiously, scanning his surroundings with the thoroughness of a minesweeper.

Part of a skull rested against a boulder, like an ossified chalice set by the rock to catch the rain. Dale turned to Manuel with a nod. "This looks like the place, all right. See if you can spot where the grenade went off."

Three minutes later they were standing by a depression created by the blast, clearly the epicenter of the shower of fragments they'd located – a femur, most of a boot, a skeletal hand. Dale walked the area and, when he had satisfied his curiosity, returned to where Manuel was waiting. "Might as well go back. If that was Magnus, he's definitely gone now."

They set up camp by the river, the approaching dusk making it impractical to try to navigate the canyon until morning. After an anxious night where few of the men slept, Dale and Manuel led them up the grade to Los Alamos, retracing the Crew's steps toward the canyon that was the final resting place of their army. The area was silent other than the clomp of the horses' hooves against the shale wash and the soft whistle of wind through the poplar trees that lined the crest.

The column picked along the avalanche area and worked its way at a crawl past the minefields, scorch marks and blast debris signaling where Bouncing Betties had detonated – not that there could be any doubt, given the skeletons strewn in telltale patterns. The ebony form of a crow lifted into the air and flapped above them, protesting with a cry the disruption of its solitude.

Manuel slowed as they neared the final narrowing of the canyon and indicated a trail at the end that led up to the top. "This is as far as we got. It was carnage – they had a Browning up there and pinned us down all through this stretch. Then they flanked us, and that was the beginning of the end," he said, his voice a whisper, as though recalling the moment like it had just taken place.

Dale nodded and gave his horse a pat on the neck, which was damp with sweat. "Might as well head up there and see what all the fuss was about. I think it's fairly safe to say nobody's left – the missing vehicles don't leave much mystery about that."

"You sure?" Manuel asked, doubt in his voice.

"We're still alive, aren't we?" Dale said, and spurred his horse forward.

The others followed, rifles in hand. The sloping trail was difficult to negotiate, narrow in spots, but after an hour of painstaking progress they reached the summit and stared down into the valley. Dale raised a pair of binoculars and surveyed the structures in the distance, and then lowered them with a grunt.

"Anything?" Manuel asked.

"Deader than Magnus," Dale said, and flicked the reins. His horse edged forward on the downhill grade, the tall grass of the valley an inviting carpet of verdant bounty before them.

Evidence of the relentless shelling was everywhere, but already the mounds of earth thrown clear of the shell craters were covered with green shoots, the cavities filled with rainwater from recent showers. They rode toward the structures at a trot, following the creek until they drew near.

Dale slowed as he approached the buildings and stopped a few hundred yards away. He swung down from the saddle and crossed the remaining distance on foot, his stride confident and measured, and his men followed. Once at the entry to the largest structure, he paused, listening, and shook his head.

"They're gone. Like we figured. Packed up and hit the road. Nobody here but ghosts now." He hesitated. "Let's look around and see if we missed anything. I doubt they could carry everything. Might pick up some clues as to how many of them made it or where they went."

Dale led them into the building, which had been partially destroyed by the shelling, and they worked their way through the rooms, empty except for beds and simple furniture. When they finished with the buildings, they entered the subterranean area the Apache guide had described, and found themselves in a series of connected vaults, all of them with working overhead lights. The relative miracle of electricity quickly faded when Dale spotted the equipment that had been left behind – presumably because there was no easy way to move it, or no time, or both.

They spent a half hour underground, and when they surfaced, Dale was frowning. "This was much more sophisticated than we thought. We underestimated them. Whoever set this up had serious expertise – which means unless they were killed, they still do."

Manuel nodded, only understanding part of what Dale had said, but getting the overall gist. "So how do we track them?"

Dale rubbed a hand over his beard stubble and took a deep breath. "We start at the highway. We know they took the vehicles. Someone might have heard them pass or seen them. Once we get a direction, we follow the trail to wherever it leads."

"What if we don't find anyone who saw them?"

Dale made for his horse, studying the sky, gauging how long it would take to return to the road. "Then we keep looking until we find the trucks or some evidence of where they went to ground."

"But we don't even know which way they went…"

"That's right, we don't. But we know where the roads are. So we follow the roads in each direction until it's obvious they didn't go that way or we learn something new. But right now the best thing we have to go on is a bunch of big diesel engines, and my bet is that someone will have heard them."

Manuel turned to one of his men. "That could take forever."

Dale stilled; when he turned to face Manuel, any semblance of friendliness was gone. "That's right. It could. Got a problem with that? Someplace you have to be?"

Manuel swallowed hard. "N-no. I didn't mean anything by it."

"You're lucky I like to work alone. If we don't trip over them in the first week, it'll be a marathon, and you boys can run home to Texas."

Dale glared at the man a final time and stalked off, keenly aware that they'd already lost too much time, the trail was cold, and they needed to make it back through the canyon before it got too dark to negotiate the mined areas safely.

Manuel, his men behind him, hurried to catch up, but if Dale noticed, he didn't say anything. He was done with them, their usefulness over now that they'd led him to the valley. He didn't need them, and they wouldn't be any help in locating his quarry.

No, that would take all his skill and cunning.

And for that kind of job, he preferred to work alone.

Chapter 9

The knock at the door of Lucas and Sierra's house echoed like a gunshot. Lucas set the pistol he was cleaning on the dining table and walked to the door.

"Yeah?" he called out.

"Lucas? It's Michael. Is Eve there?"

Lucas opened the door to find Michael on the porch, his eyes red from lack of sleep. Lucas tipped his hat at the younger man. "I think she's back with Sierra. What's up?"

"Elliot needs more blood."

Lucas's expression hardened. "Already given a boatload. Been through a lot for a little girl."

"I know. But he's close to having the vaccine ready to test, and he just needs one last donation from her to prepare it."

Lucas sighed and stepped back. "Come on in."

Michael followed Lucas inside and Lucas indicated a chair by the sofa. "Be back in a second," Lucas said, and disappeared into the bedroom area.

Sierra and Eve looked up from where the little girl was helping Sierra clean the picture windows. Sierra raised an eyebrow at his sudden appearance. "You get bored with your guns?" she teased.

"Got a visitor. Michael. Says Elliot needs Eve one last time."

Sierra frowned. "Lucas…"

"I know. He says it's important."

"It always is."

Lucas looked to Eve. "They need to draw a little more blood, Eve. What do you say?"

Eve's face was placid. "Don't worry. It doesn't hurt that much."

Sierra and Lucas exchanged a glance, unsurprised that the little girl was trying to reassure them rather than seeking their support. Eve had proven to be an unusual combination of youth and maturity, and the way she'd taken the constant demands on her had been nothing short of stoic. Sierra placed the rag she was using on the windowsill and touched Eve's arm. "You're the bravest girl I've ever met, Eve."

Eve shrugged and met Lucas's stare with her big blue eyes. "Is there a choice?"

When Lucas and Sierra emerged from the bedroom with Eve, Michael rose. "Good morning, Eve," he said.

"Morning," she responded almost inaudibly.

"Almost time for our morning walk anyway," Lucas said, reaching for his hat. "We'll head over with you. How long you figure this'll take?"

"Shouldn't be too long."

The streets were largely empty; the weather was turning ugly, as it had periodically since they'd arrived. Leaden clouds blocked the sun, and the air was heavy with the smell of an approaching squall. Sierra eyed the angry sky with narrowed eyes. "Think we'll be able to make it back before it starts pouring?" she asked Lucas.

"We might have half an hour at best, from the looks of things." Lucas shook his head. "Probably going to get wet."

When they reached the community center, Elliot was waiting for them, his face haggard with fatigue. A pair of scratched reading glasses perched on the end of his nose. The jovial, ruddy-complexioned physician was barely recognizable in him, replaced by a man who looked like he'd been to hell and back more than once.

Lucas eyed him as he shook hands. "Been burning it at both ends, huh?"

Elliot gave a rueful grimace. "We're at a critical phase. I can sleep once we're over this hump."

For weeks, Elliot had been snatching rest a few hours at a time, preferring to invest his time in refining the vaccine before winter. He spent his days racing the threat of being snowed in and thus unable to distribute the vaccine until spring. He'd become a recluse of late, leaving the day-to-day to Michael and more or less living in the laboratory he'd set up in the rear of the center.

For the actual handling of the virus, he'd built a separate facility in what had been the post office down the road, which was now off-limits to everyone. It featured his version of a Level IV clean room with an en suite bathroom, a primitive shower and disinfection stall at the inner entrance that served as a dressing room, and a second shower in a separate enclosed area that was the exit to the main building. The suite was equipped with a makeshift air filtration system that exhausted through a set of filters that were specially designed to eliminate hazardous emissions – souvenirs he'd salvaged from the Los Alamos lab, along with additional gear for handling Level IV pathogens safely, including a pair of hazmat suits.

Eve stepped forward and absently rubbed her arm in anticipation. "Hi, Dr. Elliot."

"Hello, my little treasure," Elliot said. "I'm afraid I need to ask for a little more of your blood. This should be the last time. I promise."

"I'm ready," Eve said, her posture stiff, her voice quietly resigned.

"We'll make it as quick as possible," Elliot assured her, and took her hand.

Lucas and Sierra followed them through the depths of the building to the outer area of the lab, where Elliot already had an IV bag and a butterfly needle ready. Eve hopped up onto the exam table Elliot had commandeered from one of the two doctor's offices in town, and lay with one arm hanging below her so the veins in her forearm bulged slightly.

"I keep forgetting you're a veteran at this," Elliot said with a smile as he swabbed her with alcohol.

Eve responded by clamping her eyes tightly shut, waiting for the sting of the steel shaft that would drain her lifeblood.

Ten minutes later Elliot had his precious sample, and Eve was sitting up, drinking a glass of blackberry juice mixed with water – one of Ruby's contributions, from the last of the wild fruit harvested soon after their arrival.

"How close are you?" Sierra asked Elliot as they waited for Eve to recover enough to go home.

"A few more weeks is my hope. Then we need to go into the testing phase."

"How do you plan to do that? Dogs or something?" she asked.

Elliot shook his head. "No, I'm afraid the virus only affects humans, so there's no easy way to test the vaccine other than to expose some brave folks after they've been inoculated."

Sierra swallowed. "Any volunteers yet?"

"I haven't asked."

Nobody said anything. They didn't have to. Elliot sounded confident, and the virus was his responsibility, not theirs.

Sierra stroked Eve's hair. "You up for a walk?"

She nodded and slid off the table. Sierra led her to where Lucas was talking with Elliot, and elbowed him.

"Let's make a dash for it. Maybe we can avoid a soaking," she said. Lucas nodded and tipped the brim of his hat to Elliot.

"Good luck. Duty calls."

"I perfectly understand. Thanks for bringing her so promptly. And Eve? Thank you. Very, very much."

Eve smiled, her expression lighting the room. Thunder roared from outside, and her face grew serious as her eyes drifted to the door.

"Wasn't so bad."

Lucas held out his hand to Sierra and pushed his hat down lower over his brow. "All right. Let's see if it's our lucky day or not. Ready?"

It was Sierra's turn to smile as she gripped his fingers, Eve's hand tightly clasped in her other hand.

"Race you."

Chapter 10

Elliot's senior circle filed out of the community center. He frowned, clearly displeased by the result of the meeting, as they avoided his gaze and pushed through the door. Arnold was the last to go and barely mustered an apologetic shrug as he brushed past.

When the men had left, Elliot paced the room while Michael sat watching him. The older man's increasingly agitated moods had intensified in the weeks since he'd drawn Eve's blood and put the finishing touches on the vaccine.

"If they won't volunteer, we can't know for sure that it's effective. It's a chicken-egg proposition. Are they so dim they don't see that?" Elliot fumed.

"You can't blame them," Michael reasoned. "Nobody wants to commit suicide, even if it's for the greater good."

"The vaccine's stable. They wouldn't be committing suicide. That's rubbish."

"Right. But as they said more than once, what if you're wrong?"

"I'm not," Elliot snapped.

Michael nodded. "I believe you. But obviously people aren't a hundred percent confident. You have to understand that."

Elliot sat heavily and rubbed a tired hand across his brow. Ordinarily neat and precise, since immersing himself in the final vaccine development, he'd set grooming aside and now more resembled a crazed mountain man than the reasoned leader the group knew.

"If we can't get anyone to be the first test case, I'll just do it myself," Elliot grumbled.

Michael blanched. "We discussed that. You can't. You're too vital…if something was miscalculated, nobody could rectify it if you…were incapacitated."

"You mean if I screwed up, I'm dead," Elliot clarified. "If I'm confident enough to ask one of the others to volunteer, then I'm confident enough to do it myself."

"As you've said countless times, this is more important than any one man. Confident or not, there's always a chance something might go wrong, and we can't take that chance with you."

"Maybe, but with the weather turning and no volunteers, we're dead in the water."

"I know. It's frustrating." Michael paused. "What side effects might the vaccine cause?"

"I told you. At worst, slight flu-like symptoms. You know how vaccines work – they induce a mild form of the virus so the body develops antibodies. That way when the vaccinated encounters the real thing, they're immune."

"But as Arnold pointed out, no vaccine is foolproof. There's an element of risk to all of them."

"Of course – that's why I didn't disagree. But it's small in this case. When the alternative is certain death, is there really any choice?" Elliot shook his head. "We've come as far as we can without a human trial. The computer models only go so far, and then you have to actually test it and see what happens."

"How long do you figure it will take before the vaccine kicks in and the test subject is immune?"

"A week, tops."

"You're certain?"

"The virus is virulent and disease progression is rapid. I optimized the vaccine, so the immune response is equally accelerated. I won't bore you with how I accomplished that, but I'm sure of the timeline." Elliot sighed. "Which is why we need to get people on board now. We're running out of time."

Michael sat back and studied Elliot. "When was the last time you got some shut-eye?"

Elliot waved the question away. "I don't know. It's been a while."

"Why don't you get some rest and let me hold down the fort?"

Elliot's eyes narrowed. "We've known each other a long time, Michael. What's going on in your head?"

Michael managed a wan smile. "Yes, I suppose we have. I know that no matter what you say, you're going to inject yourself if you can't convince someone to be your guinea pig. I can't allow that to happen. So I'm volunteering. Shoot me up and let's get this train rolling."

Elliot seemed taken aback. "You can't do that."

"Why not? It's either safe or it isn't. You're asking others to take whatever risk there is – hell, you're saying you'll do it yourself – but if I go ahead and I'm fine, you'll get cooperation from the rest." Michael hesitated. "It's the only way. We both know it, so let's stop pretending. Leadership comes at a price; isn't that what you always say?"

Elliot held the younger man with a fatigued stare. "Are you sure you're comfortable making that sacrifice, Michael? Think long and hard about it."

"It's only a sacrifice if you got it wrong. I'm betting you didn't." Michael looked away. "No pressure or anything."

Both men laughed nervously, the tension in the air thick as fog.

"Are you sure about this, Michael?"

"It's put up or shut up time. Way I look at it, I could have been killed when the building came down around me. I wasn't. My arm's healing, but not enough so I can really help with most chores around here yet. So I'm expendable – dead weight, for now. I'm the natural choice, Elliot. I'm young, healthy, and willing. Doesn't sound like you have any better options, so let's get this over with."

Elliot led Michael to the post office and briefed him on the clean room and its supply of fresh water, solar power, and food.

"We'll do a blood draw from you after a week and verify your antibody load is sufficient to ward off the virus," Elliot said as he prepared a dose of the vaccine. Michael sat unmoving as Elliot measured a quarter syringe's worth of amber fluid and then turned to him. "You absolutely sure about this, Michael?"

Michael nodded, his expression resolute. "Let's rock."

Elliot cleaned off an area of Michael's upper arm and injected him. Michael drew a sharp intake of breath, and then Elliot stepped back and pursed his lips. "That's it. Now go on into the clean room. I'll check on you every few hours."

"I'm on my way. In the meantime, get some rest. Nothing's going to happen for days, right?"

Elliot grunted assent. "That's right. You might feel a little run-down, at worst, for a couple days."

"Then this will be like a paid vacation in a five-star hotel. What's not to like?"

Michael entered the outer shower area and gave Elliot a wave, and Elliot watched him close the first door and open the second. When Michael was inside the room, testing the firmness of one of the cots they'd placed there in anticipation of a host of eager volunteers who'd failed to materialize, Elliot closed his eyes and felt for the wall as a wave of dizziness threatened to overwhelm him. The moment passed, and he offered the younger man another wave as he made for the door.

Once outside, he paused and leaned against the brickwork, his chest tight and his eyes burning. He forced himself to breathe deeply and pushed up from the wall with a determined expression, muttering a prayer under his breath.

Chapter 11

Houston, Texas

Six weeks had passed since the refinery uprising had been resolved with the execution of the Salazar cousins and those loyal to them; but rather than things improving, they'd grown more ominous with each passing day. Rumors of insurgence from other cities had reached Snake via the radio and by messenger, and it had become obvious that Magnus's empire was coming apart, fraying at the edges as challengers to Snake's power grew emboldened.

Snake had dispatched hit squads of his most vicious killers to deal with the ringleaders, but it was like playing whack-a-mole – for each rebellious traitor he neutralized, a new one popped up. Houston might have been stabilized once the Salazars were eliminated, but even though there were no overt signs of resistance, Snake was convinced rebellious factions were plotting his downfall, waiting for an opportune time to strike.

He'd grown progressively more erratic in his behavior, and his meth consumption increased as his agitation grew. In the past few months he'd taken to closing himself off in his headquarters, surrounded by his loyal guards, refusing to leave unless absolutely necessary. Even the weekly executions in the mammoth parking lot had grown to be a source of distress for him, and it was all he could do to attend the ceremonies, sure that there were crosshairs targeting him whenever he was exposed.

Snake awoke and his nose wrinkled at the sour smell of perspiration, the air rank in spite of the air conditioning cranked to freezing in his quarters. He groaned and blinked away the stupor of sleep, momentarily unsure of what time it was – when had he passed out? And for how long?

He checked the time and saw that it was eight o'clock. But p.m. or a.m.? The last few days had been a nonstop blur of debasement and excess – nights of drugs and sex and booze, days of continuing the party while his lieutenants contended with the daily challenges. Part of him grasped that his misbehavior was a luxury he could ill afford, but another, larger part reasoned that there was no point in being top dog if he couldn't enjoy the spoils of success.

Ultimately his baser instincts had won the internal struggle, and now here he was, unsure of whether it was day or night, trembling slightly, his head pounding and every muscle in his body transmitting pain.

He rose and stumbled to the table where his meth and stash of other drugs were scattered, and fumbled among the containers until he found a blue pill – diazepam, expired three years earlier but still sufficiently potent to blunt the worst of the hangover and leave him functional. He popped the tablet in his mouth and washed it down with a long pull from a mescal bottle, wincing as the harsh liquid seared its way down his throat, and then staggered to the bathroom, where the overhead lights sent needles of agony through his head when he switched them on.

A stream of water jetted down and he immersed himself, washing away the worst of the revelry while he considered his day – or night. He needed to figure out which it was, but baby steps. When he was done, he donned new clothes and marched to the entry door, the alcohol and CNS depressant stabilizing him enough so he could take care of business. He paused at the threshold and circled back to the table. A little hit of speed wouldn't hurt anything, he reasoned – it would just keep him alert, sharpen his senses.

He smoked a small amount, and when he made his way back to the door, he bounced on the balls of his feet as the drug surged through his system, energizing him. Snake unlocked the deadbolts and pulled the slab wide. Only two guards on duty, he noted with a frown.

"Where are the others?" Snake growled.

"Probably still asleep," one of the men answered.

Snake nodded. So it was morning. He normally didn't emerge from his chambers until nine at the earliest, so his full retinue of men wasn't there yet.

"I'm hungry," Snake announced, and turned to lock his door with a key that hung around his neck on a leather lanyard. The top deadbolt snicked shut, and he was leaning forward to lock the second when he caught the movement of a shadow in the periphery of his vision.

Snake spun as the first guard lunged at him. A glint of steel flashed in the light and then Snake had his dagger free and was driving it into the surprised man's chest, closing the distance between them in a blink – the exact opposite of how most would have reacted. He didn't pause as a warm stream of blood splashed down his arm, but instead kneed the attacker in the groin and pushed him away, knife in hand. The guard slumped to the side and dropped his blade as the second guard whipped a pistol toward Snake, who was already moving in a crouch. He hurled himself at the man before the shooter could bring the gun to bear and slashed at his crotch while head-butting him in the stomach. The wickedly sharp blade slashed through fabric and flesh, and Snake was rewarded with the sound of the pistol striking the cement floor. A gush of blood sprayed from the wound – a femoral artery gash that would cause the man to lose consciousness in under a minute.

Snake continued the offensive, stabbing the man's torso repeatedly at high speed, his arm a merciless piston powered by adrenaline and meth. When the man dropped with a groan, Snake went down with him and finished him with a thrust through his throat.

He rolled away from the guard and sat gasping for breath, staring at the man with murderous rage. After several moments he leaned forward, squinting.

He didn't recognize the guard.

It wasn't one of his regulars.

Snake pulled himself to his feet, mind working furiously as he collected the pistol.

Footsteps pounded down the hall, and Snake aimed along its gloomy length. Four guards materialized a moment later, and he recognized them as his regulars.

"What happened?" the shift leader exclaimed.

"They jumped me. Tried to kill me." Snake grimaced. "Picked the wrong guy."

The leader walked over to the first dead guard and kicked him to confirm he was dead. He moved to the second and knelt beside him.

Snake straightened and joined the leader. "Recognize him?"

"I think so…"

"Who is he?"

"I…I can't be sure. But I think he's from New Orleans."

Snake leaned over and wiped his blade clean on the dead man's shirt. "New Orleans? Are you positive?"

"No. But one of my men on the evening shift would know. He's originally from Louisiana. Spent two years there before transferring to Houston."

"Ask him to confirm." Snake reached to the door and unlocked the top deadbolt. "I'm going to clean up. Call a meeting of my council in half an hour. And make sure the room's clean and everyone is searched going in. I want no more mistakes."

"I…I didn't authorize this man to guard you. He must have killed the regular who was assigned and then taken his place."

"How did he slip by you if you were doing your job vetting them?"

"I never vetted him. Again, he must have snuck into the building and targeted the original guard. He was obviously working with this piece of shit," the leader said, indicating the man Snake had stabbed through the heart. "We'll search the building. My bet is we find the body of the guard he replaced stuffed somewhere…unless they bribed him and he left town."

"I'll be back out in thirty minutes. I want answers by then. If not, you'll be joining this pair. You understand?"

"Of course. I'm on it."

"Don't breathe a word of this to anyone, or it's a death sentence. No exceptions."

The leader nodded, his face pale.

Snake pushed his door open and slammed it behind him, his heart trip-hammering in his chest. If the leader was right, he had a problem in Louisiana, and that spelled real trouble. New Orleans was one of the main Crew strongholds outside of Texas, strategically important because of its sea access; if there was a revolt there, it would spread to other cities. He needed information and a strategy before word reached whoever had put the assassins up to it. If it was the Crew boss in New Orleans, Snake would have to move swiftly and do so completely unnoticed, or it could quickly escalate into a civil war within the Crew, and he couldn't afford that.

His instinct was to hit them hard in the dead of night. Surgical strike, in and out before they knew what had happened. Install new leadership and put the whole city under lockdown until everyone whose loyalty to Snake was in question was hanging from a lamppost.

Blood would run in the streets, and the sky would rain fire upon those who challenged his rule. Snake would handle it just as Magnus would have: he would scorch the earth.

Chapter 12

The weather was changing in the San Juan Mountains; there was a snap in the air as the nights grew colder with the approach of winter. Eight weeks had gone by since the survivors from Shangri-La had taken over Pagosa Springs, and after some adjustment, things had grown into a normalcy Lucas was enjoying, though a part of him knew wouldn't last.

Sierra had been forbearing as they'd repaired the house and outfitted it to withstand the harsh weather around the corner, but she'd become more impatient lately, reminding Lucas in a thousand ways of his promise to go in search for her son.

Following Michael's successful exposure to the virus and subsequent survival, the group's willingness to get inoculated had grown dramatically, especially once Michael was back among them, for all appearances now healthier than ever. A few more volunteers stepped forward at that point, motivated by everything from desperation to hope to altruism. And the results were the same as Michael's.

"Of course, no vaccine is going to have hundred percent efficacy," Elliott had warned when reporting the news in a community meeting. "But based on the animal and now human trials we've run, this protects the recipient against the virus as well as anything I've seen."

"Then there's a chance you could get the shot and still die?" Colt had asked.

"There's always a chance. Medicine's not an exact science,

especially when dealing with a virus that mutates. But nobody we've inoculated has shown any symptoms after being exposed. So it's benign in terms of causing any side effects and has successfully protected the volunteers we exposed to the virus over a week ago."

When the next test group emerged from the clean room without incident, Elliot had inoculated everyone in the community, foregoing any need to isolate the remainder of the population. The vaccine worked as he'd hoped – protecting without making those inoculated contagious.

Having already resigned himself to helping search for her son, Lucas had steered Sierra's name into the hat when, as part of Elliot's advisory group, he had been asked his opinion on how to best distribute the vaccine.

Now, the final decisions on logistics had to be made; the time had finally arrived to venture forth from their enclave and take the cure to the world.

Lucas entered the community center and nodded to the others sitting in a circle like attendees at a twelve-step program meeting. He resisted the urge to hold up his hand and say, "My name's Lucas, and I'm one of the last men on earth," and instead took the open seat beside Arnold and leaned against the steel backrest.

Elliot cleared his throat and sat forward. "Ladies and gentlemen, thank you for coming. The purpose of today's gathering is to decide on how exactly we're going to distribute the vaccine. I've made sufficient doses and been in contact with enough of my former colleagues to be confident it's ready for dissemination. But there are logistical issues I haven't bored you all with up until now that need to be agreed upon."

He scanned the faces around him and his voice softened. "There are three hubs where the vaccine can be replicated and manufactured. One's in Nebraska. Another in Oklahoma. And another in Arizona."

"What about the rest of the country?" Colt asked.

"Those three centers will distribute it to like-minded groups from there. But they'll act as the central distribution points for the cultures necessary for the vaccine's creation."

"Then they won't actually hand out the shots?" Arnold asked.

"No. It would subject them to too much risk – the Crew would target them as soon as it heard of the vaccine being available. What we've decided on is a decentralized approach, where several dozen distribution points appear around the country nearly simultaneously."

Lucas nodded. The strategy was smart. The old man and Michael had come up with an ingenious way to shield themselves, and their surrogates, from becoming targets. Once the vaccine was in wide distribution, the location of the new sanctuary would be moot – the virus would have been counteracted, and thus the power held by anyone looking to have an exclusive on the vaccine negated by its widespread availability.

"So why are we here?" Arnold asked.

"We've discussed the various alternatives, and we've decided that it makes the most sense to send out three teams simultaneously rather than one at a time," Michael said.

Arnold shook his head. "I warned against that. It would leave us too shorthanded here in the event of an attack."

"Yes, and we considered your input carefully, Arnold," said Elliot. "The problem is that with the weather changing, we might not be able to get teams out to the other locations if we wait to ensure the first is successful. The risk of the vaccine not getting distributed outweighs the risk of our being attacked."

"It's a mistake," Arnold growled.

"I completely agree that it's not an optimal solution, but given the choices, it's the best one we have," Elliot said.

"What if you're wrong?"

"Then we'll have to manage. But we've heard reports that the virus has taken a severe toll east of the Mississippi, and it's virulent. It's a small miracle that it hasn't spread any further, but our luck won't hold indefinitely."

"What do you think has kept it from spreading?" Lucas asked, genuinely curious.

Elliot ran his fingers through his hair. "Near as I've been able to figure, it's because it incapacitates its victims before they can make it

RUSSELL BLAKE

very far. If there were still cars and planes, we'd all be dead, but because traveling is so difficult, carriers likely only make it a few miles before they fall by the wayside."

Lucas nodded. "Makes sense."

"The problem is that with all viruses, there will be an occasional host who's asymptomatic and who will infect anyone they come across without being aware of it."

"Like the little girl?" Arnold asked.

Elliot shook his head. "Eve is a rarity – she's not a carrier, but she's got antibodies in her blood that make her immune, just as we all do now, thanks to the vaccine. No, what I'm referring to is someone who doesn't have any symptoms and is otherwise apparently healthy, yet is contagious. That person would be, quite literally, a messenger of death, wholly unaware they're spreading the plague." Elliot paused. "We're going to send three six-man teams to each hub. That's the most promising approach. Then weather won't be a risk. We've worked far too hard to let snow stop us from saving the human race."

"Besides, once the vaccine is out there, we'll be that much safer – any reason for trying to destroy us will have been eliminated," Michael said. "We'll no longer be a target."

"I think you're wrong about that. You don't think Magnus's group is going to want revenge?" Arnold snapped.

"Maybe. But it took them years to locate us. Now we're further away, and they have a thousand fewer men. Most importantly, their leader's dead, which proved that coming after us was the worst thing he could have done," Michael countered.

Elliot held up a hand to silence the debate. "How we're going to distribute it isn't the question. We're here to make a final determination of who goes."

After a half hour of vigorous debate, they'd decided on the teams – Lucas and Sierra, Colt, Arnold, and two of his top surviving fighters would travel to Oklahoma, over Arnold's objections at being forced to leave the compound.

"I'm responsible for security. I can't do much from the road, can I?" Arnold had argued.

"You've fortified our perimeter admirably, Arnold," Elliot countered. "But this is too important for us to send anyone but our best on every team."

When the meeting broke up, Arnold was still visibly agitated at the way things had gone. Lucas accompanied him outside, where he glared at Michael as the younger man departed with Elliot.

Arnold turned to Lucas and spoke quietly. "I can't believe he still listens to Michael after all the screwups during the attack."

"It's not a terrible approach, Arnold. I can see why they decided on it. And Michael did take the first bullet and prove the vaccine."

"But why send me? You can take care of yourself. There's no reason for me to leave."

"I think Elliot wants to make sure we have the best chance of success."

Arnold gazed off to the mountains and then leaned toward Lucas. "Don't look now, but you've got incoming. Too late to take cover," he said in a joking tone.

Lucas followed his stare to where Sierra was approaching with Eve. Arnold moved away as Sierra made for Lucas.

"Well?" she asked.

"We leave in two days."

Eve's eyes widened. "We do?"

Sierra knelt by the little girl. "No, honey. Lucas and I have to run an errand. We'll be gone for a few weeks."

"You do? Both of you?" she asked, her tone fearful.

Sierra nodded. "Yes."

"But why? Are you coming back?"

"Oh, Eve, of course we are. It's something we have to do. Grown-up stuff. But we're absolutely coming back. You couldn't keep us away from you."

Lucas held out his hand. "Come on, Eve. Tango needs a brushing, and he likes it when you help."

Eve took his hand, her fingers tiny in his. Sierra grabbed her other and they walked with her down the street, past homes where the occupants were hammering and sawing and salting meat in preparation for the first snowfall, which the crisp air foretold would be sooner than later. When they reached the house, where Tango and Nugget roamed the large lot, Eve seemed calmer, now resigned to the situation.

"Go get the brush," Lucas said, and when Eve had gone in search of it, he looked to Sierra. "No telling how long we'll be gone."

"I know. But to a child, a couple of weeks is abstract. It could mean anything. Don't worry. She'll be fine. I already talked to Ruby and Terry. They'll take care of her like she's their own."

Ruby had selected a house with Terry a few blocks away, and the pilot had done an admirable job of fixing it up, with Ruby providing the feminine touches. Lucas glanced at the work he'd done on theirs – bricks mortared five feet high along all exterior walls to provide protection in the event of shooting, steel plates he'd scrounged from a wrecking yard installed over the windows to create gun ports – and nodded. It might not have been pretty, but if anyone came for them, it would be hard to take the place without a fight.

Eve came scurrying back with the brush and Lucas snicked from the corner of his mouth. Tango trotted over and stood by while Lucas took the brush from her and went to work, Sierra watching with a smile.

"Nugget's next, right?" Eve asked, eyeing the mare.

"Of course. Can't do one without the other."

"I'll miss them," she said, looking at her feet.

Sierra neared and placed a hand on her head, smoothing her hair. "We'll all miss you, Eve. But you'll be with Ruby. She'll take care of everything."

Eve brightened somewhat. "I like Ruby."

"Then it's official. In two days, you'll camp out at their place and we'll be back before you know it."

Worry clouded her small face again. "But what about Ellie? She can't stay here alone. Who will take care of her?"

"Oh, honey," said Sierra, kneeling down to look her in the eyes.

"We wouldn't forget Ellie! You'll take her with you, of course. You know how she likes rooting around in Ruby's backyard for fallen crabapples. You guys will have a great time together, and we'll be back before you know it."

Lucas continued brushing, hearing Sierra's glib words, but his stomach twisted at the reality of their situation. It was six hundred and fifty miles as the crow flies to Tulsa, which even under the best of circumstances would take several weeks – and if they ran into trouble, possibly much longer, depending on what kind it was. A lame horse, an attack by scavengers, bad weather, anything unexpected...

And that was just to Tulsa. From there, they'd split off and head to Mississippi, where they'd try to confirm that her son, Tim, was either dead or alive. Which would take yet more time and was in Crew territory, increasing their risk exponentially.

Sierra viewed the world unrealistically, he thought. Or at least hadn't thought through exactly how long their trek was likely to take. With travel time, they'd be lucky if they made it back by Christmas, assuming they could negotiate the passes in the heavy snow the area regularly saw.

Lucas snuck a look at Sierra out of the corner of his eye, taking in her bronzed skin and earnest expression, and banished the doubt nagging in his gut.

Too late to back out now. He was knee deep in the swamp, and the only way out was following through on his promise to her.

For better or worse.

Chapter 13

Snake accompanied his retinue to the university hospital entrance, where Whitely and his entourage from Lubbock had organized a test of the newly developed Crew vaccine on a group sequestered in an isolation chamber. They strode down the dark halls to the stairwell that led to the basement, where Whitely greeted them with a troubled expression.

"Well?" Snake demanded.

"As you know, we exposed twenty test subjects to the virus yesterday after giving them the vaccine last week. Two of them experienced mild side effects after the shot, but that was expected in at least some cases."

"What side effects?"

"Chills, fever, muscle soreness, somnolence."

Snake didn't understand the last term, but shrugged it off as though it didn't matter. He wasn't a medical expert, having never made it past ninth grade and having stopped paying attention since sixth, but he didn't need to be – he was the head of the most powerful group in the region.

"So what's the result? Cut to the chase," Snake snapped.

"You can have a look yourself."

Whitely led him to a window, where twenty men and women were locked in a large room. Fifteen of them were huddled on one side of the room, and five were on cots as far from the rest as they could be placed. Snake's eyes narrowed as he took in the five, who were soaked in bodily fluids and laboring for breath.

He pointed at a woman who wasn't moving. Her face was cyanotic, and her hands had curled into claws. "She's dead."

Whitely nodded. "The other four will be soon enough."

"Seventy-five percent success isn't a success."

Whitely didn't budge. "I know."

"You've been directing this show for almost, how long, a year? And this is what you have to show for it?"

"Over a year. But I'm not a scientist. I'm in charge of security and of making sure the staff has whatever it needs. Magnus never intended me to direct the medical side of the project. I'm an engineer, not a doctor or a microbiologist."

"Who's heading up this effort?"

"Gabriel Kovaks. He replaced the traitor Magnus executed before...before he left."

"I want to see him."

"He's in Lubbock. He couldn't come. He's still working on the vaccine, trying to figure out what's gone wrong."

Snake's eyes narrowed to slits, and the tattoos on his face writhed like snakes. "Smart man. If he was here, I'd have him executed."

Whitely didn't respond for a long moment. "The problem is we don't have anyone more qualified, so if you do, the project's over."

"Project? You mean the string of failures is over, don't you? What has been accomplished, exactly, other than wasting a ton of time and resources?" Snake blurted.

"Magnus was told–"

Snake took a step closer to Whitely. "Magnus is dead. I'm in charge. You have something to say, you say it to me."

Whitely swallowed and took a deep breath before continuing. "He was told that with this virus and our capabilities, there was no guarantee of success. That it was a long shot. Nothing about that has changed. The researchers are doing the best they can, but it may be impossible to develop a vaccine with a higher efficacy rate than what we've got now."

"He believed that the Shangri-La team would create one that worked, and that would screw us. Why was his belief wrong?"

Whitely's tone hardened. "We have no way of knowing whether that's true or not. Until theirs surfaces – no, make that *if* it ever does – it's conjecture, not fact. They'd have to know something we don't to make a better vaccine."

"They have the girl. The Apaches told us that much."

"Which may or may not matter. We're still not sure why she was of such importance. Jacob – the scientist who Magnus executed – never explained her relevance satisfactorily. She's a question mark."

Snake spat on the concrete floor. "This is a failure. I don't need to watch the rest die to know that. Nobody in their right mind would use this vaccine, with a one in four chance of dying."

Whitely shook his head. "Not necessarily. If the odds are a hundred percent of dying without it…"

Snake turned away. The meeting was over. "It's not good enough. We both know that. Don't piss me off trying to blow smoke, or you'll never make it back to Lubbock."

Whitely waited until Snake and his guards had left before he resumed breathing. When the Crew leader had vacated the building, he moved to the technicians in the room adjacent to the experiment chamber and broke the news.

"Snake isn't happy. Let's watch them for another twenty-four hours to see if more get sick. Then shut it down and burn the bodies."

"What about the survivors?" a young tech asked.

"There won't be any. Nobody can leave that room alive. Poison their water tomorrow and then dispose of them. We can't afford any leaks on the result of the experiments."

The tech blanched but nodded, as did his companions. They understood what they'd signed up for – most against their will, but that was immaterial. They knew the job would involve distasteful outcomes. It went with the territory of live experimentation.

The test subjects had all been taken from the civilian population of Houston at random. They'd been singled out as troublemakers by Crew informants, and it had been as good a way as any to silence opposition. Whether in a public execution or a secret lab, they were all dead anyway – it was simply a question of timing.

This way, their passing would at least serve a useful purpose.

Whitely eyed the techs and then grunted. "I'm heading back to Lubbock to break the news. Marshall, you're in charge of cleaning this mess up. And I remind everyone – one word about this to anyone and the penalty will be swift and final. So keep your thoughts to yourselves."

Whitely didn't wait for a response and spun on his heel toward the door. The technicians weren't important, and he suspected there was a better than fifty percent chance that he would never see them again. Snake had seemed dangerously unstable beneath his veneer of relative calm, even more so than the last times he'd encountered the man, and Whitely had seen the telltale signs of chronic meth use in his eyes and the sallow color of his skin, as well as the barely controlled tics and unconscious fidgeting and scratching. He could easily decide that the team needed to be taught a lesson, and Whitely wanted to be well away from Houston if Snake lashed out.

Whitely had survived Magnus, who was a hothead and unpredictably violent; but compared to Snake, the former leader had been the essence of patience and reason. Snake was obviously on a collision course with disaster if he kept on the road he was on, and Whitely wanted no part of the inevitable flameout that would be the reward for his addictions.

So Whitely would return to Lubbock without announcing his departure, and deal with any consequences from afar.

Chapter 14

Clouds gathered overhead as Lucas led Tango and Nugget on foot through the early morning fog to Ruby's house, where Sierra was standing outside hugging Eve close as the little girl struggled to put a brave face on her distress at seeing the two people she was closest to in the world ride away. She looked up at the sound of the horses approaching and broke away from Sierra, surprising Lucas when she threw her arms around his waist and sobbed.

He stopped midstride, unsure of how to react, and then Eve stepped away and fixed him with her piercing blue eyes.

"Promise me you'll come back," she said with precision beyond her years. "Both of you. Promise."

"Don't worry, Eve. We'll be back," he said.

"Then promise," she pressed.

He glanced at Sierra, who nodded once, her eyebrows raised. He turned back to Eve and tried a smile.

She wasn't buying it.

He sighed and knelt in front of her. "I promise."

Eve pointed to Sierra. "And promise you'll keep her safe."

"You drive a hard bargain. You been getting lessons from Duke?"

"Promise," she insisted.

"Okay. I promise I'll keep Sierra safe and that we'll come back. And I'll do the same for Tango and Nugget. Throw them in for no extra charge. Satisfied?"

Eve visibly relaxed. "Okay."

"Behave yourself with Ruby, you hear? I don't want any reports of misbehavior," he warned.

"I'm always good," Eve said.

"I suppose you are. But I had to say it."

Ruby emerged from her front door and seemed to float toward them through the fog. "I thought I heard a ruckus out here. Why, look at how pretty you are this morning, Eve! I swear you get bigger every day. And thank you for bringing Ellie."

Sierra gave Ruby a kiss on the cheek in farewell. "Take good care of her," she whispered to the older woman.

"I intend to spoil her relentlessly. You won't recognize her when you get back."

"Thanks, Ruby," Lucas said, handing Sierra Nugget's reins.

Ruby looked him up and down. "It's time?"

"That it is."

"Good luck."

"Appreciate it."

"Don't worry about her. Terry and I will see that she gets three squares and proper beatings."

Eve's eyes widened, and Ruby smiled. "I'm kidding."

The others were waiting by the conference center. Their saddlebags had already been packed with the vaccine, which was secured in polystyrene containers Elliot had filched from a Chinese restaurant in town to insulate the contents from drastic temperature variations. Arnold nodded a curt greeting to them, and Colt grunted a monosyllable. George and John filled out their group; both were already astride their horses, obviously anxious to hit the road.

Elliot emerged from the building and greeted them. "Good morning, lady and gentleman."

"Morning," Lucas allowed. Sierra nodded.

"I've already briefed the others, so they can fill you in on the trail."

"There'll be more than enough time."

"Short version is you're confirmed to rendezvous at a compound ten miles outside of Tulsa, where my associate Reynolds has a facility ready for vaccine production. Lower tech than we are, but the method of duplication is relatively straightforward now that we've got it right."

"We just drop it off, and that's it?" Sierra asked.

Elliot nodded. "That's correct. They'll take it from there."

"And then we're free to go?" Lucas asked, more a statement than a question.

"Yes. Do whatever you need to do." Lucas had told Elliot that he'd be continuing south with Sierra once they'd fulfilled their obligation, and Elliot hadn't raised any objection. "May God go with you all."

Lucas climbed into the saddle after giving Sierra a leg up, and Arnold and Colt took the lead, the fog shrouding them so that they disappeared from view barely twenty yards along the road out of town.

Michael exited the building and walked to where Elliot stood staring at the blanket of white. "That the last group?" the younger man asked.

"Yes. Arnold and company."

"Then it's all in motion. Congratulations. Years in the making and finally coming to fruition."

"At a steep price," Elliot reminded him.

"True, but one that had to be paid for the country to survive. You were absolutely right when you said that if we're ever going to rebuild, we need to take the lead in solving the big problems so people stop acting like savages."

Elliot managed a faint smile. "That was a long time ago. You have a better memory than I."

"You also said that it's not what you accomplish that defines you, it's what you're willing to try to do – the difference you attempt to make in the lives of those around you. Yes, I remember that speech well. Some things stay with you."

Elliot nodded. "We've built a strong community, but it's underpopulated now. That's the next problem we need to address.

Too many of our best didn't make it, and we need more like-minded folks."

"True. We could go into Santa Fe again and try to recruit."

The older man shook his head. "Too dangerous. When the Crew comes looking for us, that's one of the first stops they'll make. No, I have something else in mind. Something subtler."

"Such as?"

"I'm thinking that we may be able to coerce Duke into coming out of his recent retirement and starting up a trading post a reasonable distance away, at a crossroads that sees some traffic – but not too much. He can act as a qualifying filter for us and direct promising candidates our way."

"Anyplace specific in mind?"

"I believe Alamosa's a couple of days' ride."

Michael frowned. "More like three."

Elliot shrugged. "Details."

"Duke's set for life. Why would he go back to trading?"

"To help. Boredom. Because he likes the challenge. All or none of those. We won't know until we ask, will we?"

"When would you be thinking of establishing this outpost?"

"Soon, actually. Most certainly before the weather gets bad. He won't see much traffic anywhere around there once the snow comes to stay."

Michael nodded slowly. "It could work. But it would take a long time to get our numbers back up. That's not a main artery."

"We're not after speed. We're after quality."

"And the Crew?"

Elliot looked away. "They'll do whatever they do. We're largely out of the equation now, I'd think, as long as we stay out of their way. The vaccine's been deployed, so we won that battle."

"Not until it's in widespread distribution," Michael reminded him.

"Which it will be soon enough." Elliot paused. "Assuming all goes well."

"What was it you were so fond of saying? Hope for the best but prepare for the worst?"

That drew a smile from the older man. "Hoisted with my own petard, eh? Going to use my words against me?"

Michael matched the smile. "You had a valid point."

"Well, it's too late for second-guessing now, isn't it? The teams are on the road, and what's done is done. So we'll take what we have and make a stew. Hopefully it will get us through the winter, and by spring everything will be clearer. Arnold's defenses seem thorough, so as long as we maintain discipline, we should be fine. And soon the weather will be our ally – nobody will be traveling secondary roads in blizzard conditions."

As if to underscore Elliot's statement, a low rumble of thunder shook the ground and the sky darkened.

"Looks like it'll start pouring shortly," Michael said.

"Then back in we go. We can continue our discussion under cover. No point catching our death."

Chapter 15

Snake looked up from his meal with tired eyes. The head of his Houston security team entered the dining room, which was empty save for Snake, his guards ensuring that he wasn't disturbed. Snake scowled at the man and forked another chunk of ham into his mouth.

"What is it?" he demanded.

"There's a ship entering the harbor. Looks like a naval vessel."

Snake rose, nearly upending the table. "What?"

The man nodded. "It showed up twenty minutes ago. Got the call on my two-way just now from the outpost by the port."

"But…how?" Snake blurted, his hands twitching as he tried to process the impossible news. There was no Navy any longer. No ships. No way of powering them or of manning a crew. The security head might as well have announced that extraterrestrials had landed in the main plaza and demanded to be shown to the Earth's leader.

"I don't know. It's looking like it's going to dock."

"And there's no sign of who it is?"

The man shook his head. "No." He paused. "What do you want to do?"

"Get gunmen down there now. Heavily armed. The more the better." Snake cocked his head. "Alert my guards that we're going to the port."

The security head nodded. "Will do. When?"

"Five minutes. I want to see this for myself."

The security chief left, and Snake paced for a few minutes before returning to the table and staring at his half-eaten meal. What did the appearance of a functioning naval ship mean? Obviously that whoever was operating it had access to fuel, which was surprising in and of itself – Magnus had been convinced that all the diesel had gone bad by now and had heard of no working refineries. But the presence of a vessel was proof that, like the assumption that it would be child's play to overthrow Shangri-La, Magnus had been more than mistaken.

More ominous was that Snake's tenuous hold on power might be in jeopardy. If the military was operational again and was beginning to restore order in the country...

He cursed under his breath and then stopped the panic that threatened to overtake him. He'd received no reports of the authorities reasserting themselves from the far reaches of his empire, which he certainly would have if there were a regional move to regain control. So this was probably something else. The first step in taking Houston back?

"Over my dead body," Snake growled. He hadn't connived and killed to get to the top of the heap only to have his power stripped from him, boat or no boat. If that was their plan, they'd find it harder to do than they'd ever imagined.

Snake stopped himself mid-thought.

He didn't have enough information to formulate a strategy, and he was making dangerous assumptions. For all he knew, whoever was on the boat had no idea the Crew ran Houston or what the gang's capabilities were.

Snake didn't even know who was on it.

But he would find out soon enough.

He was tempted to smoke a hit of meth to steady himself, but resisted the urge. He needed a clear head, at least for now. He speared another chunk of ham and popped it into his mouth, but it tasted like wood, and he grimaced and spit it back onto the plate, disgusted. A large swallow of his drink flushed the tang from his mouth and he crossed to the door, checking the Desert Eagle .45 on his hip and his dagger in its belt scabbard as though they were lucky talismans instead of weapons.

The ride to the port took seemingly forever. Snake and his guard detail galloped through the streets of Houston as fast as they could manage, and their horses were almost blown out by the time they reached the waterfront, where the unmistakable rumble of massive engines echoed across the port. At least three hundred Crew fighters had taken up defensive positions, big .50-caliber Browning machine guns pointed at the slate gray vessel that was now docked parallel to the concrete jetty, its artillery turrets radiating menace. A plume of smoke rose from its stack, but there was no one to be seen on its decks. Beyond the ship, the cranes and superstructures of sunken freighters that had been submerged after the collapse broke the surface of the water, a reminder of the anomaly that was an operational naval vessel.

Snake's security chief had a hurried discussion with his subordinate and then came to meet Snake, whose eyes were glued to the boat.

"We received a radio transmission twenty minutes ago from the captain of the vessel," he began.

"And?"

"He asked to meet with you. By name."

Snake absorbed that. "Who is he?"

"He didn't say."

"You didn't ask?"

"I wasn't here to ask – I was with you. My lieutenant over there fielded the call." The chief swallowed, anticipating an outburst. "He just relayed the message."

Snake surprised him by remaining calm. "What channel did they use?"

"Seventeen."

"Hail them, and let's find out what's going on."

The chief nodded and went for a handheld radio. When he returned, he pressed the transmit button and spoke into the microphone. He finished and waited. Moments later, the radio

75

crackled and a neutral voice answered.

"Yes? Over."

"Who is this? Over."

"The captain of the vessel at the dock. Over."

"Right. But who are you? Over."

A pause. "I represent a collective that has business with your new leader. Is he there yet? Over."

Snake snatched the radio from the chief's hand. "This is Snake. What do you want? Over."

Another pause, this one longer. A different voice emanated from the two-way. "My name is Lassiter. We had an arrangement with Magnus. I understand you're now in charge. It's imperative that we meet with you. Over."

"Who's we?" Snake snapped, and then remembered to finish the transmission and release the button. "Over."

"Would you like to come aboard and have a tour of the boat? I can assure you it will be worth your time. I prefer not to discuss confidential business over the open airwaves. Over."

The security chief exchanged a glance with Snake, who had just been blindsided. If he refused to go aboard, he would look like a coward and lose face with his men, many of whom in the vicinity had heard the exchange. If he did board, and it was a trap, he could be killed, and the force on the boat could dictate terms to the leaderless Crew. Snake bit his lower lip as he considered his options and then raised the radio to his lips.

"Show yourself, and I'll meet you at the gangplank. Over."

"Perfect. Over."

Snake turned to his chief. "If I go for my pistol or if they try anything with me, hit them with everything you have. Put a sniper with a Barrett on whoever shows himself, and take him out at the first sign of trouble."

"Are you sure about this?"

"They came all the way here to see me. I'm curious who they are and what they want."

"It could be a setup."

"Look at those guns. If they wanted to blow us to pieces, they could. Doesn't sound like it, does it?"

"Let me go with you."

"Fine."

Snake pushed past the line of armed Crew fighters and made his way along the jetty, the chief behind him with his Kalashnikov at the ready, as though the 7.62mm rounds would do anything but bounce off the warship's thick steel armor like hail off a sidewalk. When he reached the gangplank, he squinted against the sunlight. At the top of the ramp, a solitary figure in a lightweight blue suit stepped onto the gangplank and began the long trip down to the dock.

"I don't like this," the chief whispered from behind Snake.

"He looks like he's unarmed. Back off."

The chief stood his ground, about to protest, and Snake raised his hand halfway while keeping his eyes on the approaching figure. "I said back off. That's an order."

The security head nodded and moved out of earshot, and Snake waited as the figure neared. A Caucasian man in his forties with thinning straw-colored hair approached him with his hand outstretched. "Snake? I'm Lassiter. Sorry to hear Magnus is no longer with us."

Snake shook hands with the improbable apparition, noting that his suit looked new. His skin was bronzed, but not like that of someone accustomed to being outside for work – more the leisure tan of the prosperous and well fed.

"You knew Magnus?" Snake asked.

Lassiter nodded. "I mentioned we had an agreement. We're anxious to continue it with you. That's what brings me to Houston."

"Who are you with?"

"A group that doesn't toss its name around."

"You're going to have to do better than that. Who are you, and why do you want to meet with me?"

Lassiter sighed, as though disappointed in an errant schoolboy's inadequate answer, and nodded once. When he spoke, his voice was so soft Snake had to strain to hear. "We need you to understand how things work. As to who I am, suffice it to say that I'm someone who can commandeer one of the few warships on the seas for a personal errand and who can burn thousands of gallons of precious diesel to meet with you. Figure it out. I represent power, and power has come to Houston to cut a deal." Lassiter paused, watching Snake to ensure he was absorbing his words. "Now come aboard, and I'll show you around while we talk."

Snake shook his head. "No way."

Lassiter's eyes narrowed ever so slightly. "Two ways this goes down. Either you come aboard and hear me out, or we level Houston and there's nothing left of you within the hour. You seem smart. I trust you'll make the right choice."

"I asked you who you are. I want an answer. Are you the government?"

The trace of a smile played across Lassiter's face. "There is no such animal anymore, at least not in the sense you're thinking. No, think of us as the influence behind the throne, if that helps. A loose collection of the interested who hold the power of life and death over you, and everyone else we choose."

"That's not an answer."

"It's the best I can do, other than to say that it's obvious Magnus didn't share his knowledge of us with you, which is heartening. That was part of the arrangement."

"Riddles," Snake spat. "Last time I ask. Who are you?"

"Let's just say it's comforting to see you using one of our symbols tattooed on your head. Now follow me – this heat is stifling, and we have important matters to discuss."

Lassiter spun and walked back up the gangplank, leaving a stunned Snake staring at his back. The man didn't turn around to see whether he was obeying, and Snake hesitated for only a moment before following him up to the deck, waving the shooter off, numb from the obvious import of Lassiter's words.

Chapter 16

Once on the deck of the destroyer, Snake hesitated in the sunlight, reluctant to follow any further. Lassiter looked annoyed when he heard the Crew leader's footsteps fall silent and slowly turned toward him.

"You're...you're Illuminati?" Snake stammered.

Lassiter's expression darkened. "We go by many names. It's not advisable to mention most of them."

"Then...you're real. I mean, you exist."

"A network of like-minded folks who influence events so they turn out for the best? There have been many such groups throughout history. The wonder is that so many believed it impossible that we might be real."

"But I thought – I mean – you know, that it was more rumor and urban legend than anything."

"Magnus knew better." Lassiter paused. "The best trick the devil ever played was convincing humanity he didn't exist. That's a bit overblown, but there is much merit to remaining in the shadows."

"Was Magnus one of you?"

"Membership in our club is confidential."

"So he was? He's dead, so it doesn't matter."

Lassiter frowned. "We know he's dead. That's why we're here. To have some face time with you and come to an agreement."

"About what?"

"Magnus was helping us. In return, we helped him. It was a simple transaction at its core." Lassiter shaded his eyes from the sun. "Now let's get out of the heat. We can continue our discussion in the air conditioning."

"You expect me to just follow you in?"

"Why wouldn't you? Or more accurately, do you not grasp that you don't have a choice?" Lassiter sized him up. "Look, if we wanted to kill you, you'd already be dead. A sniper round. Or I could have had a latex mold on my hand coated with a cutaneous poison that would stop your heart in less than a minute. There are infinite ways to end a life. But you're more valuable to us alive, so relax. We're going to make you the offer of a lifetime. Now let's go. I don't have all day."

Snake bristled at Lassiter's tone but understood he was in no position to argue. And he believed every word the man said – if he'd wanted Snake dead, he already would have been.

They entered the ship, mounted the stairs, and stopped at an empty officer's lounge. Lassiter took a seat and savored the arctic blast of the air conditioning from an overhead grid and then offered Snake a drink. Snake declined, and Lassiter invited Snake to sit across from him at the table while he blotted his brow with a white cloth handkerchief from the breast pocket of his suit jacket. Snake did as asked, and Lassiter sat forward.

"Magnus was helping us with the vaccine. I can't underscore to you the importance of having sole control over it or our disappointment that he wasn't successful in eradicating Shangri-La. As long as it exists in any form, it's a threat to us, which means it's a threat to our allies – the Crew being one of our most important ones."

"What's it to you? I mean, if others get a vaccine?"

"It isn't in our best interests to have competing variants out there. Diminishes our negotiating power with other groups."

"What other groups?"

"What remains of foreign governments. Other warlords like yourself. Take your pick."

Snake looked around the lounge, which appeared to be in pristine shape. "Where did you get the fuel to run this thing?"

"We have access to refining capability, as well as the know-how to operate and maintain the vessel."

"Where are you based?"

"A number of places."

"I've heard rumors of underground cities with power and water."

"There's usually an element of truth to persistent stories."

"Then you have a headquarters?"

Lassiter sat back. "Snake, here's the deal. We'll help you solidify your hold on the Crew, as well as its territory. We'll provide you with an advisor, who will get you anything you need – although frankly you already have huge tracts of territory, so it's more likely to be guidance that you're lacking than resources. We helped Magnus obtain most of what he had, and we'll assist you as well. In return, we expect you to help us."

"Wait. You worked with Magnus to get his territory?"

"We heard of his interest in our philosophy and decided that there was a synergy there; so, yes, we did. We advised him on how to overcome any resistance, what boundaries to draw that would be sustainable, how to control the territory once he had it, and so on." Lassiter smirked. "Did you really believe he could have achieved all that on his own?"

"I always thought he did."

"Well, he had help." Lassiter paused. "Help we're prepared to offer you."

"What do you want in exchange?"

"How's your search for Shangri-La going?"

Snake looked away. "Slow. They've disappeared."

"Doesn't seem like you're putting much into finding them."

"What's the point? That was Magnus's thing, not mine. And he lost a decent chunk of our fighting force pursuing them."

"It's important that you locate them. You should make it your top priority."

"I have bigger problems at the moment."

"Ah. Yes. We've heard stirrings."

Snake's eyes darted to Lassiter's. "What have you heard?"

"Some of your hubs are no longer loyal."

Snake nodded. "New Orleans tried to assassinate me."

"And they're a formidable adversary."

"We can take them."

"But you haven't moved against them yet."

"I'm pretending I don't realize they were behind it or that they're shorting me every month."

Lassiter managed an approving smile. "Ah. A thinker. Take them by surprise. I like that."

"How do you know about them?"

"We have eyes everywhere. As your tattoo symbolizes." Lassiter shifted in his chair. "We'll give you gold with which to recruit mercenaries and to buy arms. We'll help you get one of the refineries operational so you can power your vehicles. We'll leave a top tactician with you to advise you on how best to deal with your mutiny. But you need to step up your efforts to locate Shangri-La, wherever it's moved, and wipe it from the earth."

"You can get the refinery working again? We've been trying for years."

Lassiter waved a hand as though such a thing were trivial. "I trust we have your full attention?"

Snake nodded. "What do you want me to do?"

Lassiter rose abruptly and walked to the door. "I'll be back with my man. His name is Zacharias. Zach. I'm sure you'll get along swimmingly."

Snake fidgeted, his head swimming with Lassiter's revelations about his secret group and the existence of not only a powerful force that had been responsible for Magnus's success, but limitless resources available to him. The man had spoken of gold as though discussing the weather, and brushed aside Snake's incredulousness at being able to restart a refinery as though it was self-evident that it was well within their capabilities. No wonder Magnus had been all-powerful and confident. With a group like that behind him, the sky was the limit.

A doubt nagged at Snake, though. If the Illuminati had the capability of bringing one of Houston's refineries back into operation, why hadn't they done so for Magnus?

The answer was obvious: because they hadn't had to in order to get what they wanted from him. Why give Magnus the ability to further expand his power if they wanted him as a regional player rather than a national one? They'd offered what was necessary and nothing more.

Lassiter reappeared with a bulldog of a man in tow, his face all planes, his steel gray hair cropped close to his head, and his unblinking eyes the color of lead. Lassiter introduced them and Zach's voice matched his appearance – gruff, a no-nonsense rasp that didn't waste a word.

"You mentioned gold?" Snake said, completing the introductions.

"That's right. We have a thousand one-ounce bars for you. Zach will arrange delivery to your headquarters," Lassiter said.

"Where are the rest of your men? I didn't see any crew."

Lassiter smiled. "They're giving us our privacy."

Zach turned his wedge of a head to Lassiter. "I'm going with him?"

"That's right. Help him however you can."

Zach nodded, his expression unreadable. Snake cleared his throat and eyed him. "You know where our headquarters is?"

"I'll find it. Have a horse I can use?" Zach asked.

"Sure. How long will it take to get me the gold?"

Zach held his stare. "You'll have it by day's end."

"And the refinery?" Snake pressed.

Lassiter fielded the question. "That will take some time. But don't worry. We'll make some of our fuel from the ship's stores available. More than sufficient for your immediate needs."

Snake's eyes darted around the room. "When are you leaving?"

"Once Zach indicates we don't need to remain any longer."

Snake pondered the response for several moments and angled his head at the door. "Are we done?"

"Yes. Kindly ensure that none of your men intrude on us while we're in port. My crew will stay on board, so all we require is enough of a guard that we aren't disturbed."

Snake nodded. "Anything else?"

"Zach will keep us abreast of your progress and needs." Lassiter hesitated. "Thank you for coming. Don't forget to make locating Shangri-La your top priority."

"You can bet on it."

Lassiter offered a frosty smile that never reached his eyes. "We are."

Chapter 17

After fifteen days of hard riding, Lucas's group was finally nearing Tulsa. The area they'd covered over the last few days had been surprisingly lush and green after the unvaried flatness of the high plains prairie they'd left behind. They'd spent the night under the stars, glad that the rain that had plagued them on and off the last week had abated, leaving the swell of the hills bursting with color and life.

They had skirted the inhabited settlements: Amarillo, a shadow of its former self, and Oklahoma City, the northern limit of the Crew's territory and so to be avoided at all costs. Travelers along the stretch they'd negotiated had been few and far between, and on the three occasions they'd spotted dust clouds on the horizon, they'd gone to ground and waited for the parties to pass at a safe distance.

By Lucas's reckoning, they would reach the compound by mid-afternoon, and if all went well, would be riding south toward Mississippi by evening, taking their time, posing as traders in the Crew territory and hoping that they went unchallenged in the outer reaches of the empire.

He had no firm plan for narrowing down whether Sierra's son had somehow survived the attack on the compound where he'd been living other than to make his way there and poke around. Perhaps there were people living nearby who'd heard about it or who could point them in the right direction. The alternatives grew increasingly unappealing as he went down the list, which included traveling into the belly of the beast and asking questions that would, without a doubt, have the Crew pursuing them within minutes.

The trip had been a monotonous plod across the high plains. Arnold had proved a hardy and resourceful traveling companion, though, as had Colt, George, and John, all serious men with enough trail time to avoid stupid mistakes that could get them killed. They'd kept two-hour watches throughout each night so everyone would be adequately rested as they made their way east beneath a sky as blue as the ocean.

They turned from the trail onto a ribbon of pavement, and after checking Arnold's ragged map, paused to rest and water the horses as Arnold took a bearing.

"This has got to be the road. Compound should be up another half dozen miles, no more," he said.

"Finally," Sierra said. "I was beginning to mistake the saddle for part of my anatomy."

"If we're lucky, we'll be able to re-provision and rest a couple of days before the next leg," Lucas said.

"No," Sierra countered. "I want to keep going."

His tone softened. "The horses need a break, Sierra. A day or two won't matter to us, but it will to them."

"It's already been months, Lucas."

"Which is why it won't change anything. They can't keep this up forever."

Sierra nodded, but he could tell she wasn't happy. He took her hand and pointed at the surrounding trees. "Leaves are turning," he said. She glanced at the red and orange leaves clinging to the branches with obvious disinterest.

"Probably snowing by now in Pagosa Springs," Colt observed.

"Hard to say," Arnold said. "We'll check in after we make the drop and I'll ask."

They continued riding toward Tulsa, and after another hour Colt slowed and eyed a sign by the side of a gravel drive that led to a walled collection of buildings a quarter mile away. "Barrelback Ranch. That's our place."

Lucas was the first to stop as they neared the compound's main gate. He eyed the open barrier and unslung his M4, switching the safety to three-round burst mode with his thumb as he scanned the perimeter wall. Arnold drew to a halt beside him and his eyes narrowed when he saw the gate.

"Might be trouble," he muttered, his AR-15 now in hand. The others followed suit, and they continued toward the opening at a cautious pace.

Sierra's hand flew to her mouth when they reached the gate, and she gasped and pointed to a body sprawled just inside. A vulture flapped from it, and three more took flight, clawing their way skyward before soaring away. Nobody spoke as Lucas dropped from his horse. Arnold joined him, and they edged slowly to the entrance, weapons at the ready.

The breeze shifted, and a wave of putrescence hit them with the force of a blow. Lucas's jaw clenched as he strode toward the gap, the odor of death unmistakable. Arnold's boots crunched against the gravel as they swept the area with their guns, searching for any sign of life.

They stopped at the gate and regarded the grounds, eyes flat, unmoved by the grisly vision before them. Dozens of bodies lay near the buildings: their torsos had been hacked open, and their skulls streaked with black blood. Their scalps were missing. Lucas walked toward the doorway of the largest structure and noted women and children among the dead, all mutilated in the same way. Bile rose sour in his throat as he took in the hellish tableau.

"Jesus God…" Arnold muttered, and Lucas nodded.

"Yeah. Bad as it gets."

Arnold toed a nearby body. "They haven't been dead that long. Probably last night, don't you think?"

Lucas took in a pair of tiny corpses discarded like trash by the entrance of what must have been a barn, the blood around them dried and hard. "Sounds about right."

They walked back to where Sierra was waiting outside the compound entrance with Colt and the others, their faces pale. "What is it, Lucas?" she asked.

"Stay here and watch the horses — make sure they don't run off. Colt, boys, we could use a hand."

"What happened?" Sierra repeated.

"Looks like someone attacked them. I want to search the buildings to make sure there are no survivors."

"How many?" George asked.

Lucas's deep frown told the story. "A bunch."

They returned to the interior of the compound and moved through the carnage to the main building, a sprawling ranch house of at least six thousand square feet. Inside was a disaster, and Lucas had a brief flashback to arriving at Hal's ranch only to find him dead and the place looted, the destruction as random and senseless as if a tornado had blown through it.

Half an hour later, they'd confirmed that everyone was dead. When they were through, they stood by the gate, gulping fresh air. The only sound was the low buzz of thousands of flies feasting on the remains and the occasional snort of one of the horses.

"Looks like they tried to hold off whoever did this," Arnold observed, touching one of hundreds of bullet scars pocking the mortar.

"Must have been a lot of attackers, most of the compound asleep," Lucas agreed. "They hit fast and hard and overwhelmed the sentries. Only way it makes sense."

"Some of the defenders tried to shoot it out once they were inside the walls."

"Those were the lucky ones," Colt said. "They died quickly."

"What do we do now?" George asked.

"Too many of them to cremate or bury," Arnold observed. "Whatever this was, it's a change of plans for us. We need to put some miles under our saddles or risk running into whoever did this."

"Timing's awful coincidental, don't you think?" Lucas asked.

Arnold nodded. "Yep."

"You think we might have a leak back at Pagosa Springs?" Colt asked softly.

Lucas shook his head. "Doubt it. Anyone who wanted to sell you out had their chance when Magnus attacked."

"Not necessarily."

Lucas's eyes narrowed. "Spit it out, Colt."

"The Loco – Luis – had just arrived. We know he was afraid of Magnus, but maybe he's interested in getting Pecos back for himself."

Lucas shook his head again. "I don't buy it."

"Then how could they have known about…this?"

Lucas shrugged. "That's a mystery."

"So what now?" George repeated.

Arnold kicked away a rock and sighed. "We need to find a radio so we can talk to Elliot and let him know what happened. This is his show."

Lucas retraced his steps to Sierra and the horses. He gave her a brief rundown on what they'd found, leaving out the worst of it. The skin of her face was tight as parchment by the time he finished and her eyes moist.

"Why, Lucas? Why the mutilation?" She didn't have to ask why the inhabitants had been killed. After five years living in the abyss, she accepted that there was no rhyme or reason to death – it was merely another regular visitor, like hunger, thirst, or rain.

"Don't know." He sighed. "We'll head to Tulsa and look for a trading post with a shortwave."

"And then?"

He stared off at the main road and adjusted his hat so it better shaded his eyes. When he looked back at Sierra, his face was expressionless.

"Not my call."

"This changes everything, Lucas," she whispered.

"I know."

"We should just bail now. We did our part. This isn't our problem."

Lucas looked back at where Arnold was speaking with the men in low tones and shook his head. "Tempting. But that wasn't the deal."

"We got the vaccine to where we were supposed to deliver it. I'd say that was the deal."

Lucas didn't want to argue. He walked over to Tango and patted the big horse's neck affectionately before swinging into the saddle. "Let's get this over with. Time's a-wasting."

She eyed him uncomprehendingly and then her shoulders slumped with resignation.

"Do you think we're safe, Lucas? From whoever did this?"

"Seems that way. At least for now."

Arnold led the men back toward their horses, and Sierra pulled herself onto Nugget with a wince. "I hope you know what you're doing," she said.

Lucas caught Arnold's dark expression and shrugged. "For now, playing it by ear."

"Good way to get killed."

Lucas couldn't fight her on that. "I know."

Chapter 18

Pagosa Springs, Colorado

The lights in the community center dimmed and flickered for the umpteenth time that day, and Elliot glowered at them like they were failing just to spite him. Michael clapped a hand on his shoulder in commiseration and turned his attention to Craig, who'd arrived five minutes before to report on a problem at the geothermal plant.

"Generator's failing, Doc," the engineer said, hat in hand.

"Same as last time?"

Craig shook his head. "Worse. I jury-rigged it last time. That held for a while. But ever since that pump failed, it's been operating on fewer than it was designed for. It's just a matter of time until that damages some of the other components."

"Is it overheating?" Michael asked.

"It's more complicated than that. These were experimental units, not final designs. They were never intended to provide round-the-clock power like we've been drawing."

"Would shutting it down during the day help?"

"Maybe for a while, but the basic problem is that the plant needs some parts replaced, and we don't have them."

"They must have had spares," Michael said.

"You'd have thought so. But so far I haven't found any."

Elliot reached for his hat and walked to the door. "You looked everywhere?"

"All the places I'd have expected them to be."

"Let's go have a peek. Michael, you can lend a hand, too. Three sets of eyes are better than one."

They made their way down the main street and crossed over the river swollen from the increasingly frequent rains. The bite of the cold was sharp in their lungs, and steam puffed from their mouths with every breath. At the door of the plant, Craig was reaching for the handle when an anguished scream from inside pierced the silence.

Craig heaved the door open and ran to where Miles, his assistant, was lying on the concrete floor in a spreading pool of steaming water, his hands on his face, every exposed area of his skin already beginning to blister with third-degree burns. A scalding stream of water gushed from one of the pipe connections, and Craig leapt toward it, twisted the shutoff valve closed, and then powered down the big turbine two stories below them.

Elliot and Michael stood stunned by the door for a moment and then rushed to Miles, their faces grim. As a physician, Elliot knew there was little he could do other than get the man to the hospital so Sarah could manage his pain and the inevitable shock that would follow burns of that magnitude. Elliot did a quick examination of Miles's face as he quivered like a beached fish, noting the man's eyes swelling shut. The steam had literally cooked his head, and it would be a miracle if he lived.

"Let's get him to the hospital," Elliot said. They lifted Miles carefully by his arms and dragged him to the door.

"Just when we could use ice, of course, it isn't snowing yet," Michael grumbled, and Craig frowned.

"I'll get a horse. We can't carry him all the way there."

"Be quick about it," Elliot warned. "He's already fading."

Craig showed up a minute later with an equipment cart pulled by a palomino stallion, and they lifted Miles gingerly onto the wooden bed. Elliot turned to the engineer, who was puffing from the sudden exertion.

"Ride as fast as you can. I'll stay here until you can get back." Elliot glanced up at the sky. "Warn Sarah that there won't be any power tonight, so prepare the candles and torches."

"Don't touch anything," Craig warned.

"I won't."

The engineer rolled away, leaving Elliot and Michael to consider their next step. The geothermal generator was a small one, an experimental take on an age-old concept: to use the earth's naturally heated water or steam to drive a turbine, creating electricity much like a dam, except using the pressure from the steam to drive the turbine rather than rushing water. It was reliable and stable under normal circumstances, but as the system degraded with time, the lack of replacement parts had taken its toll, and it was apparent that they were facing a significant problem. When winter hit, they'd need power to survive; and at the rate they were going, there would be none available.

Elliot eyed the system of piping and pumps that carried the superheated water from the hot spring beneath his feet to the pressure tank that drove the turbine, and his expression darkened. What would have been an annoyance in the summer months could be an existential threat to their survival after the first snowfall.

Elliot paced back and forth near the entrance, mulling over their options as Michael sat quietly, his eyes on the pipes. They were both deep in thought when Craig returned, his face grim.

"Sarah says it's bad," he reported.

"I know," Elliot said. "I could tell by looking at him."

"If he survives, he'll be blind, and he'll look like a science experiment."

"Poor bastard."

"And he'll lose some fingers. Not that it's likely. She says she doesn't think he'll make it to morning."

Elliot exhaled noisily. "I'm sorry, Craig."

"Me too." He gestured to the pumps. "And now we've got this mess to deal with. Looks like one of the seals ruptured."

"Where have you looked for parts already? We can eliminate those areas and concentrate on the most likely."

Craig described his search, and they each took a surrounding building. When that yielded no results, Michael asked Craig whether the technicians who'd monitored the system had an office elsewhere.

"I don't know. But we can look."

An hour later it was apparent they weren't going to have any luck, and they headed back to the station and studied the generator with dour expressions. Craig rubbed a weary hand across his brow and eyed Elliot and Michael.

"I can probably cannibalize some other equipment and make this limp along, but we're on borrowed time. We need a permanent solution, or there are going to be more failures."

"Can the machine shop make you any of the parts you need?"

"I have them working on a few, but you know how that goes. Trial and error. These are precision pieces; you get one thing even slightly off and they won't function." Craig surveyed the damage again and shook his head. "I'll mop this up and see what I can cobble together, but I'm not hopeful. We're going to need more than duct tape and chewing gum to keep this running through the winter. And you know Murphy's Law."

Elliot nodded. "If I didn't, this is one hell of a reminder." He glanced at Michael and then back to Craig. "Do what you can, and we'll put on our thinking caps. There's got to be a solution. We just aren't seeing it."

Michael snapped his fingers. "What about using the river water to drive a turbine? Wouldn't that work?"

Craig shook his head. "The problem is you need a lot of pressure to turn one of any size – assuming you could build one designed for that. A river won't do it. You'd need a reservoir, and then the pressure of the water backed up, released through a narrow gap, would drive it. The river's current alone won't do it. Sorry."

"Windmills?" Michael tried again.

"Sure. In theory. But where are we going to get a bunch of wind turbines to generate power? Not to mention the storage problem. See, with geothermal, you have power twenty-four seven because you always have steam. With wind? You need a really windy area, and it isn't that windy here."

"Worst case, couldn't we use wood to heat water, and the steam could drive the turbine?"

Craig opened a door and removed a mop. "Great solution. But the problem isn't that we don't have a limitless supply of hot water, Michael. So that would be perfect for a different issue."

Elliot touched Michael's arm, reacting to the annoyance that was creeping into Craig's voice. "Come on. Let's leave Craig to his work." Elliot nodded to the engineer. "Radio me if you need anything. We're going over to the hospital."

"Will do."

Chapter 19

Lucas led the group along a trail that paralleled the highway to Tulsa, periodically sweeping the landscape with his binoculars. He hadn't seen any riders or travelers on the road, which struck him as ominous this close to a sizeable metro area – generally, if people avoided travel near a hub, it was because safety was an issue. In the post-apocalyptic world, many were nomadic by necessity, either fleeing danger or pursuing opportunity, and Tulsa was large enough that he would have expected at least a little traffic.

"Why didn't the Crew take over Tulsa, too?" he asked Sierra in a low voice. "It's not that far from Oklahoma City, and then they'd have almost the whole state."

"I've never been to either place, but when I was in Dallas, I heard that there wasn't anything worth taking over. They don't devote men to an area if there's nothing to steal. Sort of like Pecos – not worth their time."

"Makes sense."

"They don't do anything that isn't about power or profit."

Arnold grunted from behind them. "Kind of like the last government."

Lucas chuckled humorlessly. Even though he'd worked for the Texas Rangers, he hadn't been blind to the inequity of the society he'd sworn to protect, where oil billionaires drove past tent cities of the homeless, insulated from unpleasantness by bulletproof glass and run-flat tires. There had been a long-running joke among his peers that if your skin was brown and you robbed a bank, you went to prison; whereas if you were white, you likely owned a bank that robbed everyone around it, and they made you the governor.

Of course that was a wild exaggeration, but it had been difficult not to see the results of a criminal justice system that was operated for profit, where the prison population was used as effective slave labor, and the vast majority of those incarcerated were minorities. Not much had changed from the days when Jim Crow laws targeted minority populations, only victimless crimes like drug possession replaced racism as the pretense for locking a large percentage of the targeted demographic behind bars.

In the old days, lawmen like his father had reacted to crimes that had victims – violence or property crime. Somewhere along the line that had shifted to where most of the arrests were for violations of laws where there was no victim, only a perp. It had skewed the role of the police to where they no longer protected and served, but rather arrested to improve their career record, and often the easiest targets were those at the bottom of the socioeconomic scale – which usually meant people of color. He'd encountered it every day on the job, and it was one of the aspects of law enforcement that he had been glad to put behind him. Now everyone was the same, discrimination a luxury few could afford in a survival-mode world where starvation and disease were greater concerns than the color of someone's skin.

Tulsa's skyline came into view as they neared, but there were still no people in evidence. The usual carcasses of rusting vehicles abandoned on the roads were everywhere, as were the ruins of homes looted in the early days before everything had run dry, but no signs of life.

"You'd think there would be farms or something, huh?" Colt said.

Lucas didn't respond. The whole area was sending a shiver of anxiety up his spine, but he couldn't put his finger on why. He was no stranger to devastation or danger – so why was the alarm going off?

Arnold pointed ahead at several columns of smoke rising from within the city limits. "At least we know somebody's home."

They fell quiet as they neared a suburb that had been flattened – by a tornado, Lucas guessed, based on the destruction: only slabs remained on many of the lots, the houses blown to the four corners.

Once they had run the gauntlet of wreckage, they arrived at the edge of the city, where three men with filthy hair and grimy skin, dressed in clothes little more than rags and holding weapons as dirty as their shirts, manned a sandbagged guard outpost on the western side of the Arkansas River.

"Whoa, there, cowboy. Hold up," one of them called. The others raised their weapons, and even at a distance Lucas could make out that their arms were so thin they were nearly skeletal. "Where you think you're going?"

"We're looking for a trading post. Something with a radio," Lucas said.

"Yeah? Where you coming from?"

"Texas."

"Why you coming this direction? Nothing here but misery, and I hear tell it gets worse the further east you go."

"Maybe so," Lucas said agreeably. "But it can't be any worse than Texas these days."

The men took in Sierra with hungry looks, and then the lead sentry's eyes narrowed. "You gang affiliated?"

"No. Just looking for a trading post."

"What you got to trade?"

"That's between me and the trader, isn't it?"

"Don't get all uppity. Just curious," the man snapped.

"Weapons and ammo. The usual."

The man's stare roamed over Tango and settled on Lucas's M4. "Nice gun you got there."

"Thanks."

"Horse looks like a winner, too. You gonna trade either of them?"

Lucas shook his head. "Not likely."

"Keep your eyes on him. Way things are these days, lot of folks would eat him just as soon as ride him."

"I intend to."

Lucas waited for the guard to decide whether to let them pass, having exhausted his questions and having no interest in discussing the weather. The man coughed a phlegmy hack and stepped back. "Well, come on in, then. It's your funeral."

"Anything we should know? Any rules?"

The sentries exchanged a glance and then laughed, treating Lucas to a view of rotting teeth and blackened gums. "Not really. You kill anyone, better have a good reason or enough to buy your way out of it. Other than that, you're on your own."

"Where's the nearest trading post?" Arnold asked, his voice flat.

"Over by the university. Can't miss it."

"Does it have a radio?"

"Did last time I was up that way."

"How do we get there?" Lucas asked.

"Cross the bridge, and then head east on Eleventh Street. It'll be on your left a ways up."

"How do we know when we're at Eleventh Street?" Sierra asked.

"It's the street right before that hospital tower," he said, pointing to a gleaming building in the near distance. "Still got street signs. But you might want to put on a jacket or something. We don't get a lot of young women as good-lookin' as you these days." The man offered an oily grin. "Wouldn't want to see you come to a bad end."

Lucas led them across the long span over a rushing brown and frothy river, and they found themselves on a broad freeway clogged with junked cars. The horses picked their way between the vehicles until they reached an off-ramp near the base of the hospital, which they veered down before finding Eleventh Street.

They rode past a pair of men with long, matted hair and faces spectral from malnutrition, who were shambling down the cracked sidewalk, pushing a rusting shopping cart filled with detritus. They looked up at the riders with the uncurious eyes of those close to death, their skin yellow and hanging loose from their skulls, and then resumed their task.

Sierra sidled closer to Lucas and whispered over the clomp of the horses' hooves, "Tell me that isn't creepy."

"This whole place is."

They passed several more pedestrians, all obviously without anything to their names, and reached an intersection where a man with a long black coat and a shabby top hat was reciting biblical verse in a loud voice to a crowd of none. When he spotted them approaching, he brightened and held up a soiled piece of paper. "Woe be to those who fail to recognize the sign! The Savior has been sent, but we have rejected our salvation, for which we are now paying! We brought this upon ourselves!" he announced, waving the paper like a talisman.

Lucas ignored the man and continued past. On the next corner, another preacher was offering his spin on the end-times to a small gathering of women and children. Sierra leaned toward Lucas. "Awful religious, aren't they?"

"Maybe this is the district or something."

"Neither Dallas or Lubbock were like this."

"These people look like they're starving. How was it in Texas?" Colt asked from behind her.

"It was bad, but nothing like this."

"Maybe that's your answer," Arnold said. "When you're out of hope and you have nothing to eat, suddenly even the worst sinner becomes a believer."

Lucas nodded. "Could be."

A child, no more than six or seven, spotted them and ran toward Lucas with a pamphlet. The boy looked feverish, his face a patchwork of scabbed sores, and Lucas recoiled when the child tried to thrust the paper into his hand. Seeing that Lucas wasn't going to take it, he held it to Sierra, who waved him away unsuccessfully. When he didn't give up, she reluctantly took it from him and he scurried back to the preacher, who looked like a mad hermit with his gray beard and dreadlocked hair, now gesticulating feverishly at the sky.

Lucas shook his head and sighed at the spectacle of so much misery. Sierra interrupted his introspection, her voice alarmed.

"Lucas!" she hissed from beside him.

"What?" he demanded, reaching for his pistol.

"Look at this."

He relaxed. "Look at what?"

"The paper that kid gave me."

"I'm a little busy right now, trying to keep an eye out so we don't get killed. Why don't you read it to me?" he said.

"You need to see it."

"Not now, Sierra. What is it?"

"It's…it's a picture of Eve. From Lubbock."

"We know they were searching for you. That's no surprise."

"No. But it's not that."

"Then what is it?"

"It says she's the…that Eve's the second coming."

Chapter 20

New Orleans, Louisiana

It was the dead of night when the destroyer idled to a stop in Lake Borgne several hundred yards from the distressed brick ruins of Beauregard's Castle, near the mouth of the channel that led to Shell Beach and its private marina, now a black hole in the shoreline. Lightning flashed within a phalanx of plum-colored clouds over the Gulf of Mexico. The air was heavy with the smell of ozone, the wetlands beyond the cut redolent of brine and decaying vegetation as the big ship drifted, its huge engines nearly silent against a background of distant thunder.

Snake watched while four tenders dropped to the water. The crew had foregone the electric winches and was lowering them manually to cut down on noise. When the boats were floating by the ship's hull, another group lowered the gangplank, at the end of which was a platform large enough for one of the tenders to tie off while loading.

"That's it. Move," he said, and the first of his fighters tromped down the ramp, bristling with weapons, their faces blacked out.

Snake had done his homework on New Orleans' defenses and learned that nobody watched any of the seaward approaches; if his force could land without attracting attention, they could be in the city center before anyone knew they were there. The warlord who ran the area was holed up in the Garden District with a retinue of twenty guards and had easily five hundred men in his fighting group, which made him a formidable threat. But Snake's best estimate had been that most of those fighters would be loyal to the Crew when pressed, especially if Snake could achieve the coup he'd planned before the sun rose.

If all went well, the New Orleans contingent would awaken to their leader deposed and Snake directing affairs until he could appoint a replacement. His hope was to avoid a frontal confrontation and present the New Orleans faction with a fait accompli – a lesson that the all-seeing eye of Providence wasn't simply a metaphor.

If successful, it would chill any further ideas of rebellion in the ranks and seal his place at the top of the pyramid.

Zach had been key in developing the plan and the ship critical to avoiding telegraphing their moves, which would have translated into a long and bloody campaign with Snake's men at a disadvantage, paying a heavy toll in blood for every yard. It was the Illuminati fixer who'd come up with the idea of transporting several hundred of Snake's gunmen via ship with no advance notice and no warning of where they were going.

Approaching by sea had bypassed the checkpoints along the roads connecting Houston with New Orleans, so there would be no radio alert to the warlord from a patrol.

The only negative was that they would have to travel the twelve miles from the shore to the city on foot, but compared to the value of surprise, that was a trivial concern. They'd calculated that most of his men would survive a skirmish at the warlord's mansion, thus leaving a formidable presence to halt any revolt against his authority by the local Crew.

The first tender filled and putted toward the inlet while the second lashed itself to the platform and the loading continued. By the time the last boat had left, the first one had returned for a second load, and soon the men were assembled near the remains of the marina, night vision goggles in place as the inky sky flashed with celestial pyrotechnics that announced the approaching squall.

Zach and Snake led the column along the rutted road that stretched to the city. A halo glow over Bourbon Street gave evidence that some things were perennial even after the end of the world. The bars and brothels there were a major source of income for the Crew and a big part of the reason Snake needed to assert control personally rather than allowing his subordinates to handle matters with a blade through the heart while the warlord slumbered. If he didn't put in an appearance and quell any speculation that he wasn't equipped to lead, his rule would be short and filled with uprisings. If New Orleans led a charge of independence from Houston, that would undoubtedly be followed by the eastern part of the state, as well as Arkansas.

Snake picked up the pace from a march to a trot as the first sheets of warm rain blew across the marsh, dimpling the lake and clouding the way forward. Soon his breath was burning in his chest, but he didn't slow. After forty-five minutes, he paused and announced a rest stop, and Zach joined him beneath the droop of a bald cypress tree, whose branches only marginally sheltered them from the downpour.

"How far do you think we've come?" Snake asked, trying not to sound fatigued.

"Maybe…four miles? So about a third of the way."

"Might be a good idea to take the rest of the way slower. No point in tiring the men out."

"Probably prudent. We have many hours before daybreak."

"And that way we'll hit them in the early hours of the morning."

"Good thinking," Zach agreed without a trace of irony, his face unreadable beneath the black face paint.

The New Orleans warlord had commandeered a massive antebellum mansion near Lafayette Cemetery and used it as his weekend headquarters as well as his home. The men resumed a faster pace once they crossed the St. Claude Avenue Bascule bridge and were within the city limits, giving the raucous Bourbon Street district a wide berth, the streets to the north of it dark as pitch. The rain beat steadily as the last of the storm blew past, masking the sound of their boots on the pavement.

Because of the inclement weather and the late hour, nobody was on the streets, and Snake was heartened to note they were closing on the mansion by three in the morning. As if by divine intervention, the downpour stopped as they neared the cemetery, and Snake slowed and had a whispered discussion with his general before motioning to Zach to remain behind as the fighters got into position.

Zach checked his watch, its face glowing in the darkness, and leaned into Snake as the men hurried past.

"They need to knock this out fast, or it'll be fighting street-to-street when reinforcements show up," he warned.

"I told Derek. He's my top commander now that Magnus's generals are toast."

Zach's tone was noncommittal. "He seems competent."

"He was a marine before he was sentenced to life. Lieutenant. Smart and ruthless."

"What did he do to get locked up?"

Snake grinned "More like what didn't he do."

"Ah. A free spirit."

"Brought the war home with him."

Zach nodded, as though speaking from personal experience. "It can happen."

"You saw action?"

Zach didn't answer. Instead, he peered down the street to their right. "Is he going to encircle the target?"

"I leave the tactics to him. He's the one with the combat expertise."

"Let's hope he does, because otherwise he could get flanked."

Snake's men vanished into the shadows, and he watched through his night vision goggles as they fanned out. Derek made a curt hand gesture, two fingers directing one group down the sidewalk toward the looming white bulk of the antique mansion, and the other to the intersection to make their way around to the back, and they split off.

Silence descended on the area, and Snake held his breath. He didn't have long to wait; less than a minute later, a shout echoed down the wet street, and the night exploded with automatic rifle fire as the warlord's guards spotted the attacking force.

Snake's gunmen returned fire, and the rattle of AKs was deafening, at least a hundred of his fighters unleashing hell on earth at the massive home. Wood chips flew from the siding as bullets slammed into it, and Zach shook his head.

"Looks like it's built out of brick. The siding's cosmetic. This is going to be harder than we thought."

Orange blossoms lit the night from the mansion windows, immediately followed by hundreds of answering rounds from the attack force, and then a grenade detonated on the front porch, blowing most of the structure to pieces and blasting the entry door to splinters. More shooting chattered from the house as at least twenty of Snake's shooters rushed the wrought-iron front gate, firing as they ran. The remainder hung back and laid down covering fire.

Three of the lead men collapsed at the gate as defending rounds found home, and then another grenade exploded in a blinding orange flash by the nearest ground-floor window, silencing the shooting that had cut them down. The rest heaved the gate open and flooded the grounds. Another blast detonated upstairs – Derek had engaged with his RPGs, shutting down the defensive fire with a single projectile.

The fighters continued across the front lawn and poured into the house, and Snake and Zach heard bursts of shooting from inside as the Crew gunmen moved from room to room. The volleys continued for several minutes, and then silence enveloped the street again, the battle over as suddenly as it had started.

Snake rose from where he'd been crouching and made his way down the street, and Zach followed, rifle in hand. When they reached the house, Derek was issuing orders to his men, preparing them for the counterattack that was sure to follow as the warlord's loyal circle arrived.

Two fighters emerged from the mansion with a wounded man between them, his white shirt soaked with blood from a stomach wound and crimson streaming down his paunchy face from a gash in his forehead. They dragged him to Snake, who sneered at the warlord contemptuously.

"Well, well, well. The mighty Victor," Snake said. "You don't look so good. Gut shot, huh? I hear that's an ugly way to go."

The warlord's eyes widened when he recognized Snake's voice.

Snake flipped his goggles up and waited until his eyes adjusted before continuing.

"Your assassin botched the job."

"You…" Victor managed with a wince.

"Yes, me. You really thought I'd let you come at me like that and there wouldn't be consequences? You must be stupider than you look."

Victor surprised Snake by spitting blood in his face. Snake rubbed the blob away and turned to Derek. "Hang him by his arms from the streetlight. His carcass can serve as a reminder to anyone else who wants to cross me of what happens when they try. Leave him up until the birds peck his eyes out. Let his men see how he shit himself as he died – the mighty Victor, now just another piece of garbage for the buzzards."

Derek nodded and gave a command. The pair dragged the warlord to an iron pole and were lashing his wrists when shooting echoed from down the block. Zach touched Snake's arm.

"Take cover. Round two's getting underway."

More shooting decided the matter, and Snake darted across the street to the cemetery, where dozens of his fighters waited quietly for Victor's men to show themselves, the night's brutal work not even close to done.

Three hours later, the sun rose over a street slick with blood. Derek had taken command of the area, and the bodies of the warlord's loyal entourage lay strewn like cordwood in the gutters. Zach and Snake strode back to the mansion. The stink of death rose from the pavement like toxic mist, the long night of death over, but Snake's even longer day of reckoning only about to begin.

"Think we're in the clear now?" he asked.

Zach nodded. "The next forty-eight hours will tell, but I'd guess so. Nobody in their right mind is going to want to wind up like these slobs."

"So we stay for only two days?"

Zach shook his head. "No. I'd remain for at least a week, maybe longer. You need to show that you're in complete control and don't

RUSSELL BLAKE

have to rush back to Houston to maintain your hold."

Snake absorbed the words and nodded. "You'll stay with me, of course?"

Zach favored Snake with an equable expression. "Of course."

Chapter 21

Tulsa, Oklahoma

"The second coming?" Lucas repeated. "Don't tell Eve, or you'll never get her to eat her vegetables."

"Lucas, I'm serious. That's what it says."

"I don't doubt it. People get all kinds of crazy ideas in their heads."

"They made a pamphlet, Lucas. That's pretty serious, in a place where everyone's starving."

"Let me see it," he said, his voice resigned. Sierra handed the paper to him and he skimmed the poorly written tract, every third word misspelled or in all capital letters and exclamation points substituting for any other punctuation. When he finished, he laughed. "Like I said. Crazy."

"But why would they put her picture on it? Why her?"

"Could be because the Crew circulated the photo, so it was one of the few they could find? It's not like they have computers in the nuthouse."

"I don't know," she said doubtfully. "Someone went to a lot of trouble."

"When things go bad, people latch onto anything. Whoever came up with this was probably looking for a way to seem important. Starting your own spin on a religion isn't a bad bet, especially when the shit's hit the fan. So they tweaked the Bible a little, inserted someone the Crew was looking for, invented a reason why, and presto, suddenly they're important. Maybe people are even offering them food and drink. Tithing them. Wouldn't be the first time."

"You're probably right. Still, you have to admit it's weird."

"No question."

He folded the pamphlet and slid it into a pocket of his flak jacket – you never threw anything away lest you find yourself needing it later, and paper was in short supply. Then Lucas picked up the pace, and they continued up the street until they arrived at the university grounds. Lucas looked around and settled on a building across the street, where a hand-painted sign with "Trading Post" scrawled across it in childish script hung above a blown-out storefront with steel bars running across it. Four toughs with rifles loitered in the shade outside, watching them ride up.

Lucas and Arnold dismounted and nodded to the men. "Afternoon, gents," Arnold said. "We're looking for a working shortwave radio we can use. There one inside?"

A large man with a bald head and a face that looked like it had been on the receiving end of a shotgun blast looked them up and down before speaking. "He rents time on it. Owner's name is Rob."

Arnold adjusted his hat. "Mind if we go in?"

"It's a free country. But you got to leave the artillery with us."

Lucas shrugged. "Here you go." He handed the big guard his M4 and Kimber and waited as Arnold did the same.

The man inspected the Kimber appreciatively and waved them into the building.

The interior of the shop was dark, and it was obvious from the wares on display that trading in Tulsa wasn't a way to get rich. They approached a counter at the back of the store and stopped when another big man, this one with the distinctive facial tattoos affected by the Crew, materialized through a door in the rear.

"What do you boys need?" the man asked.

"Heard you have a radio," Arnold explained.

"That's right. Costs one round per minute to use it."

Arnold fished three bullets from his flak jacket. "Let's try three for starters."

The man grinned, revealing gold front teeth. "Name's Rob."

"Nice to meet you, Rob," Arnold said. "Where's the set?"

"In the back."

Lucas eyed Rob. "The Crew's made it this far north?"

Rob's eyes narrowed. "Why do you say that?"

"No offense. The ink. Distinctive."

Rob nodded. "Used to be. Not anymore. That was a life I left behind." He held Lucas's stare.

"So you're not affiliated?"

"Not for two years."

"I didn't think they let you quit."

"They stay out of Tulsa. Not their turf. They leave me alone; I leave them alone. Besides, I was small fry. They don't bother tracking down their foot soldiers if they cut loose unless they stick around and ask for it. I didn't."

Arnold took off his hat and placed it on the counter. "So…the radio?"

"Follow me."

Rob led them into a smaller room where a battered shortwave transmitter sat on a table in the corner. Lucas appraised the device and the plug in the wall. "You have juice?"

The big trader nodded. "Solar. Only works during the day." He sat down at the radio, powered it on, and gave Arnold a quick tutorial. Arnold listened as though he'd never seen a radio before, his face a blank, and then took a seat in front of the transmitter and twisted toward Rob.

"Won't be more than a couple of minutes."

Rob took the hint and joined Lucas at the far end of the room. "Come on. Looks like your buddy wants some privacy."

"He's like that."

"I mind my own business."

They made their way back to the store, and Rob studied Lucas's flak jacket. "Where you from?"

111

"Texas."

"Long way."

"And then some."

"You're lucky you didn't run into any trouble. It's pretty hairy outside the city. Lot of ugly out there."

"I can take care of myself."

Rob nodded. "No doubt."

"We did run across something strange, though. Bunch of bodies that had been mutilated. That happen a lot around here?"

The trader's face could have been carved from mahogany. "What do you mean, mutilated?"

Lucas gave him a brief description. When he was done, Rob rubbed the back of his neck absently. "Yeah, that sounds about right. There's a gang of scavengers working the area that are meaner than striped snakes. They do shit like that."

"Why?"

"They say they're a cult – call themselves the Bones – but I think they're just wannabe nuts. Best I can tell, they think the mutilation makes them scarier."

"Worked for me."

"Where was this?"

Lucas shrugged. "Can't say exactly. Maybe a day's ride west."

"Damn shame to hear that. Nobody deserves to go that way."

"You must have seen plenty in your day."

"Nothing like that." He sighed. "But it makes me doubly glad I got out when I did. World's turned into hell. For good reason. All part of the plan. Like the flood in the Good Book – cleans the slate. They'll get their comeuppance for what they did. Won't be long."

"Wish I could believe that."

"You best believe it. I gave up the life when I found religion, and it's the best thing that ever happened to me." Rob tilted his head at Lucas's flak jacket. "I see you got one of those flyers, huh?"

"Oh, this?" Lucas asked, tapping the pocket where part of the pamphlet was sticking out. "Yeah. Preacher was handing them out down the street."

112

"That right there's the way to salvation, cowboy. Damned straight."

"I didn't really get a chance to look at it."

"I'd study on it if I was you. Lord works in mysterious ways. That came to you for a reason – there are no accidents. You can either ignore the call and burn in hell for eternity, or you can wake up and atone. Nothing in between."

"There's a picture of a girl. What's that all about?"

"She's the one. Read the paper. It's clear."

"Yeah? First I heard of it."

"It's spreading, brother. Can't keep it secret. Evil doesn't win this one in the end. Study on the message and you'll see – it all fits." Rob fell silent and Lucas exhaled in relief. It was just his luck to run into a zealot for company.

Arnold emerged from the back and walked toward them. "Going to need to use it again in a few hours. That work for you?"

"Sure. You manage the channel selector okay? It can be funky sometimes."

"No problem." Arnold tapped his stomach. "Anywhere we can get some food around here?"

"Few places further down the street, but they're iffy. If you're going to try them, stick to potatoes – no telling what the meat is or how long it's been stewing."

"Water safe?" Lucas asked.

"Watch them boil it. They'll tell you they do, but best to watch."

"We'll be back after we eat."

"I'm around till dark."

Arnold accompanied Lucas out the door and they retrieved their guns. Lucas leaned toward him as they walked to the horses. "Well?"

"They're going to check with Elliot's contact in St. Louis. Apparently the compound here was just helping out as a relay point."

"Did you know that going in?"

Arnold shook his head. "They don't tell me everything."

"Need to know," Lucas said.

"That's right. Smart. If we'd been captured and interrogated, all they'd have gotten was Tulsa."

"And the location of the new sanctuary."

"No plan's perfect."

The group ate in silence at a greasy spoon that had more roaches and flies per table than menu offerings. Lucas had counseled them about the trader's warning, and everyone had opted for boiled potatoes and scrambled eggs, but only once Colt had negotiated with the owner to be able to watch the cook break the eggs and boil the water. The food was tasteless and the plates chipped and stained, but after two weeks on the road it was practically chateaubriand and Pétrus.

Once they were finished, Lucas told them about Rob's enthusiastic endorsement of the second coming of Eve, and Arnold shook his head in amazement. "Maybe the virus had the right idea. The planet wouldn't be all the poorer for being rid of us as a species."

"Maybe," Sierra countered. "But the dogs and horses wouldn't have anyone to keep them company."

When they got back to the trading post, Sierra accompanied Arnold and Lucas in, uncomfortable with the leering stares of the guards outside.

Rob looked up from the counter as they entered. "Who's this?" he asked, eyeing her appreciatively.

"None of your business," Sierra snapped.

He took in the eye of Providence tattoo on her arm and raised an eyebrow. "Nice tat."

"I see you've got one too. Small world," she said.

"Let's get this over with," Lucas said.

"Sure thing, boss man," Rob said, and led them into the rear of the shop.

After another leer at Sierra, Rob left them in the radio room, and Arnold went to work. He used the default channel first, and when he reached Elliot, the Englishman offered a terse greeting and instructed him to switch to channel six.

Arnold spun the dial to ten and whispered to Lucas and Sierra,

"We add four to whatever channel he says, and we switch channels every twenty seconds or so. That makes it practically impossible for anyone to get more than a snatch of the transmission."

Elliot's voice came over the speakers. "All right. I spoke to my associate. He's sending a group to rendezvous with you in four days. He was shocked to hear about the incident, but he didn't believe it was related. Over."

"We confirmed that here, but we're not a hundred percent convinced. Over."

"Switch to channel nine."

When they were on the new channel, Elliot continued. "You have four days to get to Springfield, Missouri. It's a hundred and sixty miles. Can you make it? Over."

"Affirmative. What are the details? Over."

"Switch to channel eleven."

Arnold twisted the dial again, and Elliot filled him in on the rendezvous location and then signed off. Arnold sat back, powered the radio down, and then rose and headed for the door.

"Forty miles a day. That's aggressive for horses that have been putting in hard time for two weeks," Lucas said.

"Don't see much choice, do you?"

"We might not make it in four is all I'm saying."

"Didn't sound like that was an option."

"Won't do us any good to wind up twenty miles out with a couple of dead animals. That could happen if we're not careful, and we'd still miss the meet."

"We'll figure it out. For now, let's pay the nice man and ride. We still have some daylight left to burn."

"Getting across the city will probably eat most of that."

"Maybe the trader knows the fastest route to the eastern side of town."

"Not sure I want him to know where we're headed," Lucas said.

Arnold gave him a dry grin. "He's the last honest man, to hear your story."

"He might be, but right now I wouldn't trust my brother."

"He's a creep," Sierra added.

They pushed through the door and found Rob behind his counter, polishing a chrome Smith & Wesson snub-nosed revolver. He set the pistol down and tapped on a stopwatch resting on the glass. "You're into me four minutes."

Arnold counted out the rounds and set them in front of him. Rob pocketed the bullets and offered Sierra a smile. "Anything else I can do you for? You might be surprised at what I've got upstairs."

Lucas could see Sierra was going to reply harshly and cut her off. "We need to resupply. How are you on dry goods?"

"Not so great. I specialize in weapons and ammo."

"Where's the nearest place we could get some fixings?" Arnold asked.

Rob thought for a moment and gave them directions to another trading post. "But watch them. They're crooks."

Lucas tipped his hat and made for the entrance with Sierra, Rob's eyes burning holes in her jeans the entire way. "We're used to it."

"Study on that flyer like I said. It'll ease your mind," Rob called out after him, but Lucas was already gone, Arnold behind him.

"You boys are in a hurry, aren't you?" the trader muttered to himself, and went back to polishing the pistol. "I would be too if I had that little honey waiting on me. She's a firecracker. I can see that from a mile away." He inspected his work with a keen eye and then continued wiping at the metal with the rag. "Need to slow down and smell the flowers. Life's too short, that's for sure." He glanced up at the empty doorway and a smirk tugged at the corner of his lip. "More for some than for others."

Chapter 22

After a tense exchange at the second trading post, their saddlebags were bulging with provisions. Lucas checked the surroundings before swinging onto Tango. He'd convinced Sierra to wait outside with George and John while he, Arnold, and Colt dickered with the trader, which hadn't been hard after her experience with Rob. All of them were on edge, their sense of unease growing as they rode along the wide boulevard, and Arnold cautioned them to spread out so if anyone started shooting, they'd present more difficult targets.

"This place is giving me the willies," Colt muttered.

"Yeah. My spidey sense is tingling," Arnold agreed.

"But I don't see anything."

Arnold smiled humorlessly and looked around. "Just because you're paranoid doesn't mean they aren't after you."

The pavement was hard on the horses' hooves, limiting their speed to a slow walk, and by the time they reached the eastern edge of the city, the afternoon sun was sinking behind them. Lucas checked his watch again, did a quick reckoning, and twisted to Arnold.

"Probably got a couple more hours before it gets dark. We'll want to stay off the road once we're outside the city limits."

"I won't fight you on that, but I want to keep going as long as we can."

"I know. But if we find something defendable, we should make camp there. The ex-Crew guy warned us about the scavenger cult –

the Bones. After seeing their work, I don't want to cross paths with them."

Arnold's eyes narrowed. "Let's see what happens."

"Go ahead and take the lead, then. This is your show."

"We're all in the soup together until we get to Springfield," Arnold corrected. "But I'll ride point. Colt?"

"I'll be right behind you," Colt said.

Lucas allowed Arnold and Colt to pass and settled next to Sierra, who'd been quiet since her encounter with Rob.

"You okay?" he asked.

"Sure. Fine."

"Because you look like you just drank vinegar."

She tried a fake smile. "That guy gave me serious chills. Sorry. It was just a reminder of how…evil that bunch is."

"But he's found religion."

"Maybe so. I don't buy it. His type never do. Not really."

"Well, it's over now. You can relax."

"Spoken by the man with eyes in the back of his head."

They slogged along parallel to the highway that ran toward Claremore, using the turnpike only to cross a waterway before getting off the road again. The fields were green from fall rains, and with a breeze as mild as the temperature, the ride was as pleasant as any they'd experienced since setting off from Colorado.

They pitched their tents behind a cluster of burned-out homes south of Claremore, the ruins like broken teeth jutting from the earth against a twilight horizon, and after a hushed meal of salted meat and water, Colt took first watch with George while the rest of them crawled into their tents to snatch some sleep.

Lucas had finally dozed off when he was jarred awake by gunfire. Holes appeared in the upper part of his tent, revealing starlight outside. He dog-crawled to the entry flap, M4 in hand. A scream from nearby pierced the night as he fumbled to unzip the opening, and then he was out and rolling to the side, where the crumbled lower part of a chimney provided cover.

He switched on the NV scope, raised his rifle, and spotted a gunman fifty yards away, running toward him in a crouch. A three-round burst knocked the attacker off his feet, and Lucas shifted his aim to the next shooter. He loosed a second burst and the man jerked like a rag doll before tumbling to the ground, dropping his weapon.

"Colt! George! You okay?" Luke called as he drew a bead on yet another attacker, thankful that they were so careless they hadn't thought about cover. His M4 barked death and the man collapsed.

The distinctive rattle of Arnold's and John's AR-15s sounded from Lucas's left. George's voice answered Lucas from his right. "Colt's hit."

Chunks of brick sprayed from the chimney. He spotted the source and answered with two three-round bursts, the second of which drove the shooter backward as the rounds punched into his chest. Lucas didn't dwell on his success, instead adjusting his aim and cutting another gunmen's legs from under him, his bullets slamming into the man's unprotected thighs.

"How bad?" Lucas yelled.

More shooting interrupted George's answer, and Lucas concentrated his fire on the muzzle flashes flaring in his scope. He fired burst after burst and then ejected his spent magazine and slapped another into place, keeping his head down as he chambered a round, the brick absorbing the worst of the offensive fire. When there was a lull in the shooting, he picked another target near one of the piles of rubble and waited until the man's head was in his crosshairs before squeezing the trigger and finishing him.

More rounds snapped past and he spied a gunman firing from behind a tree. None of the shooters appeared to have night vision gear, which gave Lucas and his group a marked advantage. The attackers were firing at shadows, whereas the landscape was neon green in Lucas's scope, making it child's play to spot the gunmen from their rifles' blossoms.

Lucas made every burst count, and when his second magazine was spent and he'd rammed another into place, he held his fire, taking in the measured, disciplined bark of Arnold's rifle. Lucas swept the area with his gun, searching for another target, but there were no more. He spied movement a couple of hundred yards away and loosed a few bursts at the men who were trying to edge into the gunfight, offering them a reason to rethink their choice. The strategy worked, and he saved his rounds as the attackers retreated out of range.

He watched and waited, too seasoned in combat over the last few months to believe that the skirmish was over. His patience was rewarded when a figure with an assault rifle popped from the tall grass to his left and fired at George's position. Lucas heard a grunt near him and squeezed the trigger, stitching the figure with a burst and driving him to his knees. A final burst ended it and the man fell to the side with a scream.

A hail of rounds pocked the foundation around Lucas as another gunman emptied his rifle at him on full auto – an amateur move. Lucas kept his head down until the weapon was empty and then shot the man as he fumbled with his weapon, obviously unaware that he was visible to Lucas with the NV scope.

The intensity of the incoming fire faded over the next few minutes as Lucas and the others picked away at the attackers until there were none left, and the area fell silent as abruptly as it had become pandemonium. Lucas remained in place, maintaining his guard until Arnold's boots approached.

"I think that's it," the older man said.

"Could be. Or could be they're waiting for us to relax."

"I don't know. Must have taken down twenty of them."

Lucas spit to the side, his eye still glued to the scope. "Could be a lot more than that."

"Make 'em think twice about it, though, don't you think?"

"Depends on how committed they are." Lucas paused. "You or John take any hits?"

"Negative on me. John got one in the arm, but he's stable."

"Sounds like Colt and George are in a bad way. Where's Sierra?"

"Over by us."

"She okay?"

"Yes. I'll go check on Colt. Cover me."

"You got it."

Lucas watched for any movement in the ruins while Arnold made his way to Colt's position. The tenuous silence held for a few moments, and then Arnold returned, his expression grim. "Colt's dead. And George isn't long for this world."

"Damn. Made it all this way, too."

Arnold's expression darkened. "Wonder who they were?"

"They must have followed us from town. I knew something was off."

"What time is it?"

"Almost midnight."

"We'll wait until it's light out to reconnoiter. Don't want to get bushwhacked by a snake in the grass."

"Anything we can do for George?"

"No. He's already in shock. Took one through the throat. Nothing we can do."

"Poor bastard."

Arnold nodded. "Going to be a long night."

"For everyone."

Sierra reached Lucas several minutes later, her eyes glittering in the starlight. Lucas put his arm around her and whispered reassurance he didn't feel, his mind working on the possibilities raised by the attack – none of them good. They stayed like that until daybreak. As the sun rose, Arnold returned, and he and Lucas went to check for survivors while Sierra and John kept watch.

They counted twenty-six corpses, and Lucas was heading toward number twenty-seven when Arnold called out from nearby, "Got a live one."

Lucas came at a jog and stopped by Arnold, who was kneeling beside a shivering man in his twenties, his hair long and filthy. His chest was soaked with dried blood, and a blossom of fresh crimson from one side of his flak jacket pulsed with every breath.

"Who are you?" Arnold demanded.

Lucas pointed at an amateurish tattoo on the man's neck. "See that? A bone."

"You Bones?" Arnold asked.

The man managed a nod.

"Why did you come after us?" Lucas growled.

"Horses." The man coughed blood. "Guns."

Lucas and Arnold exchanged a glance. Arnold nodded as the man struggled for air. He straightened and eyed the wounded man without pity.

"You made your bed. This is your reward. You're just lucky we're compassionate and aren't going to gut you for fun."

Lucas nodded. "He's in his maker's hands now."

The man's eyes fluttered closed as he saved his energy. Arnold walked away, and he and Lucas resumed their search for bodies, collecting magazines and weapons as they did – a cache that could be redeemed when they came upon another trading post.

When they were finished, they'd accounted for thirty-one Bones, all male. Lucas buried Colt and George, the latter who'd expired while they'd been interrogating the wounded man, and Sierra tended to John's wound as Arnold broke camp and loaded up the dead men's horses with weapons. Once done, Lucas offered an all-too-familiar prayer for the dead while they stood by the fresh graves, and then they mounted up. The distance they had to cover was daunting, each of them was exhausted and demoralized by the loss, and the day had only just begun.

Chapter 23

Rob sat forward in his swivel chair and adjusted the radio volume as he waited for the operator on the other end of the transmission to locate Rob's handler. He'd broadcast in the middle of the night and requested an urgent meeting that morning, but apparently his superior had missed the deadline – an ominous development that spoke to declining morale and discipline in the Crew since Magnus's demise.

Rob had been sent by the Crew to open a trading post and act as their eyes and ears in Tulsa, a town at the edge of their territory that wasn't worth any resources to capture. It had nothing the Crew wanted, but the group still saw the value of having informants outside of its sphere of influence, and Rob was one of several plants in outlying areas that kept Houston posted on any developments of interest.

His cover story had been swallowed hook and line by the locals, and after several years of keeping a low profile, he was a colorful part of the landscape, his sordid past of little interest to a population on its last legs. The part he hated the most about his duty was the place itself – a dung hole inhabited by lowlifes, where nothing of note ever happened.

Until the woman had entered with the cowboys.

He'd seen her before – on a flyer that had been circulated by Magnus, along with the picture of the little girl.

He couldn't be sure, of course, but he believed it was her. There weren't a lot of women with her looks wandering around the wilderness with an eye of Providence tattoo – the Crew's brand to signify she was its property.

The speakers crackled and the operator's voice came over the air. "He's here. Are you still there? Over."

"Not many places to go in this dump. Over."

A different voice, baritone, drifted from the speakers. "What have you got for me? Over."

"A party of six rode through here yesterday. Five men and a woman. Used my radio. Over."

"And? Over."

"I monitored their transmission." Rob had engineered a tube that connected the radio room to his main room so that he could eavesdrop while anyone paying for confidential time believed themselves to be alone. "They're on their way to Springfield. Over."

"This is what you woke me up last night for? Over."

"No, you don't understand. One of them was the woman on the flyer you circulated a couple months back. Remember? With the girl? Over."

A long pause ensued, the speakers hissing softly as the handler absorbed Rob's words. When he spoke again, his voice was softer. "Switch to an alternate frequency. Over."

Rob did as instructed. It was always the same – three channels lower on the spectrum from the one the Crew monitored, and three again should the transmission go long.

His supervisor's voice drifted through the room. "Are you sure it's her? Over."

"She has our mark on her arm. Over."

"Where are they now? Over."

"They rode on. I don't know. But I know where they're headed." Rob gave him the directions that he'd scribbled down as he'd listened to the broadcast. When he was done, there was another long silence. It stretched on, and when the handler reappeared, he spoke with a new urgency Rob had never heard in him before.

"And you're sure they're meeting someone there from St. Louis? Over."

"That's what he said." Rob paused. "I could use some supplies. Rum. Anything else you can see your way clear to arrange to reach me. Over."

"Very well. I'll forward this on. Over and out."

Rob powered down the transmitter and stood. He'd done his job and, if his handler was pleased, would get a new supply of booze and drugs with which to soften life's blows or to trade to his fellow unfortunates, at his option. Rob was self-sustaining, which was a condition of his circumstance – the entire idea of the informant network was to have the benefit of reach without the cost of supporting it. Still, there were some things that he couldn't get in Tulsa at any price, and one of them was rum. Another, meth.

Both were prized by the inhabitants of the miserable place, but Rob had already decided he would keep it for himself if he got a shipment. Anything that would be a diversion from the unending sameness of each day in purgatory would be far too valuable to him to trade.

He considered the small barred window where sunlight was filtering through the grimy glass and shook off the thought. Nothing would reach him unless his information proved valuable, and he had no idea what it might mean to his betters. He knew that they'd been searching for the woman and child as part of Magnus's hunt for Shangri-La, but that had been a while ago, and word was that Magnus had found it to his detriment, so it might all be meaningless by now.

"A regular firecracker, all right," he muttered, and made his way back to the shop to begin another day of dickering with the walking dead.

~ ~ ~

The operator sat back and stared up at Raz, who ran the Crew's network of informants as part of its clandestine information-gathering apparatus. Raz shifted from foot to foot before falling still and turning to the operator.

"We need to let Snake know. Can you reach him?"

"Should be able to. They've got someone monitoring transmissions in New Orleans, just like here."

"When does he plan on returning?"

"Nobody knows."

"Springfield's a long way away from any of our strongholds. There's no way we can get anyone up there to intercept them in four days."

The operator nodded mutely and cleared his throat. "Snake might have contacts outside of our territory we don't know about. I mean, look at the ship that appeared out of nowhere. We can't make any assumptions."

"Good point." Raz's face wrinkled with a frown, the lines deepening as he came to a decision. "Call them."

Chapter 24

Sierra looked up at Lucas from the fire pit she'd built with a collection of small rocks. He smiled at her as he strode up from the shore with a stringer of plump fish. They'd reached Grand Lake O' the Cherokees an hour before nightfall, and he'd taken the opportunity to catch a fresh dinner while the rest set up camp. Arnold had approved a fire to cook if Lucas was successful, there being numerous other fires on the bank – the huge body of water was a natural source of sustenance and, as such, was ringed with people who'd taken up residence along its shores.

They'd found a promising spot on a bluff where they'd be able to see anyone approach from a good distance, and the clearing was surrounded by trees that would hide the glow of their flames from the curious. After the prior night's fight and the endless day in the saddle, none of them were feeling lucky, and all their nerves were frayed. The bandage on John's arm was seeping pus in spite of the antibiotics he was taking, and he was feverish, leaving them shorthanded in the event of another attack, and they were on edge at the prospect of a long night of sentry duty with precious little chance of sleep.

"Wow. Looks like you scored," Sierra said at the sight of the fish.

"Yep. Too bad we can't stay here a while. They practically jumped out of the water when they saw the spoon."

"I'll light the fire."

"I already cleaned them, so that's all we're waiting on."

Sierra had gathered kindling while Lucas was fishing, and felt in her vest for a disposable lighter. She flicked it to life, and the twigs began smoking after several long moments. Soon the fire was snapping and popping as the wood caught in earnest and she tossed more branches onto the conflagration. Lucas skewered a fish with a stick and held it in the flames, and within minutes it was cooked through, the smell heavenly after so many days of dry provisions.

Arnold stayed on watch while they dined on roasted white bass, and then Lucas replaced him on guard duty so Arnold could eat. John took a few mouthfuls of food but protested that he wasn't hungry, and Arnold happily consumed his portion as well. When he'd eaten his fill, he found his way to where Lucas was seated cross-legged with his back against a tree, watching the trail that led to their camp, his hat on the ground by his side.

"You want to take first watch, or should I?" Lucas asked.

"I can. I dozed some on the ride, so I'm not all that beat."

"Think you can manage five hours?"

Arnold nodded. "Gonna be just the two of us, huh?"

"Yep. John's in no shape, and Sierra…she's pretty tired."

"Rather have you on the job anyway. No offense."

"None taken." Lucas understood Arnold's lack of confidence in Sierra and had no argument of reassurance. "What do you think about John?"

Arnold shrugged. "He isn't taking too well to the pills. In the end, he'll either make it or he won't. We can't slow down because of him. This is more important than any of us."

"Kind of cold."

"Just realistic. We're talking the fate of the world here. One life or fifty is trivial compared to stakes like that."

"Not sure I'd agree with you if it was me that had to take the bullet."

"You know what I mean."

Lucas nodded. "That I do." He raised a hand to his neck and worked a kink out of it. "You really believe the vaccine's going to save the planet?"

Arnold frowned. "Elliot does. And he's a lot smarter than I am."

"Hope he's right."

"Hoping's free." Arnold sat at a tree to Lucas's right and set his AR-15 beside him. "So you and Sierra are cutting loose once we hit Springfield?"

"Yep. Heading south."

"Don't need to tell you there's little chance of success, do I?"

"You're singing to the choir."

Arnold offered a rare smile. "Man's got to do what he's got to do."

"I made a promise."

"Then honor's at stake."

Lucas squinted at him, trying to determine whether the older man was baiting him. He decided he didn't care – he was too tired. Lucas rose. "If you say so."

"Didn't mean anything by it."

Lucas nodded and fit his hat back on his head. "See you in five hours."

"Let's hope no earlier."

Sierra was sitting with John, trying to make him comfortable on his bedroll, when Lucas returned. He'd chosen to sleep without his tent, as had Sierra and Lucas. After the prior night, nobody wanted a repeat of losing precious seconds fighting their way out of a tent in the event of an attack.

"How you feeling?" Lucas asked.

"Like crap," John said. "How long till the antibiotics kick in?"

"Any time," Lucas offered, unsure of the answer but not wanting to alarm him.

"They take a while to concentrate in your system," Sierra confirmed.

"Then I won't try to amputate it while everyone's asleep," John said with a halfhearted attempt at humor.

They settled on their bedrolls near the horses, and Sierra rolled toward him and planted a kiss on his mouth. He answered in kind, and she sighed when they parted.

"Maybe we should have pitched a tent," he said.

"John's right there."

Lucas glanced over at the wounded man and smiled. "He won't mind."

Sierra swatted him with a mock frown. "We'll be on our own soon enough."

"Carrot and stick?"

"Whatever makes the mare run," she said. "But this is like Chinese water torture. I thought we'd be done by now, and we've still got three more days to go."

"Which nobody's happy about."

"Me especially." She pecked his cheek and sighed again. "Good night, Lucas."

He gazed up at the stars, bright as flares in the inky sky, and slid his hat down over his eyes. "If we're lucky."

Chapter 25

The rendezvous was to take place around dusk at the high school in Nixa, a small town just south of Springfield, and as the group made its way up the road that led to the school, the sky was painted with lavender and fuchsia. The trees on either side of the way shivered in the late afternoon breeze, rustling as they passed like nervous children in church.

All had their weapons cradled in their arms, and Lucas was studying their surroundings with his binoculars. It was a less than ideal spot for a meet; most of the tract homes along the route were still standing, creating ample opportunities for an ambush or for snipers to hide.

John's fever had broken sometime during the second night, and he was progressively improving, the angry red flesh around his wound now reduced to a petulant pink. It still hurt him to use the arm, but he was undaunted by the pain and appeared determined, with his assault rifle resting against his saddle horn.

They'd discussed reconnoitering the school grounds if they arrived early enough, but the terrain had conspired against them, and they'd had to press the horses hard just to make it in time. All the animals were showing signs of distress from the pace, but they bravely soldiered on, which they would do till they dropped.

Lucas lowered his spyglasses and leaned toward Arnold. "Up there on the right. That's got to be it."

Arnold squinted in the dying light. "Don't like the parking lots around the buildings. That place could turn into a killing field in a flash."

"We're pregnant now. Let's get this over with."

"See anything suspicious?"

"No. But with this many houses around us, we'd never see it coming."

"That's reassuring. Probably true, though. Whoever picked this wasn't really thinking," Arnold agreed.

"Or they don't have much field craft."

They rode past an overgrown playing field, and Lucas eyed the large main structure: most of its glass was missing, and graffiti marred the exterior. Sierra spurred Nugget forward until she drew abreast of Lucas.

"Where are we supposed to meet them?" she asked.

"Inside. Assembly hall."

"It'll be dark pretty soon."

Lucas nodded, the increasing danger obvious. "We're on time."

"How will we find the hall?"

"One problem at a time."

They rode across the parking lot to the main entrance, which stood open like a gaping mouth. Lucas dropped from the saddle and Arnold did the same. He looked back at Colt's and George's horses and peered up at Sierra.

"You and John wait out here with the animals. If you see anything suspicious, shoot first and ask questions later."

"I'd rather come with you," Sierra said.

Lucas shook his head. "John's got a bum wing. He'll need your help in a clinch."

She didn't look thrilled, but held her tongue.

Arnold looked to Lucas. "Let's go in and see if we can find our welcoming committee. Only got a few minutes before the sun sets."

Lucas nodded. "After you."

Arnold stepped across shards of glass littering the entryway and stepped over the threshold. Lucas followed him in, and they took a moment to let their eyes adjust to the gloom. Arnold continued forward, leading with his rifle, and Lucas did the same with his M4, the night vision scope now glowing. Arnold's boots crunched on the broken glass and the sound reverberated off the walls. They both froze when a furry form scuttled across their path, the rat scurrying so fast it was a blur.

Arnold drew a deep breath and turned his head toward Lucas before pushing on, listening intently as they descended deeper into the bowels of the building. Rusting lockers loomed in rows on either side of them, and a pool of muddy water blocked most of the passage where a skylight had failed. Arnold edged along the side of it and gestured to a sign identifying classrooms down one corridor, and administrative offices, cafeteria, and assembly hall down the other.

"Ask and you shall receive," he whispered.

Lucas said nothing, the thudding of his pulse in his ears unwanted company as he and Arnold found the way.

At the junction of halls, Arnold pointed to the left and tapped his chest, and then to the right and to Lucas, who nodded understanding. Arnold took a deep breath and swung around the corner with his rifle, and Lucas did the same, facing the opposite direction.

The halls were empty, the remains of looted cabling hanging like black entrails from gaps in the false ceiling. They continued along the passageway until they reached a set of double doors – the cafeteria – and down another hall till they spotted another set, with one standing open under a sign that announced the assembly area.

They crept toward the doorway, moving slowly so their footfalls wouldn't carry, weight on the sides of their feet to minimize any sound, and started when a voice called out from inside the dark gap.

"That's far enough."

They froze, rifles trained on the doorway, and a man stepped into view with a ten-gauge shotgun. He was razor thin, his hair cut a quarter inch from his skull, with a birdlike nose and heavy black-rimmed glasses. They stared at each other for a long beat, and then he lowered his weapon. "Code word?" he snapped.

"Elliot."

That brought a nervous smile. "Welcome."

Arnold shook his head. "What's yours?"

"Thor."

Arnold dropped the barrel of his gun so it pointed at the floor, and Lucas did the same. The man stepped forward with his hand outstretched. "I'm Lisle."

"Arnold. You alone?" Arnold asked, taking his hand and shaking it.

"No."

"Where are the others?"

"Don't sweat it. You have something for me?"

"That's right," Arnold said.

Lisle raised an eyebrow and looked Arnold and Lucas over. "Where?"

"We left our horses outside. In the saddlebags. Two containers — one of vaccine, the other of cultures."

"Well protected, I hope."

"Of course."

"Go get them. I don't want to be here a minute longer than we have to be."

"Will do." Arnold glanced at Lucas. "If you'll do the honors, I'll stay here and keep Lisle company."

Lucas departed wordlessly and retraced his path to the entry. When he reached it, the sun was sinking fast. He crossed to Arnold's horse and retrieved the containers.

"Are they there?" Sierra whispered.

Lucas nodded wordlessly and returned to the entrance, the containers under his left arm and his rifle gripped in his right hand. Lisle had been smart to keep his party hidden — assuming there was a party at all. In the event of something going wrong, he'd be the only casualty, and they could get away, depending on where they were hidden.

Which wasn't Lucas's concern. Once they handed over the containers, they were done.

Arnold was speaking in a low voice to Lisle when Lucas rounded the corner again, and they both looked up at him as he neared. Lisle eyed the containers and smiled. "Go ahead and set them down. I was telling Arnold there's not much around here, but it's probably safer in town than on the outskirts. The bandits come out after dark, and they're active. You should be okay in Springfield, though."

Lucas placed the containers on the linoleum tile floor and straightened. "That's it?"

Lisle nodded. "Thanks for bringing it. We'll take it from here."

Arnold frowned. "Need any help?"

Lisle shook his head. "I got it."

"Where do you head from here?" Lucas asked.

"St. Louis. We've got a compound there. A bunch of us saw the collapse coming years before it hit and prepped for it. We made it while just about everybody else didn't."

Lucas grunted. "A common story." He stared at Lisle. "Lot of people sacrificed everything to get that to you."

"I appreciate it," Lisle said, not moving. "Listen, I don't mean to be rude, but you should get out of here while it's still safe. We're under orders not to leave until you do, so I've got a vested interest in seeing you go."

"I understand. We're done, right?"

"Yes."

"All right. Safe travels, Lisle. Come on, Lucas. Let's ride." Arnold brushed past Lucas and strode down the hall. Lucas backed away from Lisle, reluctant to turn his back on a man with a shotgun, and felt his way down the corridor until he was at the turn.

Once back outside they mounted up. Arnold studied Lucas for a beat. "You want to make camp somewhere with us, or is this it?" he asked.

Lucas looked at Sierra and read her expression with a glance. "We'll ride to town with you and take off tomorrow. Not really on our way, but better safe, right?"

"He seemed to feel town was a good call."

"Only one way to see whether he's right."

A figure watched from the bell tower of a nearby church as the riders turned onto the road toward Springfield, and then refocused his binoculars on the school, waiting for the group that had entered two hours before to exit with the containers. He raised a two-way radio to his lips and murmured into it before setting it down, all the time focused on the school, waiting for his quarry to show themselves.

Chapter 26

Lucas and Sierra led the way north and were at the outskirts of Springfield little more than an hour after leaving the school. They were crossing an open stretch, the outlines of homes dark against the night, when Arnold called from behind them.

"Looks like a guard post ahead."

Lucas peered through his NV scope and saw a low bunker with the distinctive barrel of a machine gun poking from it.

"Good eyes. I must be more tired than I thought."

They closed the distance to a sandbagged blockade, and a voice called out when they were twenty yards away.

"That's as far as you go."

Lucas spotted the speaker – a man near the machine gun, wearing a night vision monocle. "We need to get to town."

"Not after dark, you don't. Those are the rules."

"Since when?" Arnold countered.

"Since that became the rule."

"First we heard of it."

"Come back tomorrow."

Lucas looked at Sierra. "We were told it isn't safe to camp outside town."

"That's true. But tonight you're in luck." The man pointed to the east. "There's a tent revival over yonder. Draws a lot of folks. They all camp out, so they'll have plenty of guards. Nobody messes with them. You should be fine if you bunk over there."

"We haven't eaten for a good while," Sierra tried.

"Sorry to hear that. They should have food for barter."

"Can't you make an exception tonight? We're obviously not trouble."

"Afraid not. Nobody passes. And a word of warning – the town's got fencing up, and they patrol it. If they catch you without a pass, it won't go well."

Arnold shook his head. "Friendly bunch, aren't you?"

"We been having problems with raids lately. Only not since we started closing the town at night. So think what you will."

"There's nothing we could say that would make you change your mind?" Sierra asked, her voice dripping honey.

"Sorry, lady. Rules are rules. Come back at daybreak."

Lucas and Arnold had a hushed discussion, and they agreed to try the revival. There would be safety in numbers if the guard was telling the truth, and they had nothing to lose by giving it a shot. Lucas was against the idea at first on principle, but Arnold pointed out that now they were just travelers with nothing to hide, so there was no point in avoiding people, provided they were friendly.

As they approached the field where a huge tent was raised, they could see torches burning in a ring around it and men with guns positioned every fifty yards. One of the guards spotted them and called out.

"Keep your hands where I can see 'em and ride into the light, nice and slow."

"We're here for the revival," Sierra said, and the man relaxed a little at the sound of a female voice.

"That's fine, but no sudden moves. Let's get a good look at you."

They coaxed their horses forward until the guard could make them out. Lucas tipped the brim of his hat. "Where can we tie our horses and water them? Ridden a decent ways for this."

The man seemed to like what he saw in Sierra and waved toward the tent. "You'll see the other animals over yonder. There's some boys watching them. Toss 'em a few bullets and they'll take care of yours too – brush 'em, feed 'em, whatever you want."

"Is our stuff safe in the saddlebags?" Sierra whispered to Lucas.

He shrugged and eyed the guard. "Where do we make camp?"

"You'll see where everybody else is."

"All right. Much obliged."

"No problem. Welcome, and bless you all."

"Likewise."

They rode to the far side of the tent, where a primitive corral had been created from wooden poles with rope strung between them. A couple of teenagers so thin Lucas could see their ribs through their shirts moved to help with the horses. Sierra pointed to their right, where at least fifty tents were pitched and another twenty or thirty bedrolls lay on the ground.

Lucas looked to Arnold. "What do you think?"

"Seems okay to me."

"What about our stuff?" Sierra asked. "I don't want to just leave it."

"I can watch it. Got no interest in going in there," John said.

"No? Why not?" she asked.

"Long story, but let's just say it's not my thing."

"You sure?" Arnold asked.

"Positive."

They dismounted and removed their saddles and bags, and the boys helped them carry everything to the campsite. Thirty minutes later their tents were pitched and John was sitting in front of a small fire, watching a pair of children chase each other a few rows over, darting between the rough aisles and laughing in the glow of the campfires.

"Let's see what's going on in there," Arnold said. "Maybe they have a kitchen set up or something?"

"Worth a shot," Lucas allowed. He unslung his M4 and laid it inside his tent, noting the bullet holes from the other night. "Not going to do well in the next rain."

"Mine's fine," Sierra said. "I don't mind sharing."

"That's the spirit," Arnold said with a wink at Lucas, more relaxed now that he'd completed his mission.

They walked together to the entrance, where music was emanating from inside – by the sound of it, a bluegrass band, complete with fiddler. A pair of men with the faces of undertakers stood at the entry and nodded a greeting to the newcomers.

"Howdy, folks. Welcome, welcome," one of them said. "Be three rounds apiece, all you can eat, free entertainment. A bargain at twice the price."

"What's on the menu?" Lucas asked.

"Beans, stew, juice, lemonade, fresh baked bread with honey. All the fixin's. Like grandma used to make."

Lucas counted out nine rounds of the 9mm he used for barter purposes and handed them to the greeter. The other man tied a length of dirty red string around their wrists and stepped back to allow them to enter. "Enjoy. Preacher starts up in about fifteen minutes. He's amazing, he is," the man said with a Creole accent.

"Good to know," Lucas said, and ducked into the tent with Sierra, Arnold tailing them.

Inside were several hundred people, most of them gaunt from the deprivations of the post-collapse life, but wearing clean clothes, the men's hair roughly cut and most with it greased back, the majority of the women with kerchiefs over modest braids or modestly trimmed styles. Many wore long dresses that were obviously homemade, and a few clutched Bibles to their chests, eyes burning with inner light as they studied Sierra with disapproval.

Lucas knew they looked like they'd been dragged behind the horses, but removed his hat as a concession, as did Arnold. Sierra ignored the scrutiny of the females and nudged Lucas in the ribs. "Smell that? Food! My mouth is already watering."

"Let's take a look at what they've got."

They walked to the side of the tent where collapsible tables had been set up and a line of stern-faced women were ladling out heaping portions. They stood in the queue and collected dented metal plates from the end of the first table, and a boy with grubby hands set a square of yellow bread on each. "Corn bread," he explained. "Honey's over yonder."

"Thanks," Sierra said with a smile, which faded when she met the gaze of the first serving woman.

"Beans?" the server snapped.

"Please."

The woman dipped her ladle into a steaming pot the size of a beer keg and dumped a portion onto their plates. The next did the same with the stew after answering Lucas's question as to what kind it was with a tight frown. "Meat."

They found a spot on a wooden bench and Sierra went for lemonade. She returned with a pair of red plastic disposable cups, set one beside Arnold, and then sat next to Lucas, who had waited for her to begin eating. Arnold mumbled a thanks as he mopped up beans and stew with a wedge of bread and stuffed it into his mouth.

The food was better than anything they'd had since they'd left Colorado, and they cleaned their plates in record time – just as a buzz went up from the crowd and people began heading toward the folding chairs in the center of the tent. Lucas and Sierra lifted their heads, and Arnold leaned toward them. "I feel like I'm going to explode. Enjoy yourselves. I'll be outside keeping John company."

He rose and carried his plate back to the serving women and asked where the latrines were, and then trundled toward the exit, patting his stomach. Sierra and Lucas did the same with their plates, and Sierra took Lucas's hand and pulled him to the chairs. He shook his head, but she gave his fingers a tug. "Come on. I've never been to one of these. Maybe it'll be interesting."

"Been a long time since I had a full night's sleep, Sierra."

"Just a little while. I promise."

He saw the pleading in her eyes and acquiesced, reckoning that it had been a while since either of them had done anything that wasn't drudgery or risking death. They took a seat at the back of the gathering just as a tall man in a frock coat entered through a flap in the back of the tent and strode purposefully to a podium that looked like it had been liberated from a local school.

The preacher's assistants led the crowd through a few hymns, and when everyone had quieted down, he ran his fingers over his balding head and glared at the gathering like they'd stolen his wallet.

"The devil walks the earth, ladies and gentlemen. Just as the Good Book said he would. Lucifer! The Bringer of Light! Prince of Lies! Old Club Foot! He's here with us right now, in this very room. Can you feel him? Can you feel his cold fingers on your heart?" he cried in a loud voice that increased in volume as he spoke. "You are all, every one of you, his helpers! He's visited his wrath upon all of you as your punishment for not having the strength to cast him out."

"Oh, brother," Lucas whispered, and Sierra kicked him.

"Now I don't have to tell any of you all what happens when you get into bed with the devil. You can just look around and see it everywhere. You get the four horsemen. You get your disease, your pestilence, your famine…and his right-hand man, the grim reaper. That's your reward for having sin in your hearts. And you all do. You know it, I know it, your neighbors know it." The preacher slammed his hand down on the Bible he'd placed on the podium and lowered his voice. "You have consorted with the king of the underworld, the number one demon, and he's punishing you for your trouble. That's fact, just as plain as day, so understand what brought this about. We been wicked for so long our Father hardly recognized the place, so he turned his back on us and said…"

The crowd hung on his pause, holding its collective breath.

The preacher leaned forward, his eyes blazing with righteous fury. "To HELL with you!"

The throng gasped, the hook set.

Lucas's neck tingled and he looked around, searching for what had set off his alarm. At the far side of the gathering, a rough-looking man with black hair was staring at him and quickly averted his eyes when Lucas spied him. Lucas frowned and looked back at the preacher, who was raising a hand over his head in preparation for another spellbinding volley.

The watcher's interest could have been nothing – he and Sierra were obviously road-weary, dressed differently, and thus would arouse the curiosity of locals. But Lucas wasn't in the habit of dismissing his instincts so blithely, and his hand reached for his Kimber.

The oration went on for an hour, and by the time the sprightly preacher had finished, Lucas had been subjected to enough fire and brimstone to last him into his next life. He had to hand it to the preacher, though – he had mastered the art of hypnotic delivery, and Sierra had, like the rest, seemed entranced by his every word.

The man who'd been staring at him hadn't shown any further interest in them, and Lucas had gradually relaxed, ascribing the scrutiny to benign curiosity. A hat was passed and the crowd dropped bullets into it while the final hymns rose from their lips, and Lucas took the opportunity to rise, reaching for Sierra.

"You coming?" he asked.

She took his hand. "I suppose it's that time."

They made their way from the tent under the disapproving glowers of the faithful and emerged into the cool of the night. Lucas waited for his eyes to adjust, enjoying the breeze after being cooped up in the stuffy confines of the tent, and Sierra inched closer.

"So what did you think?" she asked.

"I'm hell bound."

She smiled. "Hopefully not quite yet."

"Matter of time."

"Well, then, might as well have some fun in the meantime," she said, her eyes dancing in the starlight.

"I'm listening."

She pulled on his hand and began walking toward the camp area, an impish smirk on her face. Lucas had no choice but to follow, banishing the thoughts he'd had during the sermon about the ease with which he'd taken to ending the lives of his fellow men, and instead marveling at his good fortune in having found something worth fighting for in Sierra.

Chapter 27

The following morning Lucas and Sierra packed their things before joining Arnold and John in a subdued breakfast of leftovers from the prior night's feast, now available for the discounted price of a bullet per plate, presumably as a concession to the lack of refrigeration. They opted for only corn bread, preferring to avoid botulism from stew or beans that had turned.

"How's the arm?" Sierra asked John as she finished her portion.

"Better every day. Thanks for patching me up."

"No problem. Just keep it clean and keep taking the pills until your course is through."

"Yes, ma'am."

Arnold popped the last chunk of the dense bread in his mouth and chewed with gusto. He swallowed from his canteen and turned to Lucas. "So how many days you figure it'll take you to get to Vicksburg?"

"Reckon about ten."

"Crew territory really starts for real in Arkansas?"

Sierra nodded. "Yes, but from what I heard, there isn't much in northern Arkansas for them to police. Their main hub is Little Rock, which we'll avoid – obviously."

"And once you make it to Vicksburg?"

Lucas shrugged. "See what we can learn."

"That's on the east side of the Mississippi River, right? The virus side," John said.

"Right. But we've had the vaccine. We should be fine," Sierra said.

"That's one way to test it," Arnold observed.

"Yeah, well, we aren't planning on staying there long," Lucas said. "How about you? Back to Colorado?"

"Yep. Assuming we can make it and it's not snowed in by the time we get there."

"What if it is?" Sierra asked.

"Then we'll sit it out somewhere like Santa Fe."

"Ah."

Lucas ate his last bite of bread and stood. "Time to hit the road, fellas. Best of luck making it back in one piece."

Arnold also stood and shook Lucas's hand. "Thanks for the help. We did it."

"Seems that way," Lucas agreed.

"You two be careful. I wouldn't want to be heading into the belly of the beast like you."

Lucas lowered his voice. "Makes two of us."

Sierra frowned as she rose. "I heard that."

They carried their saddlebags to the corral and retrieved their horses and tack, tipping the boys before mounting up. Sierra waved at Arnold and John while Lucas scoped out the area, looking for his admirer from the night before. He didn't see anyone watching them, so he led Sierra down the dirt path toward the highway, aware of his surroundings as they rode.

"You seem tense," Sierra noted when they turned south.

He told her about the prior night. She shook her head.

"Probably was staring at me," she said. "Not that you're not worth a second look."

"No, he was eyeing me."

"Maybe he was interested."

That drew a tight smile from Lucas. "Takes all kinds to make a stew."

"Well, I don't see anyone following us, so we're in the clear."

"Still got all the usual suspects to watch for."

"Their bad luck if they try to get the jump on you."

"It's the trying that can get you killed. We'll stay off the roads, same as ever." He looked to his right. "And here's a trail. Time to put that into practice."

They picked their way through the high grass to a track that stretched toward an abandoned farmhouse with a broken wind vane and half the roof gone. Tango veered left along another trail and Lucas let the stallion have his head while he checked behind them, the nagging sense that all wasn't well still with him from the night before. Seeing nothing, he lifted his binoculars and swept the trees just to make sure.

"Anything?" Sierra asked.

"Nope."

"Maybe what's bugging you is your guilty conscience."

Lucas sighed and dropped the spyglasses back against his chest. "I'm not proud of the men I've killed, Sierra. It eats at me every day."

She gave him an odd look. "I was thinking more about us living in sin."

Lucas's face flushed slightly. "Oh." He chuckled. "Not feeling too guilty about that just now."

"We're going to hell."

"Way I read the preacher's sermon, we're already there."

"Still time to turn it around."

Lucas shook his head. "Problem is, if I manage to sneak past the pearly gates, I won't know anybody. All my friends will be in the basement."

"You're irredeemable."

"Set in my ways," he agreed.

"There's always the chance I could make an honest man out of you yet."

Lucas held his tongue, marveling at how differently their brains worked. He was running scenarios, calculating the odds of making it to Vicksburg without getting killed, trying to figure out their next step, and Sierra...well, Sierra was considering other matters.

She fell silent for several minutes, and when she spoke again, her voice was earnest and hushed. "Thanks for doing this, Lucas. You're a man of your word. That means everything to me."

"Even if I'm a sinner?"

It was her turn to smile to herself. "There's worse things."

He nodded. "At least the hours are good."

That brought a laugh. She studied his profile: the worn straight-brimmed hat pulled low over his brow, eyes continually scanning, skin tanned the color of burnished copper. "Why, Lucas, if I didn't know better, I'd say you're developing a sense of humor."

"Tango will tell you I've got a great one."

They quieted, leaving only the sound of birdcalls from the trees along the trail and the clumping of hooves as they made their way toward enemy territory and the unknown.

Chapter 28

St. Louis, Missouri

Dr. Charles Darby looked up from his desk at his assistant, who'd offered a courtesy tap at the lab doorjamb and was standing at the threshold with an excited expression.

"Yes, Colleen?" he asked, setting his reading glasses down and fixing her with an expectant stare.

"They're here," she said.

"Wonderful!" he exclaimed, and pushed back from the desk. "Let's go see what goodies they brought, shall we?"

Darby was a distinguished man in his early sixties, lean with a full head of salt-and-pepper hair and a perennial expression of mild bemusement, as though puzzled by the continual folly of the human condition. An oncologist by training, he'd parlayed a chain of free-standing radiation treatment centers into a waterfront home in the Hamptons he would never see again, as well as this walled compound on the outskirts of the city that was now home to a thriving colony of like-minded survivors – the remnants of a militia cell that, like he, had prepared for the worst and who'd agreed to share resources with him and fight against the encroachment of the gangs who'd ridden roughshod over the land since the collapse.

Darby followed Colleen from his office down the hall to the building entrance. Originally a lodge for corporate retreats before it had fallen on hard times and been bought for a song by Darby, it was perfectly suited to its new role as the headquarters of the militia, whose numbers had swollen to fifty over the years as new recruits had joined.

The nucleus of the compound was walled, making it easily defendable, and had ample land surrounding it for vegetable gardens, along with a grazing area for the cattle and sheep they'd acquired through trade. The outbuildings surrounding the main house served as bunkhouses, and one of the original rec halls had been converted into a passable medical clinic and lab, as well as Darby's offices and storage for all the necessities and equipment he'd accumulated over the years. An ample solar array provided power, a well sufficient potable water, and regular hunting parties reasonable variation in their menu.

The perimeter wall was eight feet tall, crafted from brick and mortar and reinforced to stop even armor-piercing rounds, with turrets at each of the four corners that were manned at night by pairs of sentries with assault rifles and night vision gear. An electrified fence encircled the property, whose battery banks stored sufficient charge to fry anyone unwise enough to try to take them on.

With Darby's help, they'd created a sustainable enclave of sanity in a mad world and had been able to stave off attacks by miscreants to the point where the compound was avoided as a death sentence by the gangs that still terrorized the area.

Darby stepped out into the afternoon sun and shielded his eyes with his hand as a half dozen horsemen rode through the open gate, Lisle in the lead. When the younger man saw his mentor, his face lit with a grin.

"We did it!" he exclaimed, and reined his horse to a halt, slipped down from the saddle, and strode to Darby to shake his hand. Darby embraced him and patted Lisle on the back, ignoring the road dust that covered him.

"Well done. No difficulty?"

"None. We made decent time and avoided the problem spots."

"Excellent news." Darby eyed the rest of the party. "Where is it?"

Lisle unbuckled the straps of his saddlebag and withdrew the containers, still taped shut, and presented them like gifts to the doctor.

"I didn't open them."

"Let me get them into the lab so I can verify they're fine. Good work, Lisle. It's a proud day for us all."

Lisle flushed at the praise. "Glad I had the opportunity to contribute something."

"We couldn't have done it without you." Darby studied his face. "Get cleaned up, fed, and grab some sleep. You look worked."

"It was a long one."

"No need to explain. I can imagine."

Darby handed one of the containers to Colleen and escorted her back to the lab. There he carefully removed the tape from the containers and lifted the lids to peer inside, where rows of sealed vials fitted into cavities in the polystyrene greeted him.

A note was taped to the inside of one of the lids, and Colleen peeled it from the container and read it aloud.

"Charles. Greetings from paradise. Each vial holds ten doses of vaccine, which has been tested as discussed via radio. The other container holds the relevant cultures. Reach out if anything's in question. Good luck, and God bless. You hold the future of the world in your hands. Elliot."

Darby smiled and nodded like he'd listened to his favorite symphony's opening measures. "Elliot's always been a bit melodramatic," he explained.

"Well, it's a big day. Nothing wrong with a little hyperbole," she said with a wink. Colleen was twenty going on fifty, razor sharp and possessed with a particular charm Darby fought daily to resist. He routinely encouraged her to find a suitable mate among the young men of the militia, but she dismissed his prodding with complaints that they were all immature clods and dullards.

"Future of the world, eh? Well, perhaps not that much of an exaggeration if the virus spreads any more than it has."

"But didn't you say that was unlikely?"

"Of course. But nothing's impossible. This is our insurance

against the unthinkable happening. Which, given our recent history, isn't as far-fetched as we'd like to think. All it would take is one carrier traveling west. Or someone weaponizing it, God forbid."

"Why would anyone do that?" she asked.

"We as a species have been killing each other since we could hold a rock or a club, so I have little faith that our nature has changed much. Wherever there's a thirst for power, death follows."

"But the world's a shambles," Colleen protested.

"That it is. But no more than it was when the Mongols or Visigoths swept the land. The poor condition of the planet didn't stop them from butchering everyone in their path." He shook his head. "No, the truth is that we're a warlike tribe, and if there's an atrocity that can be imagined, it will be carried out by someone."

"Well, thank goodness you're here to stop this one."

"Or do my best."

Colleen studied her shoes as Darby removed a vial and studied the seal on it. "Will there be anything else?" she asked.

"What? Oh. No. Thank you. I'll just inventory these and finish up my work. Go ahead and take the rest of the afternoon off. I won't be much company, I'm afraid."

"I don't mind staying."

Darby shook his head, pretending not to notice the undercurrent of pleasant tension neither of them overtly acknowledged. He hummed to himself as he walked to a workbench and searched for a felt-tip pen, and Colleen's shoulders slumped slightly as she made her way to the door.

"Let me know if you need anything," she said. "I'll be in the mess hall helping my mom."

"Perfect. Will do."

Darby stole a look at Colleen's departing form and exhaled heavily. "Youth is wasted on the young," he whispered to himself. Much as he was tempted by her thinly veiled overtures, he was the leader of the compound, and she deserved someone young and vital with whom she could start a family, not a broken-down doctor who had socks older than Colleen. He'd tried to steer her toward Lisle, but she'd been uninterested – a shame, as he needed a companion, and even if not of robust physique, he was certainly possessed of a strong moral character and keen intellect.

He sighed and found the marker he'd been after, and pushed libidinous thoughts from his mind as he turned to the work he'd been waiting for years to begin.

~ ~ ~

Night had fallen and the compound was dark, the sentries in the turrets drowsy as they neared the end of their shift. An owl hooted from one of the trees by the eastern wall and then flapped away, frightened by a loud pop from a nearby thicket.

One of the two sentries' heads exploded from a custom-loaded subsonic slug, splattering his partner with blood and brains. The surviving guard froze at the drenching, and then his upper dental plate shattered from another round.

The area fell silent again, the other three turrets far enough away that they hadn't been alerted by the sound of the suppressed shots. The moon disappeared behind a cloud, and a score of gunmen in head-to-toe black ran from where they'd disabled the electric fence and made for the wall beneath the neutralized turret.

When they reached the wall, one of the point men hurled a grappling hook secured to a length of knotted rappelling cord over the top, and after confirming that it was secure, scaled the sheer surface in moments and dropped in a crouch on the other side. He swept the area with his night vision monocle and, seeing no movement, jogged to the gate while keeping to the shadows, and slid the two heavy bolts securing the steel barricade open.

The gunmen were inside in a blink, and the sharpshooter who had taken out the two sentries climbed the iron rungs to the tower as his companions took cover below. Once he was in the guard post, he pushed one of the corpses to the side and unslung his rifle to dispatch the other sentries.

Two pops in quick succession neutralized the watchers in the northern tower, and then a warning shout sounded from one of the darkened bunkhouses, followed almost immediately by the staccato bark of an AK-47. Rounds snapped around the sniper's head and pocked the exterior of the tower, and he ducked down – the game was about to become much harder.

One of the attackers below him ran in a beeline to the bunkhouse and tossed a grenade through a window. The glass shattered with a crash, and then the structure plumped like an overcooked hotdog and flames erupted from within. A militiaman staggered from the doorway, firing on full automatic, and an answering volley cut him down as another blasted away from the interior of the building. A second grenade sailed through the door and detonated, and the shooting from the bunkhouse fell silent, replaced moments later by a barrage from the second building.

Several of the attackers fell to the onslaught, their ceramic body armor failing after multiple hits from high-velocity rounds, and they tumbled backward as the rest took what cover they could and pressed the assault with relentless fire at the new shooters. Up in the tower, the sniper saw his chance as the sentries directed their aim below, and shot both of the southern tower gunmen during the confusion from the blitzkrieg attack.

The fighting continued with more grenade blasts and gunfire until the second bunkhouse was silenced. Only a dozen of the attackers were left standing, but they wasted no time and made for the main building's entrance. Once inside, the fighters worked their way through the interior until they reached the last room, where they were stopped by a steel door.

~ ~ ~

Darby stood in the near darkness of his lab beside the refrigerator containing the vaccine samples. Awakened by the shooting and explosions, he'd peered out his window to see the main bunkhouse destroyed and a paramilitary force attacking the second with disciplined fire and grenades.

He'd intellectually prepared for this moment, knowing there was a chance that it would come, and had agonized over how he would react if it did. Watching his people slaughtered with cold, calculated precision told him that his worst fears had been realized – the attackers that had somehow breached their impenetrable defenses were anything but the unruly gangs of predators that abounded beyond the walls.

Which meant that somehow Lisle had been followed or a tracking device had been planted in the containers. He cursed as he felt along the workbench and slid open a drawer – he hadn't thought to check the boxes. The idea that he might have been responsible for the death of those he cared about was like a physical pain, but he shrugged it off at the sound of someone trying the door handle.

He was under no illusion that the barrier would hold indefinitely, and he knew what he had to do. Strangely, all his fears that he might be paralyzed into inaction proved to be in vain as he felt in the drawer for the metal orb that would deny his adversaries the two things they'd come for – the vaccine and his know-how. Any doubt was replaced by a deep calm that surprised him more than anything else that night.

Before he could second-guess himself, he pulled the pin and tossed it and the spoon aside, and then walked unhurriedly to the refrigerator and opened the door, holding the grenade over his chest, where it would vaporize the contents of the fridge as well as his body.

He said a quiet prayer for forgiveness at his deed, which he hoped would be interpreted as dying in battle and not suicide, and then the world relinquished its hold on him in a blinding flash just as another detonation blew the lab door off its hinges.

Chapter 29

New Orleans, Louisiana

Snake bit back his fury as Zach relayed in a dispassionate tone the message he'd just received from his headquarters. The compound in St. Louis had been raided by a mercenary group employed by the Illuminati, but the assault had failed and they were no closer to their objective than they had been a month before.

Snake eyed the man like he was insane, and then forced himself to breathe deeply. When he finally spoke, he sounded reasonably calm.

"So no vaccine, and no leads on where the Shangri-La survivors are?"

Zach nodded. "Correct."

"They didn't follow the group that dropped off the vaccine?"

"Yes, but when they split up, they had to make a decision who to go after. They opted for the pair that went to Springfield."

"And?"

"And sometime over the last week, they must have gotten wise that they were being tailed, and they lost them."

"How?"

"I have no idea. I wasn't there."

"So where does that leave us?"

"Waiting for your tracker to turn up a lead in New Mexico."

"He hasn't located the vehicles. He's at a dead end," Snake said.

"For now. He needs to keep looking."

"Which is what he's doing. But it's a big area. They could have gone anywhere. And the weather's gone to hell. There was a blizzard a couple of days ago."

Zach's brows narrowed. "That's unfortunate."

"Yeah. It is," Snake said, wondering how the man could remain so detached about the failure in St. Louis. "And there's no way to pick up the woman's trail?"

"None that I can see, unless she's spotted again by one of your people."

"No ideas why she might have separated from the other two?"

"The obvious is that she wanted to go somewhere else."

Snake couldn't suppress the sneer that twisted his lip. "Even I figured that out. The question is where, and why?"

"Two questions," Zach corrected.

Snake bristled but didn't snap back. He'd gotten accustomed to the Illuminati man's deadpan delivery and had noticed that he evidenced no emotional responses to anything. So he wasn't trying to goad Snake with the correction – Zach was clarifying that he'd posed two questions rather than one.

"Why did they send vaccine to St. Louis? I still don't understand."

"Assuming that's what it was."

"It's a fair bet."

"Yes. Well, probably so it could act as a distribution point for the region."

"Then we're screwed no matter what. If they've got something that advanced, we're spinning our wheels." Whitely's latest report on the Lubbock effort hadn't been encouraging, and Snake was beginning to suspect that developing a foolproof vaccine was beyond the Crew's abilities.

"No, until we see what it is that they've created, we can't assume anything."

Snake frowned. "We have to do something."

"You're right. Issue the woman's photograph to the field again. It's possible she'll surface, and if her face is fresh in everyone's mind, the odds of one of your men recognizing her go way up."

Snake nodded. "I will, but it's a long shot. Only a fool would dare set foot back in our territory once she's escaped."

Zach studied a spot on the wall, an expression on his face like a thought was flitting just out of reach, and then he turned back to Snake with his usual unreadable stare. "Maybe. But it can't hurt, and it's not like you have a lot of options." He didn't have to say, "Just do it and shut up."

Both he and Snake perfectly understood the nature of his advisory role. His masters had bailed Snake out and solidified his leadership position, and the presence of their warship on the horizon served as a constant reminder of the Crew's ability to reach virtually anywhere, as far as his men were concerned. Reports of insurrection had all but vanished since he'd taken back New Orleans, and that had been handed to him on a platter.

Snake nodded agreement to the Illuminati man. He would find out where Magnus had gotten the photo and put someone on distributing the flyer again. It would take time to circulate, due to the realities of traveling by horse, but it was better than nothing – although not much.

Snake cleared his throat. "Lassiter mentioned getting the refinery in Houston back online so we can manufacture fuel?"

Zach blinked once. "Then he will."

"Any idea when?"

"He hasn't confided in me."

"It would speed up our ability to help you if we could run our trucks. He also mentioned giving us some of his ship stores so we could…"

"I'll let him know next time I talk to him."

"Maybe I should?"

Zach's lip twitched. "I wouldn't try his patience. Better to let me."

Snake swallowed hard at the obvious warning. "Whatever you think's the right way to do it."

Zach nodded and made for the door, his message delivered. Snake waited until he was gone and shook his head in frustration. He ran the most powerful gang in the country, and now he had a boss he had to answer to? Snake couldn't understand how someone as volatile as Magnus had put up with it. After only a few weeks, Snake was already considering arranging for Zach to have an accident.

He dismissed the thought. He would do what he had to in order to consolidate his power. He could play along with the best of them and lull Zach into believing that he'd capitulated. In the meantime, he would build his organization and get what he needed out of Zach's masters – and the refinery would be just the first of their concessions; he'd see to that. Because right now they needed him. Their mercenaries had blown it in St. Louis, which left them nobody to turn to except the Crew.

And they'd soon learn the Crew didn't work cheap.

Chapter 30

Lucas and Sierra arrived at the banks of the Mississippi River across from Vicksburg, Mississippi, on a cloudy afternoon eleven days after leaving Springfield, the air heavy with humidity as a front pushed north from the Gulf of Mexico. They'd spent the night in a decrepit barn outside of Tallulah, one of the easternmost bastions of the Crew, occupied by two dozen miscreants who preyed on the surrounding countryside for amusement and sustenance.

They'd skirted Little Rock, Arkansas, and stuck to secondary roads and trails from Missouri, trading with isolated locals whenever they could for produce or eggs. Lucas honed his prowess with his fishing tackle when there were no other options. There had been several anxious moments on the trip when they'd had to outfox Crew patrols, but Lucas had found doing so not particularly hard – the cartel thugs were clearly out of their depth in the wilds, their experience as urban parasites failing to translate well outside the city.

Sierra's anxiety had grown as they'd pushed deeper into Crew territory, although she'd tried to hide it, and Lucas sympathized with her. He couldn't imagine what it had to be like returning somewhere she'd been a slave, and a part of him suffered with her every step of the way. Then again, everything had a price, and nobody was forcing her. He just hated to see someone he had feelings for pay so dearly.

The river was at least a half mile across at the narrowest point he could see, swirling past like liquid chocolate. Lucas studied the pair of bridges that spanned the Mississippi from Louisiana to Vicksburg through the binoculars and shook his head as he lowered the glasses.

"They've got a roadblock in place," he said. "Bunch of Crew. So much for crossing here."

"But there aren't any other bridges for three days' ride in either direction. And the compound my cousin and Tim were at is only a few miles south of the Vicksburg airport, Lucas. We have to figure a way across. Maybe we can distract them or something? Blow something up and sneak across while they're dealing with it?"

"Not sure that would work. I mean, there isn't a lot out here, and the chances that everyone deserts their post to check on what happened are slim and none." He hesitated. "I thought you said the compound was attacked by a rival gang in a territorial fight."

"That's right."

"But Mississippi isn't Crew territory?"

"Not anymore. Since the new virus, they pulled back to this side of the river and let the other bunch have it – assuming there's anything left of them now." Sierra's lip twitched. "We have to get across somehow."

"I know, Sierra. Come on. Let's see what's south of here. Maybe we'll get lucky."

"How?"

"If I knew that, we wouldn't need luck."

They turned inland until they were out of sight of the bridge and then rode toward the water along a dilapidated secondary road. Mile after mile of marsh stretched before them, but the river was far too wide to cross, even with a strong swimmer like Tango beneath him, and the current was likely treacherous. He didn't know much about the Mississippi but figured that amount of water running out to sea had to have some momentum behind it, and he didn't want to risk their lives any more than they already had.

Their prospects didn't improve over the next hour as they rode along the levee, farmland to the west of them, swamp and marshland to the east along the river. They were crossing a gravel road that led toward the water when Lucas stopped abruptly and cocked his head.

"What is it?" Sierra asked.

He shushed her and then motioned to her to follow and spurred Tango down the gravel road. Sierra goaded Nugget after him and they disappeared around a bend just as a Crew patrol rode into view, their horses' steel shoes clacking on the levee like ball-peen hammers.

Lucas guided the big stallion onto the grassy shoulder and Sierra followed, the color drained from her face at the prospect of being stopped so close to their objective. She looked like she was going to speak and Lucas held a finger to his lips, his stare unflinching. She nodded silently, the message received, and they made their way farther from the road, the river only footsteps away.

After thirty seconds he paused and listened, breathing evenly, and leaned forward to pat Tango reassuringly. When he didn't hear any sounds of pursuit, he tilted his hat forward and coaxed Tango along the shoulder toward a collection of abandoned homes by the water, their tin roofs dull under a slate gray sky.

He dismounted at the last house in the line and rested a hand on Sierra's leg. "Let's take a break. The horses can eat – there's plenty of grass in that field."

"Why don't we keep going?"

"Because I want to nose around, and if there are Crew patrols actively working the area, that changes things."

"Wonder what they're looking for?" she asked, almost to herself.

"I've been thinking about the roadblocks. That's probably how they've kept the virus at bay – it's not to keep people from escaping Crew territory. It's to keep travelers from crossing from Mississippi."

She nodded. "Makes sense. But I'm not sure how that helps us."

"It doesn't. But it tells us they're afraid of whatever's over there." He regarded her. "If they're afraid, maybe we should be, too."

"We've gotten the vaccine."

"Right, but remember that Elliot said no vaccine's a hundred percent." Lucas looked away and sighed. "I suppose it's a little late to worry about that now. Take a load off Nugget and let her graze."

"What are you going to do?"

"Like I said. Look around."

Chapter 31

"Sierra!"

Sierra twisted toward where Lucas was waving at her from beside one of the houses. She stepped around the horses, who were munching on grass, and walked toward him. As she neared, she saw a smile on his face.

"What is it?" she asked.

"Help me drag this out of the garage," he said, motioning to something in the dark interior. Sierra peered inside and her eyes widened.

"It's a boat."

"Makes sense," Lucas said. "What's the point of having a waterfront home if you're not going to play in the water?"

They moved inside the garage and she studied the skiff – maybe eighteen feet long and fashioned from aluminum. Lucas reached over the transom and began unscrewing the outboard motor from the hull. "We aren't going to need this. The gas will have gone bad a long time ago."

He lifted the motor free, set it down next to the wall, and then tested the weight of the boat, which was resting on a rusting trailer, its tires disintegrated to piles of black dust. Sierra hefted the bow and nodded. "We can do this."

"On three," he said, and gave a quiet count.

They heaved the boat free and carried it onto the dirt. Sierra barely made it out of the garage before giving a small cry and dropping the bow. "Sorry," she said. "It got away from me. It's heavy."

"I know. Don't worry. I can drag it down to the water from here."

"How are we going to get across, though?" She looked inside the boat, empty except for a couple of filthy vinyl cushions.

"There's a pair of oars in the garage. Can you grab them?"

"Sure."

Lucas didn't wait for Sierra, instead hauling on the yellow nylon rope tied to the bow, his boots digging into the moist soil. The bass boat scraped along the dirt until he got it onto the grass, his work suddenly easier as the friction reduced by half. Sierra came at a half run, carrying a pair of wooden oars, and he continued pulling the craft down the bank, maintaining his momentum as she followed him to the river.

Once in the water, he climbed into the boat and she handed him the oars. He fit them into the oarlocks, testing them with a tug to make sure they were secure, and then stepped out of the boat and gave her the rope. "Hang onto it while I stow Tango's and Nugget's kits."

"What are you going to do with the horses?"

"They seem happy enough in that field. There's a fence around it, so that should keep them from wandering too far. Plenty to eat, and there's water in a cement cistern near the gate. Owner kept horses, that's for sure. They'll be fine for a day or two."

Sierra gave him a worried look. "What if it takes longer?"

Lucas frowned. "No way to get them across, so we'll just have to make sure it doesn't. Besides, it's not like they'll die if we're not with them. They won't run out of food or water with the rain and amount of grass here."

Lucas was gone for fifteen minutes. When he came back, he was carrying his M4 and the night vision monocle, and his tactical vest bulged with extra magazines. Sierra climbed into the boat while he held it steady, and then he pushed it away from the shore and hopped in, his legs and boots soaking.

The current carried them south, and Lucas pulled on the oars to steer them toward the far bank, but the further into the middle they drifted, the faster the rush carried them downriver. Sierra pointed at a large industrial complex on the Mississippi side about half a mile south of them, its cranes reaching for the sky like skeletal arms.

"That's where they used to make oil rigs. I remember it from my trip here. They'd build them over there and tow them down the river to the Gulf."

"Long way," Lucas said, twisting to get a look at the massive buildings on the bank.

"My cousin's compound is north of that. If we can make it to the landing there, it shouldn't be that long a walk–"

She was interrupted by the crack of a rifle from the Louisiana side, and a fountain of water plumed skyward ten feet away. Lucas heaved on the oars with all his might while crouching as low as he could manage and yelled at her from the awkward position.

"Get down!"

~ ~ ~

The leader of the Crew patrol was urinating near the water while his men took a break beneath some trees on the bank when he spotted an aluminum boat in the middle of the river, maybe three hundred yards away. Fishing on the river was allowed, with permission from the Crew – at a cost – but crossing to the Mississippi side wasn't, and it looked to him like that was what the boat was doing that far from the shore.

He finished draining his bladder and buttoned up, and then raised his binoculars to get a better look. There were no fishing poles that he could see, but that didn't necessarily mean much – they could have been using hand lines.

A man wearing a cowboy hat was rowing hard, fighting the current, and it was obvious that he was no fisherman, judging by the rifle strapped to his back. He adjusted the focus and his eyes narrowed at the sight of a woman in the bow, her back to him as she gestured at something ahead of the boat. He could see from her slim curves and athletic frame that she was young, probably in her twenties, and his interest quickened when he spotted a tattoo on her bare arm, her olive wifebeater offering an ample view of tanned skin.

She turned to speak to the rower and his breath caught in his throat. He recognized the face – it was the woman on the flyer they'd received a few days before.

He called out to his men as he made his way up the bank, and they came at a run.

"What?" one of them called.

"Out on the river. It's the woman Houston's looking for."

"You sure?"

"Positive. She's got the mark."

The man eyed the boat. "They're making for the Mississippi side."

"I know."

"Out of range for these things," the gunman said, holding up his AK-47.

"Maybe out of accurate range, but the bullets keep traveling. We can adjust our aim by watching where they hit the water," the leader said, and snatched the rifle from the man and jogged back to the shore. He took up position behind a tree and used the trunk to steady his aim, and then flipped the firing selector to single shot and drew a bead on the boat.

The first shot went wide, and he cursed. He'd misjudged the distance, which was growing longer by the second. They were more like four hundred yards, judging by how badly he was off. Any chance of an accurate shot discarded, he switched the rifle to continuous fire and called to his men.

"Empty your rifles at them. We throw enough bullets their way, we may hit something," he ordered, and then opened up, the assault rifle bucking in his hands like a wild animal.

~ ~ ~

Sierra ducked down as the river around them erupted in a spray of water. She cringed as the chatter of rifles from the western shore reached them a moment later.

"Oh, God, Lucas…"

"Stay down," he said, but got cut off by a bullet punching through the transom and exiting through the bow not eight inches from where Sierra was crouched. "Lie as flat as you can on the bottom. That's the safest place," he said, and renewed his effort on the oars, aware that at any moment a round could end his life.

More slugs peppered the river around them as he strained, his arms burning from the exertion, sweat coursing down his face. He didn't dare look over the hull to see how far they were from the shooters, leaving only his arms above the boat as he followed his own advice and lay on his back as he rowed, Sierra's legs beside him.

Another hole appeared in the back of the boat, and then another, and Sierra screamed in fright.

"Are you hit?" he hissed from between clenched teeth.

"N-no."

A round punctured the hull beneath the waterline and a brown stream began filling the boat. Lucas swore under his breath but kept rowing – reaching the Mississippi side was now their only hope.

"Hang in there," he said.

"We're sinking," Sierra said, panicked.

"Just a little leak."

"No, really, we are."

There was a lull in the shooting, and the next barrage was more scattered as they crossed the midpoint of the river, now well over six hundred yards from the gunmen. Every foot they were able to put between the Crew and the boat increased their survival odds, and Lucas offered a silent prayer that the current carry them to safety.

Spray geysered skyward ten yards behind them, and then five, but the pattern was wide, and none of the rounds struck the hull. Lucas continued stroking with the oars, willing himself to greater effort, ignoring the water sloshing along the bottom of the boat, easily three inches and rising rapidly.

When it became obvious they were out of range, the shooting stopped, and Lucas risked a look over the transom. He guessed that between the current and the rowing they were over a thousand yards past the shooters. He felt in his vest for his bandana, and when his fingers snagged it, he pulled it free and called to Sierra.

"Scoot down and hold the oars while I plug the hole."

"They stopped shooting."

"Yep."

She did as he asked, and he maneuvered around so he was facing the transom. Lucas rolled the bandana as tightly as he could and jammed it through the hole. The fabric saturated instantly, but the flow eased to a trickle, and he sat up to study the damage. The hull looked like Swiss cheese; it had been hit at least a half dozen times. That neither of them had been wounded was a miracle, and he thanked his maker for that favor.

"Okay, let me have the oars. Hard part's done – we're way more than halfway there now," he said. Sierra relinquished them and scooted back to the bow, keeping her head down as she did, wary of another volley of shooting.

"That was too close," she said with a shiver.

"We're lucky they're bad shots and don't carry anything better than AKs. If they'd had my Remington or something with a decent scope, we'd have been toast." He fell silent and resumed rowing, keeping the bow pointed at the oil rig plant, the reality of the danger they'd willingly subjected themselves to quashing any banter. The only sound present was the sloshing of muddy water in the bottom of the boat, the creak of the oars, and his breathing, rhythmic as a metronome with each pull.

Chapter 32

The bow scraped onto the bank just south of the manufacturing site, around the bend and out of view of the Crew, and Lucas pulled it from the water with Sierra's help and dragged it into the dense underbrush so it wouldn't be easily spotted should the Crew decide to launch a river patrol looking for them. He had no reason to believe they would, but he couldn't be sure, and prudence dictated that they have a means of getting back to the Louisiana side.

Lucas removed his soggy bandana and studied for a moment the bullet hole through which the water had leaked, and then selected a nearby sapling. He unsheathed his Bowie knife and sliced off a branch, trimmed it so that it tapered, and walked back to the boat.

"What are you doing?" Sierra asked, eyeing the stick. "Making a spear?"

"No," he replied, kneeling and jamming the thinner end through the hole until it wedged firm. "Buying us a little insurance." He sawed the excess branch from the exterior of the hull and pounded the wood to set it firmly in the gap, and then straightened and inspected his work. "That should hold. It'll swell with water, and the external pressure will keep it in place." He toed it with his boot. "Not going anywhere."

"They nearly got us."

"Like being nearly pregnant," Lucas countered. "Ain't so until it is." He tried a small smile. "You okay?"

"Just shaken up. I get that way when about a thousand bullets almost hit me."

"I know the feeling." He paused. "You said your cousin's compound is near here?"

"That's right. Maybe a mile up the main road."

Lucas checked the time. "Got about an hour of light, tops. Want to fan this until tomorrow?"

She shook her head. "Let's get it over with. With no tent, we're just as exposed no matter where we go. Maybe there's a spot where we can spend the night safely."

Lucas didn't offer his thoughts on that possibility. "Then let's go."

They walked together, he with his M4 at the ready, she with her AR-15 in hand. Once off the plant access lane, they turned north along the road that traced the course of the river. The ground was still spongy from a morning cloudburst, and the air was fragrant with the scent of blooms, decaying vegetation, and wet earth. Vines and moss hung from the trees that lined the strip of cracked asphalt, now overgrown in many spots, the pavement having largely given up its battle against nature's encroachment.

A rustle sounded from a tree to their right, and Lucas spun to face the source, only to relax when a curious squirrel leapt from one branch to the next. Sierra grinned nervously and they resumed their march, the sound of their boots muffled on the grassy shoulder. Lucas wore a serious expression after the near miss on the river. His gray eyes roamed over the road ahead, his senses on alert and his nerves clamoring a warning with every step. He realized that his disquiet was a function of residual adrenaline burning through his system. but that didn't make it any less real, and he continually swept the area ahead with the barrel of his M4, the safety off and his finger on the trigger guard.

Half an hour later Sierra slowed, a frown in place, and stared at the remnants of a drive on her right. "I think this is it," she said in a hushed voice.

"Okay."

They veered off the road and followed the driveway for fifty yards until they arrived at a gate partially ajar, hanging off rusting hinges attached to a high wall on either side. Lucas noted the bullet marks marring the surface and nodded once – the evidence of an attack was as clear to him as though captured on film.

"This look familiar?" he asked.

Sierra's voice was barely audible. "Yes."

When they entered the compound, it was immediately obvious that it had been long deserted: the walls of the buildings were cracked and dark with mold, the roofs staved in, and the windows shattered. More bullet gouges pocked the areas around the openings, the doors ruined by termites as well as gunfire. Sierra gasped at the sight, and Lucas put his arm around her, trying to offer comfort but failing. She shrugged him off and made for one of the far buildings, and Lucas tailed her, his steps more deliberate than hers, taking in the surroundings with a wary eye.

Her boot kicked an empty can hidden beneath a carpet of leaves, and the walls echoed with the sound when it bounced off the nearest building. Lucas winced at the noise, but Sierra ignored it and continued her beeline to the structure. She hesitated at the doorway, and Lucas whispered to her, "Let me go first."

She shook her head and pushed past the half-open rotting slab of door to the dark, dank interior. Beetles scuttled away at her intrusion, and a juvenile water moccasin slithered into the shadows, its patterned scales shining in the dim light.

Lucas entered and nearly ran into her. Sierra stood in the gloom, shoulders heaving as she sobbed quietly. He didn't try to quiet her this time, intuiting that she needed to vent her grief and frustration at a fruitless end to their quest – it was clear nobody had survived to tell any story, and there would be no leads found in the rubble. If her son was alive, the answer to where wasn't in the haunted ruins, and she'd now be forced to confront the hard fact that they had no plan to find him and, absent one, little room for optimism.

"This was where my cousin and Tim lived. The last time I saw them was at a little dining room table over there, when they were waving goodbye to me." She gestured to a corner of the room, where any dining set had in the intervening years been looted or ground to fragments by termites.

"There's nothing here, Sierra. I'm sorry," Lucas said quietly.

"Their room was over there. I want to look inside, Lucas." She didn't say she had to. She didn't need to.

Lucas nodded. "Be careful. I saw a snake."

Her voice was hollow. "It doesn't matter."

"It will if it bites you. Remember Colt. Just watch your step."

She moved woodenly to the doorway of the room and stared through it, stopping at the threshold as though unable to enter. The room was a shambles, the floor covered with soggy leaves and mud. The cheap beds were nearly unrecognizable as such, the mattresses rotted through and the metal frames rusted to dust.

Sierra stood transfixed until Lucas broke the spell with his hand on her shoulder.

"It's nearly dark, Sierra. We need to find someplace to spend the night."

She nodded mutely, her thoughts elsewhere, and Lucas's heart lurched at the nightmare of recriminations that must have been playing through her head. He couldn't even imagine what it was like to lose a child. To revisit the place she'd last seen him – where he'd probably died – had to be excruciating.

Sierra wiped away her tears with the back of her arm and sniffed loudly. "I'm sorry. I don't know what I was expecting. I mean, I knew in my head, but in my gut…" She trailed off, losing the thread.

"You don't have to explain. Come on. Let's go."

She nodded, her body radiating defeat, and Lucas guided her from the building, the sky darkening by the minute. A mockingbird trilled from a tree near the wall, its call echoing through the brush, and Lucas checked his watch.

"Where to?" Sierra asked.

"Maybe back to the river? I don't think–"

"Drop your weapons," a male voice called out from behind them.

"You heard him. Now," another voice ordered from near the gate.

Sierra gasped and Lucas's eyes darted around the compound, but the shadows were too deep for him to see who was there.

"Sierra," Lucas whispered, "listen to me. Put your gun on the ground."

"Lucas—"

"Just do it," he insisted.

"You heard him, missy," the voice behind them ordered. "Drop it or you're dead."

Sierra slowly knelt and placed her AR-15 on the leaves at her feet, and Lucas did the same. He straightened and held his hands above his head, and Sierra followed his lead.

"Now your pistols. Use two fingers. Index and thumb. Nice and easy, or it'll be the last thing you do," the voice behind them warned.

They did as instructed and laid their handguns by their rifles.

"Now what?" Lucas asked.

"Stand still while we figure that out," the voice said. A third man emerged from behind one of the buildings, his pump shotgun pointed at Lucas. The gunman from the entry moved into view, supported by an improvised crutch beneath one armpit, his left leg terminating in a stump, but the AKM in his right hand steady.

Lucas heard the leaves rustle behind him, and the owner of the gruff voice drew closer. "I say we shoot 'em now and be done with it," he said.

"What are you doing here?" the man with the shotgun growled.

"Looking around, that's all. Didn't mean any harm," Lucas said.

"Why?"

"My...my cousin used to live here," Sierra managed, her voice tight.

"Your cousin?" the voice behind them demanded.

"Yes. Her name was Amy. She lived here with my son."

The man with the crutch limped closer and regarded Sierra with milky eyes. His unruly beard was a mat of gray and black, his face deeply lined and burned the color of toffee by the sun. He studied her for a long beat and then nodded and looked over her shoulder. "You can see the resemblance. Looks a lot like Amy." He considered Sierra for a long moment before speaking. "What was your boy's name?" he asked, his voice now gentle.

"Tim."

"That's right. Of course. He used to play with my grandson, Eddie. I remember him well."

"You do?" Sierra blurted.

"Of course. Just 'cause I'm a half-blind cripple doesn't mean I'm daft. Remember it like it was yesterday."

"But…you're alive. How?"

The old man nodded like it was painful to do so and exhaled sadly. "That's a longer story than we've got time for." He motioned to their weapons. "Get yer guns and follow us. Be nightfall soon enough, and you don't want to be out after dark." He hesitated. "Name's Eli. That's Ned," he said, indicating the man behind them. "And that there's Frisco. Don't let 'em scare you. Their bark's worse than their bite."

Chapter 33

Eli lived a twenty-minute hike from the compound, on the river side of the road, and night had fallen by the time they reached his home. The men had horses, but were limited by Sierra and Lucas's walking pace and seemed visibly nervous as they rode.

They turned off the road onto a barely discernible track and found themselves in a densely overgrown area that appeared impenetrable. Ned dropped from the saddle and approached the wall of vegetation, felt around, and then something popped behind the leaves and he heaved a stainless steel chain-link gate open, its hinges groaning like a drunk after a three-day binge. Eli spurred his horse through the dark gap, and Frisco followed him through. Ned motioned to Lucas and Sierra with his rifle.

"Go on. Ain't got all night."

They moved through the opening and found themselves on the far side of a tall fence woven with vines and creepers, the cover completed with strategically placed hanging moss. Fifty yards away was a modest house with a metal roof, where two other men sat in collapsible lawn chairs by a small fire, rifles in their laps, one with a sweat-stained baseball cap emblazoned with a chewing tobacco logo.

Eli demonstrated surprising dexterity considering his age and limitations and was off his horse in moments and removing his crutch from a sling attached to his saddle. He limped to the men and had a muted discussion, and then waved Lucas and Sierra over.

"Have a seat," he said, indicating a pile of lawn chairs folded near

174

the fire. "This here's Art and Kenny. Boys, meet Sierra and Luke."

Sierra had introduced them on the trek, and Lucas didn't bother correcting Eli. He tipped the brim of his hat and nodded. "Gents."

"What's for dinner?" Eli asked.

"Hog stew," Kenny said. "Again."

Eli nodded. "Plenty for guests, I reckon."

"Enough to feed an army," Art said.

Eli explained to Sierra as she unfolded a chair, "Woods around here are teeming with feral hogs. Things are the size of small cars. They've overrun the area – probably happy as hell most of the humans got their walking papers."

"How's the stew?" Lucas asked.

"Tasty enough, I reckon. Only one way to know, right?" Eli said.

Ten minutes later they were spooning the pungent concoction into their mouths, the gruel surprisingly good in spite of the somewhat strong flavor of wild pig. When they'd eaten all they could, Sierra sat forward in the fire's glow and began asking the questions that had been nagging at her since meeting their hosts.

"So you lived with Amy?" she asked.

Eli nodded. "That's right. We all did."

"How did you survive the raid?"

"We were on a hunting expedition. Got back and found the place destroyed."

"What happened?"

"Near as we can reckon, the Crew decided to make an example of what happens to folks that cooperate with their enemies. At the time, the Crew claimed this part of Mississippi, but the Red Devils outta Mobile and Jackson did, too. So one day the Crew came in and wiped out our home and, with it, everybody there. Sending a message."

"How do you know it was them?"

"They lost a bunch of men. We recognized 'em easy enough from their markings. Mansfield clan outta Alexandria."

"Mansfield?" Lucas asked. "I thought they were Crew."

"That's right. They run Alexandria. They're a chapter of the Crew. That's how it works in the boonies."

"So they killed everyone?" Sierra asked.

"All the adults. My daughter Kris. Your cousin Amy. About twenty-five others."

"I didn't realize the compound had gotten that big."

"Yeah. Word spread we had a good thing going, so lots of folks wanted in. Probably one of the reasons the Crew took us out. Got too big for our britches, and became a target." Eli paused. "That's why we keep a low profile now. Ain't good for yer health if too many know 'bout you."

"The territory's still being contested?"

"Oh, no. Ever since the second round of the virus hit, that's over and done. Crew wants nothing to do with Mississippi anymore, and can't say as I blame 'em."

"But…you're fine."

"We keep to ourselves. Hunt, fish, stay off the roads. Not that there's many out and about these days."

"The new virus…"

"Wiped out Jackson like the wrath of the Almighty, from what I hear tell. Red Devils managed to stop it before it got to Mobile."

"How?"

"Shot anyone tryin' to get in."

Lucas nodded. "That'd work."

"Last I heard, it did. But that was spring. For all I know, someone slipped through and Mobile's gone by now, too." Eli shrugged. "Ain't seen anyone to ask about it since then. Which is fine by me."

Sierra frowned. "Wait. You said they killed all the adults. What about the children? My son? Your grandson?"

Eli stroked his beard as he considered his response. He grunted and held up his cup. "You want some moonshine?"

Sierra shook her head, and Lucas did as well. "No, thanks."

"Ned?" Eli asked. Ned rose wordlessly and rematerialized a few minutes later with a jug. He poured a stream of amber into the old man's cup and recorked the container, and then set it by his side and sat back down.

Eli took an appreciative sip and smacked his lips. "Don't that just beat all. Whoo. Feel like a new man on that. Yessirree."

"You were saying, about the children?" Sierra prodded.

"We found the bodies of the adults and a few of the young'uns. My grandson, for instance, shot twice, execution style. Best we could figure it was 'cause he put up a fight – he was older than your boy."

"But they didn't kill everyone?"

"We didn't find all the bodies, if that's what you mean."

"My son? Tim?"

"Nope."

Sierra eyed Lucas. "So he *is* alive. I told you. I knew it!" she said.

Eli fiddled with his cup. "Well. Could be."

"Where did they take them?"

"Don't know. I mean, probably Alexandria, but there's no way of knowin' for sure."

"You never went after them?"

He shook his head. "Lost my foot to a snake the week after the massacre. I'm in no shape to go anywhere, much less into Crew territory. Besides, they shoot anyone from this side of the river on sight."

"Why would they take the children?" she asked.

"The girls? Easy to figure that one out. Now, the boys, that's a different story. Best we can figure, they probably have 'em workin' the cane."

Lucas frowned. "The cane?"

Ned nodded. "Sugar cane. They got a rum plant there. There's a big demand for cheap rum, but it's backbreakin' work harvestin' it and such."

Sierra's face fell. "They use them as slave labor?"

Eli stared into the fire like it held the answer to her question. "We heard rumors before they wiped us out. But that's all they were. Stories." The old man raised his head again to Sierra. "Where you been holed up all this time? Been, what, year and a half, at least, since they hit Amy's place..."

"I was in Lubbock."

Eli grunted. "Crew territory."

"That's right."

"How was it?"

Sierra was silent for a moment. "Some places have it harder," she said. "All in all, somewhere south of horrible and north of hell."

That drew a cackle and another swig from the cup. "Seems like we never learn, do we?"

"How's that?" Sierra asked, not understanding.

"Before the virus, we had a bunch of liars pretendin' to care about us, but doin' not much besides robbin' us blind and stickin' our asses in jail at the drop of a hat, usin' us for slave labor, just like the old chain gang days. Mother Nature wipes the slate clean, and we got a different bunch doin' basically the same thing. Makes you wonder, don't it? Not much has changed. I was born dirt poor, worked my whole life, and got nothin' to show for it, just like my daddy and his daddy before him."

"What did you do?"

"Anythin' I could. Sharecroppin' like my daddy. Worked on a tug crew. Did my share of rig work till I got too old for it. Fixed lawn mowers, cars, refrigerators. You name it." He looked at Lucas. "How 'bout you, young feller?"

"I was a lawman."

He nodded slowly. "That figures. Didn't take you for a banker or a doctor. But you look like you can handle yourself." He took a pull on his drink. "Heard shootin' earlier down by the river. That you?"

Sierra nodded. "Crew patrol."

"You come over on a skiff?"

Lucas answered. "They shot it up pretty good."

Eli took in Lucas's face, the deep tan, the dusting of beard, the steel gray eyes beneath a furrowed brow. "Goin' back in the mornin'?"

"Probably," Lucas allowed.

"Headed Alexandria way?"

"Maybe." Lucas gave Eli a hint of a smile. "Always wanted to see how they make rum."

Eli laughed, the sound dry. "Well, you got some balls on you, I'll give you that." He tapped on the jug and held his cup aloft. "Sure you don't want a taste?"

Lucas shook his head. "My grandfather used to make white lightning, but I never warmed up to it. Not my thing."

"Put hair on your chest. Not that you strike me as no choirboy."

"Just never got the taste for it, is all."

Eli shrugged. "Suit yourself. More for me."

"Think we'll have any problem getting back across?" Sierra asked.

"Dunno. Never tried. But if I was to give it a shot, I'd want to get over before sunup. No point makin' it easy for 'em, is there?"

"Do they patrol the water? With boats?" Lucas asked.

"Those lazy bastards? Nah. No way they'd break a sweat rowin'. Easier to watch the bridge and patrol the roads."

Lucas's eyes narrowed. "Don't suppose you have an alarm clock."

Eli's eyes danced in the flames. "I'm an early riser."

"You mind waking us?" Sierra asked.

"No problem. You're welcome to take some stew, too. Should keep another day or so."

Sierra swallowed hard. "Um, that's very generous of you."

"Don't worry. We salt it before we cure the meat. You won't get sick." He looked at Ned and Frisco and smiled, revealing nothing but gums. "At least, not most of the time."

"That's mighty kind," Lucas said. "Let's see how we feel tomorrow."

They continued picking the men's brains for information on Alexandria, but quickly realized they had nothing material to add to what Eli had shared. Frisco had been to the city before the collapse, so was able to give them rough directions, but beyond that they would have to rely on their wits and Lucas's compass.

The men retired one by one, the moonshine obviously an effective sleeping agent. Frisco announced he'd take the first watch and strode off toward the gate with his rifle and a canteen of water.

As the fire died down, Eli showed them to an area inside the house where they could sleep, and fetched a thick blanket to use as padding on the hardwood floor.

"Sorry. We don't get a lot of guests overnightin'," he said.

"This is great," Sierra said.

"Where do you get your water?" Lucas asked.

"Collect it in barrels when it rains, boil river water when it doesn't. But this time of year, it rains a fair amount."

"Can we top off our canteens before we leave?"

"Be my guest."

Lucas lowered himself onto the blanket and removed his hat. He looked up at the older man. "Thanks for the hospitality, Eli. Kind of you."

"Nah. It's nothin'," he said.

"You short of anything? Got some extra ammo I've got no use for," Lucas tried.

Eli waved the offer away. "Mostly use bows to hunt. Been savin' the bullets fer bigger game. We're fixed up fine."

"You sure? Got some 5.56mm and 9mm. It's yours if you want it. Just say the word."

He appraised Lucas and then turned to Sierra. "You keep it. Sounds like you'll put it to good use where you're headed. I wouldn't know what to do with it." He hesitated. "Where's your boat?"

"Down by the oil rig plant."

Eli nodded. "You should be okay on the road before dawn. Ain't too far."

"You have raiders and scavengers here too? Even with the virus?" Sierra asked.

"Little lady, what we got is human nature. And something like this brings out the worst in folks, even the good ones. So yes, we got our share of cutthroats working the roads. Just watch yourself and you should be fine first thing, though. They like to sleep in, generally speakin'. That life don't attract the hard workin'."

Eli limped off to the sleeping quarters, leaving them to themselves. The interior of the house was dark except for the glow from the starlight outside that filtered through a nearby window. Sierra scooted closer to Lucas and gave him a kiss, which he returned. When she pulled away, her eyes were bright.

"I told you he was alive."

Lucas closed his eyes and nodded. "That you did."

"We're going to do this, aren't we?"

"If it can be done, we will."

"You'll find a way."

He sighed, amazed at her faith in him, and smiled in the dark.

"One way or another."

Chapter 34

New Orleans, Louisiana

Snake's subordinate stood staring at his boots as he delivered his report. Zach sat nearby with Whitely, who'd arrived two days before to explain why the vaccine effort had stalled yet again and to assist Snake in dealing with Zach on the refinery issue. Snake didn't understand most of the reasons Zach had given for why the Illuminati hadn't yet gotten the refinery operating, and Whitely was his technical expert, chartered with negotiating with Zach and Lassiter to arrange for the plant to be brought online.

"The transmission came in last evening. The woman was spotted near Vicksburg, in a boat on the Mississippi," the subordinate said.

"Why am I only hearing about it now?"

"It was received by Houston late in the day. There was nobody available to make a call on whether to disturb you until this morning."

Snake's eyes hardened. "Disturb me? I left orders that anything related to the woman was of top importance."

"The radio operator received the information and tried to track down the security chief for that region, but he couldn't find him until a few hours ago. He received the report at five a.m. He radioed us at six, after verifying a few details."

"Only two hours ago," Whitely said. "Continue."

"They opened fire on the boat but were unable to stop it. It's possible that it was hit multiple times, but they lost it once it was out of range."

"So she was within reach and they flubbed it?" Snake growled.

Whitely shook his head. "Sounds like they did what they could. Remember we're talking a field patrol with AKs. In the middle of nowhere. Can't really expect much more than what they managed." Whitely ignored Snake's obvious agitation and continued. "A better question is why there, why now?"

"Who cares?" Snake snapped.

The subordinate cleared his throat. "They said the boat appeared to be heading to the Mississippi side."

Zach spoke for the first time. "But why? Why travel from Springfield to Mississippi – a state overrun with the virus? That's a death sentence. Why do it willingly? It's common knowledge."

Whitely drummed his fingers. "Must be some damn good reason." He stood. "I need to use the radio and talk to my people in Houston, see what we have on the woman's background."

Whitely hurried from the room and returned twenty minutes later with a deep frown.

"Well?" Snake demanded.

"Her son was in a compound on the Mississippi side, near Vicksburg. Apparently we took him prisoner, and he's working on a plantation in Alexandria."

Zach nodded. "She's after her son." He threw up his hands at Whitely. "Why are we only now getting this information?"

Whitely shrugged. "I can't be everywhere at once. I have nothing to do with this new effort to find the woman. I've got my hands full with the vaccine development in Lubbock, our pharmaceutical manufacturing, and security in Texas – and now, the refinery issue, which we're making precious little progress on, incidentally."

Snake nodded slowly. "It's not Whitely's fault. But I'm going to make it his problem now." He shifted his focus to Whitely. "I want you to personally head up the effort to capture her. She's our best lead to where Shangri-La has relocated. I want her taken alive."

"So you want me to drop everything and focus on this?" Whitely asked, his tone even.

"No, I want you to add this to your pile."

"The refinery. The vaccine. Security. And now this as well," Whitely said quietly. "I'm good, Snake, but I'm not superhuman. If I'm to prioritize this, the others will have to wait."

Snake waved a hand. "I want you to go to Alexandria. Set a trap." Snake looked to Zach. "And Zach, I want you to go with him and help. We can't let this woman get away."

"We don't know that she'll show up in Alexandria," Zach said. "She wasn't headed there on the river, that's for sure."

"It's the best we have. Whitely? Arrange for a team to head to Vicksburg, too. See what they can find on the other side of the river."

Whitely stiffened. "That's a death sentence for whoever goes, and we both know it. You're not going to find any takers."

"Dammit, Whitely, stop throwing up roadblocks and figure this out," Snake screamed. "Do whatever you need to do, but I want this woman taken alive. Do you read me?"

"I'm just pointing out the obvious."

Snake's voice quieted to a dangerous purr. "If you can't manage this, I'll find someone else who can."

"I didn't say that. I pointed out that you can't expect anyone to sign up for a suicide mission into virus territory. The men are loyal, but nobody will voluntarily put a gun to their head and pull the trigger. I'd expect that anyone we order over to that side will simply disappear."

Zach nodded. "He's right."

Snake's expression turned even more sour. "I don't want to argue. I want you to fix this, Whitely." He glowered at Zach. "And I want you to see to it that he gets everything he needs."

"That's not really what I'm here for," Zach observed.

"You're here to help me and advise me. To ensure we locate the Shangri-La survivors and kill them. This is our only hope of doing that. Am I missing something? Find the woman, drag the truth out of her, and your problem's solved. Seems clear to me."

Zach seemed about to protest, but apparently thought better of it. "How far is it to Alexandria?"

"About a hundred and seventy miles," Whitely said.

"Then it will be at least four or five days."

Whitely exhaled. "No. We can have fresh horses waiting along the way, like the Pony Express. We can go faster and cover more like eighty miles a day instead of thirty or forty."

Snake nodded. "Then do it. Make the calls. Whatever it takes, am I clear?"

"She may not show up," Whitely warned again.

"I'm tired of discussing possibilities. Do as I say. Now."

Whitely gave a small shrug and made for the door. Zach rose and followed the older man. "I'll need to use the radio before we go. I have to keep Lassiter abreast of developments."

Snake frowned. "Whatever. Just don't stall. If she shows in Alexandria and you weren't there because of delays, there'll be hell to pay."

"We should radio ahead so they're on alert," Zach said to Whitely as they left Snake's chambers.

"No. Worst thing that can happen is we bring more people into this than already know. We tell those clods in Alexandria what's going on, and they'll probably blow it. These aren't the best or the brightest, in case you haven't noticed by now."

"And yet you work with them?" Zach asked, studying Whitely's profile.

"They're the only game in town, and I like breathing."

Zach turned away to conceal the smile that traced his lips. "Good call."

Chapter 35

Fog hung over the river road as Lucas and Sierra made their way back to the oil rig plant, the going awkward in the predawn. When they reached the boat, there was no sign of it having been disturbed, and he wasted no time in pushing it down the slope and into the water.

"Hold the bow," he said to Sierra, handing her the bow line as he climbed into the craft to inspect the branch with which he'd plugged the leak. A quick look showed it to be firmly in place with only a few drops of water oozing from the edges, and he nodded in approval. "Push off and hop in. I'll do the rest," he whispered, and Sierra did as asked and clambered into the boat.

The trip back to Louisiana was less exciting than the row from its shore had been. The only sound other than the rush of the water was the methodical splash of the oars. The sky was aflame over Mississippi as they reached the bank and leapt from the skiff, Lucas pausing to kick the branch from the bullet hole before pushing the boat into the current to meet its fate.

They hiked for two hours along the bank before arriving at the scattering of homes by the river, and Lucas slowed as he neared the field's wooden gate, which he'd closed when they'd left, but which now stood open. Sierra whispered to him, "What is it?"

"Someone's been here."

Lucas slid the M4 strap from his shoulder and flicked off the safety, and then snicked for his horse as he strode toward the opening. A snort followed by a whinny greeted him from the trees, and Tango trotted into view, apparently none the worse for wear. Lucas patted the stallion's neck as his eyes scanned the field and whispered to him, "Where's Nugget?"

"Good question," Sierra said, pointing to the muddy ground, where a hoofprint led away from the field. "Maybe she got spooked and forced the gate open? Looks pretty flimsy."

Lucas studied the rope that looped over a fence post as its crude closure mechanism and shook his head, hand tightening on the rifle grip. "No. Someone opened it."

"But Tango's still here."

"Tango wouldn't have let anyone take him." He eyed the big stallion. "Let's see if the saddles are still here. I hid them pretty well, so I hope they are."

He hurried to the hiding place and breathed a sigh of relief when he felt in the bushes. The saddlebags and saddles were right where he'd left them. Lucas hoisted his and strapped it onto Tango, and then leapt onto the animal's back.

"Stay out of sight," he cautioned. "I'm going after Nugget."

"We don't know how long ago they took her."

"Those tracks look fresh."

She eyed him doubtfully. "Be careful. It's not worth getting killed over a horse. We can always get another one."

"Tango can't carry you to Alexandria, and we can't take the chance that anyone has a decent horse to trade. If I can get Nugget back, that's best."

Lucas rode off, following the tracks with Tango at a canter. Half an hour later he slowed, and Lucas spotted Nugget tied to a post by the ruins of a shack. Two boys, maybe ten or eleven, looked up at him in alarm from their position by the hovel's entrance, and one of them pulled a pistol from his belt and stood.

Lucas held his M4 aloft so they could see it. "Drop the gun. I don't want to shoot anyone, but if I have to, I will. There's no way you'll get close with that thing, and I can hit you with my rifle no problem from here, so it's a bad bet, kid."

The boys exchanged a worried look, and the one with the pistol reluctantly lowered it and tossed it on the ground.

Lucas nodded. "Good thinking. Now keep your hands where I can see them."

He spurred Tango forward, his weapon pointed at the children, watching them closely as he neared in case one of them had another gun. When he was a dozen yards away, he dropped from the saddle, never taking his eyes off them, and approached. "Turn and put your hands on the wall so I can make sure you're unarmed," he instructed, and the boys did so, the smaller one visibly afraid. Lucas frisked them and then scooped up the pistol – a filthy Chinese .32 revolver. He thumbed the cylinder open and dumped two cartridges on the ground.

"We didn't mean no harm takin' the horse," the younger boy stammered. "We thought she was wild or somethin'."

"Shhh," the older one hissed. "I tol' you to keep it shut."

"You know they used to shoot horse thieves where I come from," Lucas said.

"Didn't know she was yours," the older boy tried.

"You thought she might have locked herself in?"

"Never know."

Lucas took in the boys' emaciated frames, their ribs washboards beneath their filthy shirts. "Where are your folks?"

"Don't have any," the older boy said.

"Just you two?"

"What's it to you?"

The younger one's voice had a tremor. "You gonna shoot us?"

"Got a good reason why I shouldn't?" Lucas asked.

"Bullets ain't cheap," the older one said. "Besides, there's your horse. No harm done. We was just watchin' her, keepin' her safe, is all."

"That's one way to look at it." Lucas stepped back. "How long you been on your own?"

"Maybe a year."

"What happened to your people?"

"Our pa crossed the Crew."

"The Crew leave you alone?"

"We stay outta sight when they come around."

"How often is that?"

"Couple times a week. You can hear 'em from a mile away."

"When did they last come by?"

"They was here yesterday shootin' up the river."

Lucas nodded thoughtfully and glanced at Nugget before focusing on the boys. "All right. Here's what I'm going to do. I'm going to take my horse and leave. You're going to stay where you are, and your lives are a gift from me to you. Which means you owe me. I catch you stealing horses again, I take the gift back. You read me?"

The boys mumbled yesses and Lucas stifled a grin. He hastened to Nugget and untied the mare, and then led her to Tango and climbed into the saddle. The boys were still leaning against the wall when he rode around the bend, and he shook his head at the world he inhabited, where desperate children were forced to carry guns and described the murder of their father with the nonchalance of discussing the weather.

When Lucas reached the field, Sierra emerged from the trees and came running. Lucas told her about the pair of ruffians who'd taken Nugget, and she was visibly relieved at the source of their temporary woes.

"Hard to blame them, isn't it?" she said.

"I'd have done the same at their age."

Sierra helped him with the saddle and bags, and by the time the sun was melting the ground fog away, they were riding west. Alexandria was a solid four days away, assuming no complications. The risk involved was an obvious one: they'd be riding through Crew territory the entire way and, because of the marshy terrain and lack of a map, would be forced to stay near established routes, which raised the risk of discovery.

Clouds rolled across the sky as the morning transitioned into afternoon, and when the rain came, it did so with a vengeance, pelting them with drops the size of marbles. The horses drove forward through the deluge, and the trail grew treacherous as the downpour intensified, the mud sucking at their hooves and slowing their progress.

When they set up camp for the night by a stream, the rain having finally abated, Lucas estimated that they'd covered no more than thirty miles. After stringing tripwires to alert them to intruders, he settled down with Sierra for the night, and he reckoned that this leg of their journey would be the hardest yet.

"Didn't get far as I'd like, but we'll be there soon enough," he said as she nuzzled his chest.

"I can't wait for you to meet Tim. You'll like him," she murmured, already half asleep.

He didn't give voice to the thought her comment spurred, namely that the life expectancy of a juvenile slave working the cane fields for the Crew was likely less than ideal, and not to get her hopes up.

Because he knew from their ongoing discussion that if they didn't find her boy, it would destroy her.

And while he couldn't shield her from that reality, he could delay the day of reckoning until it was unavoidable. That, at least, was within his power.

Which was enough for now.

Chapter 36

Elliot hummed to himself as he worked on his computer, calculating the rate at which the hubs could produce and distribute a quantity of the vaccine sufficient to inoculate the surviving population of the country, when the lights dimmed alarmingly and his battery backup screeched like an angry bird. He quickly saved the data and was powering down when the lights went out, plunging his workspace into darkness.

He felt in his lab coat and twisted a penlight on, and then made his way to the door. The pump fix that Craig had come up with had appeared to be stable with the loads the town was drawing – although the engineer had warned Elliot that it would only be fine until it wasn't. Elliot hoped this was just a minor glitch. The weather had been getting colder with each day, and it was just a matter of time until the snow turned from an inconvenience to a matter of survival.

Elliot pushed into the outer room and turned the flashlight off, enough sunlight streaming through the windows to be able to make out the furniture. He walked to the entrance and swung the door wide, bracing himself for the bite of cold he knew would assault him. A second later his expectations were rewarded by a blast of icy wind, and he was reminded again how quickly the moderate autumn could turn to winter.

He fumbled in his pocket, removed a two-way radio, and transmitted a call to Craig. The engineer answered thirty seconds later.

"This is Craig. Over."

"Power's down. Over."

"Pump gave out. Over."

"How long until you can get it back up? Over."

"I'll come by shortly. Over and out."

Elliot frowned. Craig taking time out from any repair didn't portend well. When he showed up a half hour later, his face was long.

"It's not good. We lost the pump, as I said, but there's no way to jury-rig it anymore. The seals blew. That's it – game over," he reported.

"Surely we have material we can use, or we can bypass it and put less load on the generator?"

"No. These are specialty pumps – subject to extremely high heat and pressure. I can't just cut up a crumbly tire or whatever and make seals – they won't last five minutes. And as to bypassing it, I already tried that – it isn't enough pressure to drive the turbine."

"Then what's the solution?"

He frowned. "You're not going to like it."

"Try me."

Craig explained the options, and when he finished, Elliot's dejected expression mirrored his.

"You were right. I don't like it. But you think it's possible?"

"It's our best shot."

Elliot nodded and waved to Arnold, who was walking with Duke and Aaron toward one of the nearby lodges. Arnold returned the gesture and the trio trudged to the community center, their breath steaming in the chill.

"Lost power, I see," Arnold said when he arrived.

"Yes," Elliot said. "Craig here says the only way we can get the juice flowing again is to go on a little expedition. I thought I'd enlist your help."

"How little?" Arnold asked.

"There's another geothermal plant about a hundred miles north of us," Craig said. "It's mothballed, but we should be able to cannibalize it for parts."

Arnold's eyes widened. "A hundred miles? That could be a week each direction, depending on the terrain."

"It won't be easy," Craig agreed. "But it's the only way. Either that, or plan on spending a long winter without power."

Elliot eyed his security chief and then shifted to the trader and his assistant. "So what do you say, gentlemen?"

Duke blinked, reminding Elliot of a startled cave dweller exposed to a bright light. "What do you mean, what do we say?"

"Are you up for an adventure?"

Duke frowned. "You mean us?"

Elliot nodded. "Arnold and Craig need backup. A hundred miles is a long way, and they can't keep reasonable watches with less than four people, as we all know."

"Why us?" Aaron asked.

"You're both trail savvy and have been through your share of firefights," Elliot said. "I don't have a lot of people anymore I can say that about."

Duke eyed Elliot skeptically. The physician had approached him the prior week about setting up a trading post as a recruiting station for the new Shangri-La. Duke had punted, saying he needed to think about what he wanted to do now that he was a wealthy man. Elliot had agreed to wait as long as it took for his answer, the truth being that there was nobody else with Duke's trading expertise who could do it, so he had no choice other than to be patient. "What do you think, Aaron? You in the mood for a ride?"

Aaron met his gaze. "Hell, it was getting pretty boring around here with nobody shooting at us. Why not?"

"When do you want to leave?" Arnold asked Craig.

"Sooner we take off, sooner we'll be back."

"I need half an hour to pack my kit," Aaron said.

"So meet back here in thirty minutes?" Craig asked.

Arnold looked at the sky. "We probably have another four hours of light. Better use all of it we can."

The men departed and Elliot watched them go, the sanctuary's future in their hands. Without power, it would be difficult, if not impossible, to continue his work on survival projections, which was his latest project now that the vaccine was in the field.

The only troubling issue was that St. Louis hadn't responded to any transmissions for well over a week. That was extremely unlike Darby, who was meticulous and prompt in all matters. Elliot had to assume the worst, which was why he was devoting his time to the scenarios where the virus couldn't be stopped in the Midwest for another six months.

With Darby off the playing field and his contacts exhausted, Elliot had no plan B to fall back on. That was a huge problem for a large chunk of the country if the virus flared up and began moving – a likelihood that was always at the front of his thoughts.

Michael came jogging up, his expression annoyed. "Lost the power again, I see."

Elliot explained the situation, as well as the solution. Michael pursed his lips in displeasure. "No power, no radio. So if disaster strikes, we'll have no forewarning."

"We can rig a few of the solar panels we scrounged. That should give us enough to operate the radio, at least during the day."

"Agreed. But it's a bad situation if they don't get the parts they need. Half the town will freeze to death with no power."

"Well, not to put too fine a point on it, but we can always hole up in the lodges with the hot springs. They emit more than adequate heat, and we should be able to run PVC pipes to the rooms and create some sort of passive radiation system."

"A hundred people all crammed into those lodges for four months?"

"It's not an elegant solution. But if freezing is the only other option, you'll grow to love thy neighbor, I'm sure."

Michael studied the houses in the near distance, his face dark. "What do you think the odds are they can fix the plant?"

Elliot frowned. "Right now I'd say you better start working on your social skills, because barring a miracle, we're dead in the water without a paddle."

"But Craig was optimistic?"

Elliot looked away. "He said that was the only option other than freezing. If you want to view that as optimism, you're a better man than I."

Chapter 37

The trip to Alexandria took the full four days Lucas had feared it would, though fortunately had been uneventful other than dodging a Crew patrol as they neared the city late in the morning. The contingent of riders had been large compared to what they'd seen at the Mississippi River: ten men armed to the teeth, with prison ink visible on their faces and shaved heads. Lucas had heard their horses before they appeared around a bend and taken evasive action, hiding behind a grove of trees, his and Sierra's rifles at the ready as the riders flew past in a blur.

Now they were on the outskirts of Alexandria, headed toward the rum factory grounds. They'd met an old woman selling fruit by a hovel on one of the secondary roads, who'd directed them to the sugar cane fields adjacent to the plant. She'd pointed to a plume of smoke corkscrewing into the sky and said it was from the factory's smokestack, and then cautioned them to stay clear of the place unless they wanted an express ticket to the promised land. Lucas had nodded solemnly at the warning and rewarded her with a round of 9mm, and she'd seemed delighted with the exchange.

When they were near the edge of the first cane field, they dismounted in the brush and tied the horses to a low-hanging branch before making their way toward its edge. The sugar cane stood tall in the sun, planted in long rows that seemed to go on forever. In the distance was the factory, a dull gray sheet metal structure with only a few broken windows at the second-story level and a ground floor consisting of loading docks and pedestrian entries that were bleeding rust.

"The fields are huge," Sierra whispered as they crept to a promising tree to climb and use as a vantage point.

"It's a big area. Rum must use up a lot of sugar cane."

"How many acres would you guess it is?"

"Maybe…a hundred, at least? Could be more."

They scaled the tree, and through his binoculars Lucas surveyed the field, where he could see gunmen on horseback with wide straw hats along the edge of the cane, watching the workers in the rows, some of whom were chopping with machetes while others were tilling at the roots. He counted six guards in all, and when he was satisfied there were none on foot, handed the glasses to Sierra so she could look for her son.

It was a humid day, and the sky was a gray sheet, the heat cloying with no breeze. Sierra gazed intently through the binoculars in silence as Lucas contented himself with keeping watch with his M4 in hand. Now that they had arrived, the magnitude of the challenge was obvious, and Lucas had not the faintest inkling as to how they would free her son in the unlikely event they actually found him.

The morning dragged on with no progress, and Lucas proposed that they skirt the field and find another location from which to observe the workers.

"It's a big area, Sierra. If he's not in these nearer groups, he might be at the other end. See the riders over there?"

She nodded silently and Lucas felt his heart lurch at the expression on her face. While not defeated, the odds of finding her boy were hitting home, and her eyes told the story of the stark realization.

They edged two hundred yards further along the perimeter and climbed another tree, this one lower, and Sierra went to work with the spyglasses again. After a tedious hour, Lucas was going to suggest a different vantage point when Sierra gasped and nearly lost her balance. She grabbed his arm with her free hand to steady herself and whispered, her voice tight, "I think I see him!"

Lucas didn't say anything. She continued peering at the field and then nodded slowly.

"It's him. He's bigger now, and his face has changed some, but I'd recognize him anywhere. He's alive, Lucas. Tim's alive, and he's down there."

Lucas's face was impassive. "Where, exactly, and what's he wearing? Describe him."

"He's got brown hair, like mine, cut short, and he's wearing a brown long-sleeve man's shirt with the sleeves half rolled up, and canvas pants, both hanging off him. He's working a hoe, it looks like. About a hundred yards down that second row – the guard's three rows away from him."

"Give me the glasses," Lucas said.

She took another long look through the binoculars and then did as he requested, pointing at the spot she'd called out. "See? There are about twenty kids there."

"I see them. But most of them are dressed the same, Sierra. It's kind of hard to tell them apart."

"Brown hair, brown shirt. Dark brown. Button up, open most of the way. You can see his chest. He's rail thin."

Lucas scanned the boys, all of them emaciated. "How far down the line?"

"Maybe…three quarters."

He adjusted his focus and saw the boy who sort of fit the description. "Dirt on his left cheek?"

"That's him, Lucas! That's Tim."

Lucas swept the area with the glasses, marking the guards' positions relative to the boys. The good news was that the horsemen didn't seem to have much inclination to move in the muggy swelter, preferring to sit on their horses and watch over the laborers, only occasionally goading their steeds to bark orders at the slaves before ambling back to what Lucas presumed were their assigned stations.

"You have to get him," Sierra whispered, her voice almost frantic.

"Also got to get away without us getting killed," Lucas answered reasonably, continuing to watch the nearest guard.

"Can't you sneak near him and tell him to follow you out?"

"That would work until one of the others sounded the alarm."

"Why would they? They're all in the same boat."

He didn't want to have to explain his reasoning to Sierra – that the other boys would be punished if Tim disappeared, possibly executed for not alerting the guards. Instead, he offered a terse response. "Don't want to risk it."

Sierra's voice hardened. "Lucas, we came all this way and found him. You have to do something."

He slowly lowered the glasses. "Sierra, we'll get him out of there. But we're not going to rush in and get caught. That won't accomplish anything, so cool your jets and let me think this through."

The resolve in his tone seemed to calm her, and she nodded mutely. He raised the binoculars again and scanned the rows, calculating how he could get to the boy without being seen by the guards or any of the other crews. After twenty minutes of patiently watching the boys' progress along the row, he handed Sierra the glasses and lowered himself down the tree trunk.

"You figure out how to do it?" she asked.

"Guess we'll find out soon enough."

"What do you want me to do?"

"Wait here. If they start shooting, make for the horses and get out of here."

"I'm not going to leave you and Tim."

"Won't do anyone much good dead. Better to live to fight another day, Sierra. If you've learned anything from me, that should be it."

"I hate it when you lecture me, Lucas."

Lucas didn't respond, already focused on the task at hand. He edged away, crouching in the brush as he made his way toward the field, wondering to himself what the hell he thought he was doing, trying to penetrate a guarded field in broad daylight.

It took him five minutes to creep to where he'd spotted a promising area of the fence that ringed the property, and he eyed the sagging barbed wire, a shred of fabric stuck to it where some unfortunate had presumably made a run for freedom – no doubt with disastrous results. That gave him further pause. If anything tipped off the guards, he and the boy would be dead meat. There was no way they'd be able to escape on foot with six mounted gunmen giving chase, especially while it was light out.

He debated returning to Sierra and explaining the harsh reality of their situation, but thought better of it. He'd at least give it a shot and see how close he could get. The guards weren't watching to ensure nobody tried to sneak into the slave camp, which was his only edge – though a slim one at that.

Lucas spread the wire until he could comfortably make it through the opening and dog-crawled to the first thick row of cane. Once up close, he saw that the row was impossibly dense, and realized that his idea of finding a gap in the cane was misguided. That left him with crawling in full view of any interested guards to one of the openings through which crews could traverse the rows, which would be suicide.

His thoughts were cut short by the sound of hooves from his left, one row over. A guard was making his way along the row – whether routine or not, Lucas didn't know, but if it wasn't, he had only seconds to take action.

Lucas scurried back to the gap in the fence. His boots were disappearing through the hole when the sound of the horse turning into the row vindicated his decision. He freed his M4 and lay still, holding his breath, a trickle of sweat working its way down his face as he prepared to engage.

The hooves neared the breach in the fence and stopped a few yards away from where Lucas was hiding. His finger moved to the trigger, his pulse thudding in his ears. The horse snorted irritably, and then boots hit the ground and walked to the gap.

A radio crackled and Lucas heard a raspy voice from nearby.

"I thought they fixed the fence over by L section. Over."

"They said they did. Over."

"Did a piss-poor job. Get someone out here and do it right. They didn't string new wire. Over."

"I'll add it to the list. You must be bored today. Over."

"Not too bored to whup your ass. Just do it. Over and out."

A pair of boots stood facing the gap. Lucas lay on his back only a few yards away with his rifle pointed at the guard's shins and his legs spread so his feet were concealed by the brush. He waited for what seemed like a small eternity, and then a stream of fluid splashed onto the fence wire.

The guard finished relieving himself with a sigh and trod back to his horse, and Lucas resumed breathing. He waited for the hooves to recede before pulling himself slowly further into the brush, the miss too near for his liking.

When he returned to Sierra, she was frowning, her worry clear. Lucas told her what had happened, and her expression changed from concerned to shocked.

"Oh, my God, Lucas…"

"Yeah. Don't want to do that again."

"Then how…"

"We're going to watch and wait. Once we know when the shift ends, what the guards do, and where they take the kids, we can see if there's a better way of approaching this. But right now I'd say there's zero chance of making it out alive trying something during the day."

"So we're just going to watch?"

Lucas nodded. "It's called planning, Sierra. You want your son back alive, we have to do this right. Otherwise he and I will die because we didn't do our homework."

Sierra's brow creased and she resumed staring through the glasses at her little boy laboring in the relentless heat, close enough to reach out and touch, and yet as inaccessible as if he'd been on another continent.

Chapter 38

It was dark when Lucas and Sierra descended from their perch and returned to the horses. The slaves had been herded toward a low building connected to the main plant, their tools confiscated before they entered, Lucas had seen through his glasses. Sierra's impatience was palpable, but he was still on edge from the close encounter with the guard, so he ignored it, determined to be systematic in his casing of the factory.

They moved closer to the buildings and settled in for the night where they could watch the guard shifts. Sierra eventually drifted off, leaving Lucas to his vigil, and he passed a sleepless night.

An hour after dawn the laborers, children and adults alike, filed from the building, and bowls of gruel were distributed to them. After ten minutes to eat, the guards passed out the tools and directed them to the fields for a repeat of the prior day.

Lucas watched the boys go to work, and when Sierra awoke, he whispered to her, "No point in spending all day monitoring this again. We have to move at night. Let's find someplace secure, and I'll try to get some sleep."

"I want to watch Tim."

"Sierra, the tiniest slip of any kind and they'll come for you. Then we're screwed. We can't afford that. I'll make my move tonight, but I need sleep, and I can't do so if I have to worry about you getting an idea and acting on it while I'm out."

He'd read her intentions accurately based on the dark look she gave him. He was too tired to engage further and walked to where Tango waited. Sierra reluctantly followed him and climbed onto Nugget, and they rode for a half hour until they found a secluded spot near a stream where the horses could drink and graze and Lucas could rest.

The day passed quietly, with Lucas snatching sleep in one- and two-hour bursts. Once it was dark again, they rode back to their observation spot and Lucas briefed Sierra on his plan.

"There are only two guards outside the building where Tim's being kept. If I can take them out silently, I can find him, detonate a grenade, and we can slip away in the chaos. By the time they figure out one of the boys is gone, we'll be in the clear."

"Won't the grenade lead them straight to you? Why alert anyone if you don't have to?"

"I may not have to set it off, depending on how the sleeping quarters are set up. But I'm assuming that they're all in one big room, in which case the others will see me. Like I explained earlier, there's no chance that the boys will stay quiet once I leave with Tim. I want things confused for as long as possible. So yes, I'm drawing attention – but by the same token, the kids will be terrified and the Crew distrustful of anything they say, which buys us time." He paused. "Hopefully enough to get a good head start."

Lightning veined the sky and a peal of thunder rumbled several seconds later. Lucas eyed the sky.

"Smells like rain's coming. That could work in our favor. I need you to wait here with the horses. Under no circumstances move, or leave, unless I'm not back by morning. Promise me you'll do that, Sierra. Please. If you want to see Tim alive, you have to do as I ask."

"I promise."

"Good."

She looked into his eyes. "So you're going?"

"Not yet. I'm going to wait until they're nearing the end of the first watch shift. The guards will be tired by then. And if we're lucky, it'll rain by then, which will serve as cover for me."

"How long?"

"Just before midnight."

They settled in for the wait, and the hours crawled by. Lucas's wish for rain was rewarded when a cloudburst sent sheets of water blowing across the cane fields, dropping visibility to a matter of yards. At eleven thirty he removed his crossbow and four quarrels from his saddlebag and handed Sierra his M4. She took it wordlessly, and he strapped his night vision monocle into place and switched it on.

"You're not going to need your rifle?" she asked.

"No. Whole point to this is to get in and get out silently."

"What if you have to shoot it out?"

"Doesn't matter what I'm armed with at that point, Sierra. There are way more of them than me. This isn't that kind of plan."

Worry crossed her face. "Are you sure?"

He leaned into her and kissed her on the lips. When he drew back, her eyes were moist. He flipped the monocle down so it was in his field of vision and turned from her, whispering as he did, "Don't worry. I can do this."

She watched him cock the crossbow and load a quarrel, and then he disappeared into the rain, his boots leaving puddles in his wake.

Lucas darted to the gap in the fence and slid through it, thankful that his bet that the Crew had been too slothful to fix it had proved a safe one. He leapt to his feet, the rain rinsing the mud from his clothes, and crept along the row until he reached the opening that would take him to the next channel. He repeated the process until the rum factory loomed above him in the darkness, the rain now lessening to a steady drizzle.

He'd noted the guards had bolted the access doors to the sleeping quarters the prior night, and was guessing that they were less to prevent intruders from penetrating than a precaution against the slaves trying to escape. That impression was confirmed when he spied the first guard standing in the shelter of an overhang and turned toward the building rather than the fields.

Lucas spotted the second guard at the far corner of the building, seated on a crate, a rain parka draped over his torso and his gun in his lap. This man was looking out at the field, making him the first target for Lucas's crossbow. Lucas edged along the row until he figured he was no more than twenty yards from the guard, and then parted the cane until he could see him through the haze of precipitation.

The thwack of the bow discharging was masked by the curtain of sugar cane. The quarrel drove home through the guard's chest, and he slumped forward as he clutched at the shaft with dying hands. Lucas waited a few beats before cocking and loading another bolt, and when he was sure the guard he'd shot was dead, he retreated to where the first guard was standing, as yet unaware of his companion's demise.

Lucas stepped from the nearby gap and crept along the cane until he was close enough to be confident of a head shot and loosed the bolt. The quarrel skewered the man's skull through his temples, and he dropped like a building in free fall, his AK 47 clattering beside him.

Lucas was in motion before the guard hit the ground, sprinting through the rain, thankful for the cover of darkness and the storm. Just as he reached the dead man, the sky brightened with a flash of lightning, and his ears popped from the explosion of thunder that immediately followed. He froze at the sound and then drew the crossbow and fitted a bolt in place before heading for the door.

He worked the bolt free and grimaced at the loud scrape it made. He repeated the maneuver with the second bolt at eye level with the same result and then pulled the door open, unsure what he would find inside.

A corridor led into the building, flanked by industrial metal doors on either side of the long passage. Lucas took a tentative step over the threshold, dripping water as he went, and approached the first door. He reached down and twisted the corroded lever handle and swung the door inward, leading with the crossbow, and gagged at the odor of human waste: he'd stumbled across what passed for the latrine – holes cut in the floor – the area foul beyond comprehension.

He was turning away when a flashlight beam struck his monocle from the end of the hall, blinding him.

A voice called out, "Freeze."

Lucas blinked away stars and debated reaching for the Kimber at his hip or firing the crossbow blindly at the voice, but decided not to when he heard multiple sets of boots rushing toward him.

"You go for the pistol, I'll blow your balls off," another voice warned, and Lucas stood motionless, obviously outnumbered.

A truncheon slammed against the side of his head, knocking the monocle ajar, and strong hands wrenched the crossbow from his grasp as his knees buckled. He felt his Kimber being removed from the hip holster, and then the original speaker was standing over him.

"Take him to the solitary cell," the man ordered. Lucas winced in pain as a pair of men hauled him to his feet and frisked him, taking his knife, grenade, and flak jacket. They handcuffed his hands behind his back and then half dragged him down the hall, stumbling and disoriented. At the end of the corridor they stopped and threw him into a room with a barred window, the glass gone, the air putrid and stifling. The men stood aside and a tall figure entered, his tattooed face and shaved head identifying him as Crew.

"Where's the woman? Sierra," he demanded.

"Don't know what you're talking about."

"We know you're after the boy. Where is she?"

"Boy? What are you talking about? I was after rum."

The man moved so fast Lucas was unprepared for the kick to his ribs. He grunted at the pain but made no other sound, and the man stood back and studied him before turning and making for the door.

"You'll wish you'd told me," the man said quietly, and then the steel door slammed shut behind him, echoing off the walls with the finality of a gunshot. Lucas pulled himself to a sitting position, leaning against one of the rough brick walls, his mind working furiously as he waited for his captors to reappear, this time prepared to interrogate him in earnest. He had no illusions that he wouldn't be subjected to the tortures of the damned, and mentally steeled himself for the ordeal to come, cursing silently that having survived everything that life had thrown at him, he would meet his end at the Crew's hands over a fight that wasn't even really his.

Lucas closed his eyes and prayed that Sierra would honor her promise, and when he didn't show come morning, would abandon her reckless crusade, but he knew her too well – this would be the end, not only for Lucas but for her, and likely her son as well.

Chapter 39

The mountains around the second geothermal plant were white with fresh snow as Duke, Aaron, Arnold, and Craig made their way up a trail to the valley where the hamlet and the hot springs that hosted the plant were located. Three-quarters of the way into their trip, a storm had blown through and dropped over a foot of snow, the relentless blizzard assailing them as they'd hunkered down overnight. Now, on the last day of their trek, the going was slow and treacherous, and what should have been a four-hour ride had taken most of the day.

"Don't want to be on this trail after dark," Arnold said, looking to his left where a ravine dropped to the silver rush of a swollen creek below.

"Shouldn't be too much farther," Craig assured him from his position in the lead.

"So we spend the night here and then head back in the morning?" Aaron asked.

"Assuming we make it," Duke grumbled, unhappy at having to slog through the snow rather than enjoying the warmth of his new home in Pagosa Springs, a fire crackling in the hearth.

An arctic wind off the mountain carried with it a mist of snow, the tail end of the storm lingering like a bad taste. Craig braced himself against the onslaught, the cold burning his exposed cheeks, a bandana tied over his nose and mouth like an old Western bandit to shield them from the worst of it.

"This sucks," Duke added as he lowered his head, his eyes slits, his appendages freezing in spite of the extra layers he'd donned. He'd spent too much time in the Texas sun – the cold affected Aaron and him more than the pair from Shangri-La, who were accustomed to the vicious winters of the New Mexico mountains.

"No country for old men," Aaron joked, his voice deadpan.

"Who you calling old?" Duke snapped.

"If the shoe fits is all I'm saying."

The snowfall intensified as they climbed the grade, and at times the sky was white, visibility down to nothing, which slowed them further. When the storm remnant passed, it left the landscape covered and the trail even more treacherous. The horses picked carefully along, their footing unsure in the slippery coating.

Arnold never stopped scanning the pine trees around them, his AR-15 in hand out of habit. They had no idea what they were walking into, although Craig had guessed that the plant would be deserted, the systems mothballed just prior to the collapse, based on the reports he'd discovered in a work journal of one of the engineers at the Pagosa Springs plant. Still, that was just a hunch, and Arnold was naturally cautious and refused to let his guard down, even for an instant.

Dusk was an hour away when they rounded the final bend. Arnold spurred his horse forward, pulled even with Craig, and whispered to him, "Hold up. I saw something move on our right."

The group stopped, and Arnold swung down from his horse and handed Craig the reins. "Stay here," he said, and disappeared into the trees. The valley with the plant and a scattering of houses still lay at least a quarter mile ahead.

Arnold plowed through the calf-high snow, weaving among the conifers as he pushed toward whatever had drawn his eye. When he reached a small clearing, he spied a young man digging in the snow with a hoe. Arnold took in his appearance – wild hair, ragged and torn clothing – and stepped from the tree line, rifle trained on him.

The man looked up with an expression of shock and stood motionless as Arnold drew near, his eyes wide. When Arnold was no more than fifteen feet away, the young man spoke in a low voice.

"I haven't got anything worth killing me over."

Arnold gave a half shrug. "Wasn't planning on killing anybody today. What are you doing out here?"

"Trying to salvage what's left of our vegetable garden. We have a bunch of crops planted and didn't expect a freeze so soon. Thought we had a few more weeks, at least."

"You live here?"

"That's right." The man studied Arnold. "Why? You sound surprised."

"I am. It's just that we thought...nobody would be here."

"Yeah, well, my family and I live here. In peace, until recently."

Arnold tilted his head at the last words. "Yeah? What happened?"

"You headed into town? You'll see soon enough." The man frowned. "You're going to need that rifle. I'd just turn around if I was you."

"Why?"

"Two months ago a gang of scavengers showed up. Meaner than dirt and violent. They camped out at the hot springs and terrorized us into doing their hunting and fishing for them." The man paused and looked away. "And I've got three sisters. Youngest is only eleven."

"Oh."

He ground the toe of his boot absently in the dirt. "Yeah, it's been bad."

"Why don't you leave?"

"And go where? Besides, they said they'd kill us. I believe them. They're animals."

"Just you and your family...and them?"

"That's right."

"Whereabouts do they stay? The scavengers, I mean."

"There's some kind of generator building by the springs. They took it over because it's always warm inside."

Arnold cursed. "Think you could describe the layout for me?"

"Why? What's it to you, anyway?"

"We need to get some parts from the generator."

"For what?"

"You ask too many questions."

"Taking them on is a death sentence, stranger. I'd get out of here while you can."

"I don't know about that. I had two sisters myself before the collapse. Hate to think they'd have been fair game to a bunch of miscreants if they'd survived."

"You hard of hearing? There's ten of them, and one of you."

"Not really. More like four." Arnold studied the man. "What's your name?"

"Sal."

"You must know the layout like the back of your hand, right?"

Sal nodded. "Of course."

"You'd be better off without your unwanted guests?"

"Are you kidding?"

"Here's what I propose. You tell me everything you know about the plant – the approach, their habits, their weapons. In exchange, we clear them out for good."

"How do I know this isn't a trick?"

"What kind? We're on the side of a mountain, and you're rooting around for turnips. What do you think I'd be tricking you out of?"

Sal leaned against the hoe, considering Arnold's hard expression and obvious familiarity with his weapon. "First thing you have to know is that you have no chance until nightfall." He continued speaking for five minutes. Arnold interrupted him several times, but Sal proved thorough in his descriptions, anticipating most of Arnold's questions. When the young man finished, Arnold regarded him with a half smile.

"One last question, Sal," he said.

"Yeah? What?"

Arnold studied the young man's lean form and angry eyes.

"How are you with a gun?"

Chapter 40

The cell door opened and Lucas looked up, the blood now dried on the side of his face. A powerfully built man with gray hair cropped close to his skull stepped into the cell and closed the door behind him. Lucas regarded him, pausing at his face, which was unblemished by the prison ink the Crew members sported. The man nodded as he approached Lucas and stood just out of reach of his legs, obviously reading the intent in Lucas's eyes and avoiding the sweep kick he'd planned.

"Doesn't look very comfortable," the man noted, eyeing Lucas evenly.

Lucas stared vacantly at him.

The man smiled. "We know you're Sierra's accomplice. We know this because we expected you, and you didn't disappoint. But the question is, where is she? And who are you?" Zach paused. "Although the latter isn't of that much interest."

"I told the other guy I don't know what you're talking about."

"Yes, I heard." Zach appraised Lucas, taking his time. "Have you ever been waterboarded? Probably not, I'll guess. I hear it's the closest to dying you can get. You basically drown – your body goes into panic mode and your lungs fill with fluid. Again and again and again. Like an unending hell."

Lucas remained silent.

"The problem is that torture rarely generates reliable information. That's a problem the unsophisticated ignore at their peril. Don't get me wrong – it's certainly cathartic for all involved, but in my experience a tortured man will say anything to make it stop, invent anything, confess anything. Not that inconvenient facts will stop the Crew from doing it, mind you. They tend to be a hammer that sees all problems as nails."

"You're not Crew?"

"No."

"But you're working with them."

Zach crouched down and eyed Lucas, maintaining a safe distance. Lucas could see the man was seasoned, his eyes cold.

"I know all about your Shangri-La. About the vaccine. About Sierra's son. I know it all."

Lucas's expression remained neutral. "Then why question me?"

"I need to know where she is."

"I have no idea who you're talking about. I told the other goon, too. I was after rum."

"You carry a Kimber and killed two guards with a crossbow, and you expect anyone to buy that ridiculous excuse? Maybe I give you too much credit for intelligence."

Lucas went to a peaceful place in his mind, anticipating the pain that was to come. Zach seemed to intuit what he was doing, and his voice changed from hard to reasonable.

"Everything you think you know is a lie." He spoke the words slowly, as though revealing a great secret. "You see things as black and white. The Crew is bad. Your leader, Elliot, is good." Zach smiled at the flicker in Lucas's eyes. "Yes, that's right, I know all about Elliot. I'm sure you see this as a struggle between ultimate good and ultimate evil. Don't get me wrong – the Crew is without a doubt a bunch of thugs and sadists and as evil as the devil himself. But they're just a cog in a larger machine. They're meaningless in the scheme of things." Zach paused. "Am I getting through to you?"

"You're talking in riddles. I was after rum."

"Please don't insult me with that story. It's almost worse than if you said nothing. It's so bad it's painful."

Lucas's lips narrowed to a thin line. "Fine. You know everything.

And you're working with the Crew, who are really great guys if you can get past the mass murder and slavery and all."

"No, they're despicable. But we're forced to use them."

"Forced," Lucas repeated.

"Let me tell you a story. I'll start off with the version you've been told and then tell you the truth. You were told that Elliot was selflessly developing a vaccine to save the world because he's a great man, and it's the right thing to do. That Magnus was trying to stop him because he was a power-hungry monster who wanted to control the vaccine himself so he had the power of life over death, which, of course, he would abuse to enrich himself. Does that sound familiar?"

"It's your dime, buddy."

"Parts of that are true. Magnus was a monster. And he was certainly power-mad. The problem is that the real world isn't your black-and-white construct – it's shades of gray. Your Elliot is not without sin in this. I know you and the rest of his acolytes believe he's wonderful, but the truth is that we reached out to him years ago to assist him in developing the vaccine, and he refused. The reason is anything but selfless. You see, he could have had it developed far sooner, and many innocent lives would have been spared in the interim. But he didn't want that. He didn't want to work with anyone else. No, your Elliot wanted all the credit for himself – because he is also thirsty for power, and as the savior of the world with his vaccine, he will certainly be a revered figure, will he not?"

"You say *we*. Who are you?"

"It doesn't matter who I am or what my affiliation is."

"Does to me."

"Why? So you can prejudge us based on other half-truths and distortions? It's not useful. Think of us as the power behind the throne. We've been that, and more, for a long time. It's useless to resist us, and we're anything but evil – the truth is that your concept of good or evil is entirely relative and doesn't apply any longer…if it ever did. It was a comforting morality story, a fairy tale to keep the young and dim from misbehaving. We are neither good nor evil. We simply are, and always will be, because we correctly foresaw the collapse and took measures to ensure our survival."

"You're telling me this because I'm a swell fellow?"

"I'm telling you because you're working for a zealot and a madman who would watch thousands die so he can take credit for something that could have saved them. That's your good, in your simple-minded good versus evil equation."

"Why is it so important to find out where he is?"

"The virus is mutating. We need his help. The vaccine he's created will be useless against the new variants, and mankind's existence is at risk."

"That's why Magnus tried to destroy him?"

"Magnus was a fool. He took matters into his own hands. He, like you, didn't understand the full story and thought it was all about seizing more power. He was wrong, and he paid for being wrong, and the world's better for it. But we still need to reach an agreement with Elliot; and to do that, we need to send an emissary to negotiate a truce. There are international repercussions as well – what they used to call national security. There's a strong possibility that a hostile actor will use the current state of affairs to seize the country and eliminate us all."

Lucas shook his head. "I can't help you."

Zach's face softened. "They'll kill the boy, you know. In front of you. Filet him and make you eat his heart while it's still beating."

Lucas shrugged. "Haven't had a hot meal for a while."

Zach smiled again. "Here's the alternative. Help me and you'll go free. So will Sierra. She'll be reunited with her son, and bygones will be bygones. We'll remove you from Crew custody and transport you to our closest enclave. It's safe, has water, food, power, fuel – everything you could wish for. You'll be given a large property, free and clear. Wealth beyond your wildest dreams." Zach eyed him. "Women. Girls, if you like. Or boys. Doesn't matter. You'll live like a god."

"And if I don't?"

"The boy will die in front of you, and then they'll cut you to pieces after they've abused you in ways you can't even imagine."

Zach straightened and moved to the door. "Think about it. I'll be back shortly, and when I return, your decision will determine the rest of your time on earth." Zach wet his lips. "I can't even begin to explain how horribly they'll violate little Tim before they kill him. So if you're thinking you'll tough it out, trust me when I say there's nothing on earth quite like what they'll do to him while you watch. They're sadistic butchers, and they live for this. Which you look like you know."

Zach swung the metal slab wide and exited the cell, leaving Lucas to stare at his back before a guard slammed it shut and bolted it. Their footsteps receded down the hall, and Lucas closed his eyes again, his mind roiling.

~ ~ ~

"Well?" Whitely demanded upon Zach's return.

"I don't think he bought it."

"That's a problem."

"Yes. I realize that."

"So what next? The boy?"

"I'm not sure killing him in front of our friend will accomplish anything. I recognize his type. He's seen too much."

"Then we torture him until he talks."

Zach shook his head. "He won't."

"They all do."

"Oh, he'll talk, but you won't know what's true and what isn't. He'll mix truth and lies together, his ultimate revenge to leave us with nothing we can use. You can see it in his eyes. He's already resigned to dying, and he honestly doesn't fear it."

"Snake will have us both executed if we fail."

Zach frowned. "I'm not sure he'll do that. But I agree he'll want a scapegoat, and you're probably it."

Whitely paced, his brow furrowed, and then stopped abruptly, a look of wonder on his face. "There's another way."

"Which is?"

"We let him go, and he leads us to the woman – or even better, to wherever this Elliot is hiding."

"Just like that? Are you mad?"

"Hear me out. I know all about the operation in Lubbock where Sierra was captive. I can tell him that I'm part of the rebel faction, working against the Crew for the good of humanity, and in charge of security here. If it's rushed enough, he won't have time to question it. I can show up with the boy, hand him back his weapons, and guide him to an exit – where you can be waiting to pick up his trail."

"You don't think he'll see through the deception?"

"He took a blow to the head. Plus the alternative is being tortured and killed. My story is entirely non-disprovable. Under the circumstances, it's a lifeline anyone would grab."

Zach nodded. "You'll need something to convince him, something you would do if you were genuine, or he'll smell a rat."

"I'll have to kill a guard outside the cell. That would do it."

Zach snapped his fingers. "No, wait. He shot two guards, didn't he? One in the chest. We'll drag that one in, throw a new shirt on him, and you can cut his throat."

"He might be stiffening up by now."

"Won't matter. The hall's fairly dark."

"We'll need some blood. Smear it all over him for effect."

Zach nodded again. "We'll slaughter a hog."

"It has to be soon. I'll go get the boy and the weapons; you handle the body. But for God's sake, be quiet, or he'll hear you getting it into position. Give me fifteen minutes."

"The boy can't see you."

"You can leave him by the north gate – tell him not to move. He's conditioned to obey. He'll stay put."

"If he doesn't, it all falls apart."

It was Zach's turn to pace. Halfway across the room, he spun to face Whitely.

"Tie his arms and legs, then. I don't care. You have fifteen minutes."

Chapter 41

From his hiding place down the road, Sal pointed Arnold's 9mm Heckler & Koch pistol at the geothermal plant. The interior of the building glowed with torchlight, and smoke drifted from the open windows along with steam from the hot springs. Darkness had fallen two hours before, and Sal had agreed to rendezvous with Arnold's party at an abandoned home nearby. He'd reappeared on time, and Arnold had introduced him to the others and given him the pistol, showing him the safety and quizzing him to verify he wouldn't shoot his foot off.

"They never sleep. I mean, not all at once. There's always a couple of them that stay up," Sal said.

"Think the rest might be asleep by now?"

"No way of knowing. Some nights they're out after they eat, others they're all up half the night."

"Would they freak out if you knocked on the door?"

"I've never done that."

"Can you think of some reason to draw them out? Maybe a problem with one of your sisters?" Arnold asked.

Sal's face clouded. "They couldn't care less."

Arnold sighed. "Then we do this the hard way." He turned to Duke and Aaron. "We'll sneak in through the back door. Sal, you and Craig take cover out front. Any of them come through that door, let them have it."

218

Sal nodded, and Craig grunted assent.

They'd discussed a frontal assault but had discarded the idea – too many of the scavengers slept well away from that area. The rear entrance made the most sense, although it involved more risk. If the cold from the outside alerted anyone, they'd be in a drawn-out gun battle, and that didn't work in their favor, given the two-to-one odds.

Arnold led the pair of traders around the building, sticking to the trees in case anyone was paying attention inside. When they reached the back, Arnold nodded to Duke and tried the doorknob.

It turned soundlessly, and he switched his AR-15 to burst mode, took a deep breath, and cracked the door open just wide enough to slip through.

Aaron followed him in, and Duke brought up the rear. They found themselves in a small utility room, as Sal had described. Reassured the young man hadn't led them astray, they crossed the room with cautious steps, and Arnold pointed to the door that opened onto the main pump area, where the scavengers slept on bedrolls, warmed by the steam from the hot springs.

"Ready to do this?" Arnold whispered.

Aaron nodded, his expression determined, and Duke did the same.

"I'll open the door. Aaron, you go in low and move right. Duke, I'll go next, and you cover us from here. The wall should stop any rounds. Fire when you acquire targets."

"Be careful not to shoot us in the back," Aaron said.

"Don't put ideas in my head," Duke whispered.

Arnold reached for the lever and Aaron got into position, ready to enter the room in a crouch. Arnold closed his eyes for a moment, gathering his thoughts, and then twisted the handle and pushed the door wide.

A jumble of metal pipes rose from the floor and twisted to one of the walls, and Aaron crept into the room, leading with his rifle. Arnold was halfway through the door when a warning cry sounded from the far side of the space, and then the still of the night exploded with shots as Arnold and Aaron engaged.

RUSSELL BLAKE

The sleeping men scrambled for their weapons while Arnold's first two bursts slammed into the shooter by the front door who'd fired at them, knocking him against the wall and shattering the ceramic plate in his flak jacket. He slid down the wall, leaving a red streak, his eyes wide in shock. Aaron blasted at his companion, who'd thrown himself to the ground in order to make a more difficult target, but his rounds missed and ricocheted off the cement floor, spraying chunks of concrete into the air as they whined past the gunman.

Three of the other scavengers opened up with their weapons, and Duke's rifle barked three-round bursts from the doorway. One caught a crouching shooter in the upper chest and throat, blowing him backward. Aaron cried out in pain from Duke's right, and Duke stitched three bursts into the shooter Aaron had been trying to hit.

Arnold darted behind the pipes and ducked around to unleash a barrage of fire at the scavengers. His rounds found home more often than not, cutting the legs from under one gunman and shredding through the torso of another. Slugs pinged off the pipes and snapped past his head, and he emptied his magazine into the remaining men, who'd taken cover using the bodies of the fallen to block his fire.

He ejected the magazine and slapped another into place as Duke continued drilling the scavengers whenever one showed himself in the gloom, and Arnold heard the breech of the trader's AR-15 lock open as he ran out of rounds. Two of the scavengers took the opportunity during the lull to make for the front entrance and rushed through the door, only to be shot to pieces by Craig and Sal when they emerged.

Duke and Arnold mopped up the remaining scavengers in thirty more seconds, and then the shooting stopped, all the scavengers neutralized. Arnold rose from his position behind the snarl of pipes and slowly walked into the main area. The floor was slick with bright red blood. One of the scavengers moaned and reached for his dropped weapon with a trembling hand, and Arnold finished him with a burst to the head.

Arnold moved from body to body, confirming that each was dead,

220

and was at the last corpse when Duke's voice hissed from across the room.

"Aaron's hit bad."

"Damn," Arnold said, his face grim. He turned and made for Duke, who was kneeling beside Aaron. The younger man's flak jacket was soaked crimson, and Aaron gasped for air as blood pooled beneath him. At least two rounds had penetrated his body armor…and his lungs.

Aaron grabbed Duke's hand, clutched it weakly, and tried to raise his head. Duke inched closer. "No. Don't try to move."

"This…this is…it…" Aaron managed, and then let out a long groan and shuddered before lying still, pinpoint pupils locked on the ceiling as though it hid a secret only he could see.

Duke's shoulders heaved and he reached forward to close his friend's eyes. Arnold left him to his grief and walked to the front entrance to let Craig and Sal know it was all clear.

"Don't shoot. It's over. They're dead," he yelled through the door, and then stepped back, knowing that nerves could do strange things in battle and not wanting to get hit by inadvertent friendly fire.

Craig entered first and Sal trailed him in, pistol pointed at the ground. Arnold held out his hand for the weapon, and Sal nodded numbly and gave it to him before approaching one of the dead and spitting on his face.

"His name was Zeke. He…my youngest sister will be glad he's dead."

"No loss to the world that any of them is gone, sounds like," Arnold said.

"No."

"Aaron!" Craig exclaimed when he saw Duke by Aaron's body and rushed to him. Duke looked up with red eyes and shook his head.

"He didn't make it."

"Oh…God, Duke. I'm sorry."

Duke didn't answer and, after a long pause, pushed himself to his feet and turned to Arnold. "Let's get what we're after and get out."

"You can stay with us for the night, if you want," Sal offered. "There's a house next door that's still got its roof. Might not be too bad if you start a fire."

Arnold nodded. "Thanks, that's mighty kind of you, but we're not going to want to spend any more time here than we have to." He looked to Duke. "We'll bury Aaron in the morning before we leave."

Duke shook his head. "No. I'll do it now. No reason he should lie out all night. You don't need me anymore. Craig can get his precious parts and I'll take care of it." Duke made for the back door.

"Where are you going?" Arnold asked.

"To get a shovel."

"Ground's hard as brick," Sal said.

"I need the exercise."

Sal nodded. "I've got a pick. I'll help."

The men left Craig and Arnold to scrounge for the pumps Craig needed, and returned shortly to haul Aaron outside. It took the engineer a half hour to remove the pumps and seals, and he carried them to his horse. The snow flurry had ended, but the air pricked his skin like needles. Arnold joined him and gestured to where Sal and Duke were finishing up Aaron's grave. They walked over and Duke said a prayer, choking on the last words and barely managing an amen.

They hung their heads in silence for several moments, and then Arnold looked to Sal. "Where's your place?"

"On the edge of town."

He led them a few hundred yards from the plant to a cracker-box home that appeared to be barely standing. A young woman with a frightened face peered out from inside; when she saw Sal, she burst from the doorway and ran to hug him.

"You're okay!" she said, and then stared fearfully at the strangers.

"I am. And they're history," Sal said. "These are the men I told you about. Duke, Arnold, Craig, this is Liza, my oldest sister." Two more faces peeked from the doorway. "That's Cody, and the youngest there is Cas."

Arnold touched Sal's arm, and Liza released her brother. Arnold led him a few feet away and spoke in a low voice. "We have a nice setup where we are. Power. Water. Well defended. If you're of a mind, you and your sisters are welcome to join us."

"We...that's a hell of an offer," Sal said, and then frowned. "But we don't have any horses."

"Don't the scavengers?"

"Oh. Right. Sure they do."

"Then they're yours now. So are their weapons and ammo. That should give you a good start on a new life – you'll have something to trade for anything you need."

"I have to talk to my sisters, but they'll do whatever I decide," he said. "How far is it?"

"Four days' ride."

"And you're sure it's safe?" Sal gestured at the plant. "Nobody like that bunch there?"

Arnold gave Sal a reassuring grin. "If there was, I'd have personally blown their head off."

Sal nodded and offered his hand to shake. "Then consider us in."

Chapter 42

Lucas stirred when he heard the bolt on the door screech open and prepared for the ordeal to come. He'd always known the risk he was taking, and now it was time to pay the piper – in blood. That Tim would wind up dying horribly was an abomination, but it was too late now to do anything. He knew that he and the boy would be killed whether or not he gave them what they wanted, so there was no point in doing anything but tuning out and seeking refuge in the deepest recesses of his mind, where nothing could reach him.

The door opened and Lucas looked up. An older man with a neatly trimmed gray beard and a gray shirt covered in blood stepped in. A satchel hung from his shoulder, and he clutched a holstered gun in one hand and a key in his other. He hurried to Lucas and knelt beside him.

"Lean forward. I'm going to uncuff you," he said.

"Who are you?"

"Name's Whitely. I'm one of the rebels fighting the Crew. From Lubbock. I was tight with Jacob and Eddie."

The right cuff snapped open, and Whitely went to work on the left. When it dropped on the floor, Lucas flexed his fingers, trying to coax the circulation back. Whitely grabbed one of his arms and helped him to his feet, and then handed him the holstered gun.

Lucas's eyes widened when he saw that it was his Kimber. Whitely reached beneath his loose shirt, removed Lucas's big Bowie knife, and gave it to him. "Sorry I couldn't get your night vision gear, but it's broken, so wouldn't do you a lot of good."

Lucas strapped on his pistol and checked the magazine – full, he could tell from the weight. He verified that a round was chambered and then slid his belt through the slots in the knife sheath and buckled it.

Whitely looked over his shoulder at the door. "Hurry up. We need to get out of here. They'll be coming for you any minute."

Lucas eyed him suspiciously. "How are Jacob and Eddie doing?"

"They…they didn't make it. I'm sorry. Nothing I could do to save them."

Lucas nodded and followed Whitely to the door. Whitely poked his head out, cast his eyes about, and then took off down the hall toward the rear of the building. Lucas took in the blood-covered form of a guard on the floor and kicked the man as hard as he could, verifying that he was dead. Satisfied, he trotted to where Whitely was waiting.

"What's the plan?"

"I'm going to lead you to one of the loading docks. They expect you to go out the north dock. You're going to go out a different one."

"I don't understand."

"I convinced them that the only way we'd find Sierra was to break you out and then follow you to her."

Realization lit Lucas's eyes. "They think you're working with them. This is all part of a ruse."

"Correct. What they don't know is that I actually *am* with the rebels, that it's not just a cover story."

"Won't it be hard on you when things don't go the way they're supposed to?"

Whitely shook his head. "Things never go as planned. Entropy and chaos. Not my fault." He stopped and peered around a corner, and then took off again. When they reached another steel door at the end of the corridor, Whitely grimaced. "Besides, you're going to conk me on the head with your gun, so it'll look like you overpowered me once we were at the loading dock. That way it will seem like I was out cold and had no idea you were going to double-cross me."

Lucas nodded. "Dangerous game."

"I'll have the wound to back my story."

"What about the boy? I'm not leaving without him."

Whitely pushed the door open and motioned for Lucas to follow. "I didn't think you would."

"You killed the guard?"

"No. That was faked."

Lucas nodded again. "I could tell. He'd been dead for more than a few minutes."

"You actually killed him – he was the first man you shot."

"Don't suppose you have my crossbow, do you?"

"Negative. Just be glad they went for my idea. Otherwise they'd be slicing and dicing you and the boy as we speak."

Whitely led Lucas across a warehouse filled with plastic crates containing rum bottles. He pointed to one of the roll-up doors. "That's where you're supposed to duck out. They've got a party in place to track you." Whitely turned and pointed to the far end of the warehouse. "Go out through that door, make for the south end of the fields, and you'll avoid them completely."

"And the boy?"

Whitely indicated a stack of crates. "He's behind those. I had to tie him up to make sure he didn't run off. He's scared and doesn't trust anyone – for good reason."

A thought occurred to Lucas, and he unbuckled his belt and slid off his sheath and holster. He withdrew the blade and closely examined the leather of the sheath, feeling with his fingers along the inside as far as he could, and then repeated the inspection on the holster. When he was done, he nodded. "Eve had a tracking chip on her."

"You should check the boy, too, just in case."

"I plan to."

Lucas crossed to the crates and looked behind them. Tim was on the floor, his hands bound behind him along with his ankles, clearly terrified. Lucas crouched down and whispered to the boy.

"Your mom sent me. My name's Lucas. I'm here to get you out of here." He studied the boy. "Understand?"

Tim nodded, though his eyes were still distrustful. Lucas saw the look and leaned in closer. "Look, you have to stay quiet or we're both dead. Your mom's waiting not far from here. Do what I say, and you'll be with her within an hour. Make a sound and you screw the whole thing up."

"What's her name?" Tim asked.

Lucas smiled. "Sierra."

"How do you know her?"

"I rescued her from the Crew, same as I'm doing with you."

Tim's eyes narrowed. "You own her?"

Lucas shook his head. "More like she owns me. It's complicated. But no. We're all free. Nobody owns anybody."

Tim grappled with the explanation and nodded again. Lucas withdrew his Bowie knife and severed his bindings with the razor-sharp edge, and then sheathed it and lifted Tim to his feet. The boy couldn't have weighed more than fifty pounds, and Lucas frowned at the mistreatment that would result in a boy his size being so thin.

Lucas did a methodical search of the child's clothes and reassured himself that there was no obvious tracking device, and then turned to Whitely and pulled his Kimber free. Whitely's eyes tracked it and he winced. "I suppose you have to make it convincing. Let's go over to the loading dock so there's no mistaking you clobbered me as I was leading you out."

"Fair enough."

The older man walked to the door. "Good luck, Lucas."

"Same to you. Turn around and close your eyes."

Whitely did as instructed, and Lucas clubbed him in the side of the head with the butt of the Kimber. Whitely dropped heavily to the floor, and Lucas caught him before his head could strike the ground. He set him down gently and leaned down to check his pulse, and then straightened and held out his free hand to Tim, eyeing his homemade sandals.

"Gonna have to get you some boots," Lucas said, and Tim

reluctantly took his hand. "Remember. Not a sound."

And then they were running for the door, Tim's small feet pattering on the concrete at twice the rate of Lucas's, the area so dark they could barely see except for the glow of ghostly light drifting from the high windows.

Chapter 43

Outside the plant, Lucas pulled Tim along toward the far left cane field, his eyes adjusting to the dark as they ran. The ground was soft and spongy from the rain, which had abated at some point during the night, but distant pulses of lightning foretold more downpours to come.

They paused at the first gap in the tall sugar cane, and Lucas whispered to the boy, "You know these fields pretty well?"

Tim nodded.

"Get us to the fence the fastest you can. They're waiting for us over there," Lucas said, indicating the field to their right. "So we need to go the opposite direction."

"Okay. This way."

Now it was Tim's turn to lead Lucas, who wasn't thrilled with the idea of his life being in the hands of a ten-year-old. They stayed low as they ran, the ground giving beneath their feet, and Lucas silently damned the rain for creating an environment where their tracks would be obvious. His only hope was that it started pouring again before the Crew picked up the scent, because otherwise they'd be in a race that they couldn't win.

Tim directed them through a gap and they jogged along another row of cane. Lucas checked over his shoulder periodically to ensure they weren't being followed, though the loss of the night vision monocle had eliminated an important edge he'd counted on having when they escaped.

His plan in tatters, he allowed a child to pull him through the night, praying that the boy knew what he was doing – because Lucas could only play it by ear now. They reached another gap and Tim didn't hesitate, dodging through it and continuing in a westerly direction, away from the area where the Crew lay in wait.

They reached the fence and Tim stopped, panting from exertion, and looked up at Lucas. Lucas peered in the gloom at the barbed wire and spotted a fence post where the steel was wrapped around the wooden pole. He moved to the support and pushed against it with his foot, and it gave a few inches. He kicked it, and it shifted again. As he'd hoped, the post was driven straight into the mushy ground, with no concrete base to stabilize it. He stepped nearer and heaved at it, working it back and forth as he lifted, and after an agonizing few seconds the wood stake slid from the soil with a sucking sound.

He laid it flat on the ground and pointed at the wire. "Mind that. You go first."

The boy obeyed, and Lucas followed him across before turning and righting the post. Tim whispered in the shadows, "Why are you doing that?"

Lucas drove the pole back into the hole and pushed down with all his might. When he was sure it wasn't going anywhere, he whispered back to the boy, "No reason to leave an easy trail."

Lucas took the lead again, and they skirted the fence and drove deep into the brush, eventually arriving at a trail that led back to where Sierra was hopefully still waiting a mile away, the rasp of Tim's labored breathing the only sound. Lucas ran with an easy grace, pacing himself for endurance, and Tim did his best to keep up. He fell behind and Lucas slowed. When Tim caught up to Lucas, he looked at the ground. "Sorry," he whispered.

"No problem. But you need to do your best to run as fast as you can, okay? Just until we make it to your mom. We have horses, so you're home free from there."

"I'll keep up," Tim said, his tone determined.

Lucas resumed his race to Sierra, slowing slightly in deference to Tim and also because without the monocle he had a difficult time being sure exactly where he was. They continued running for another ten minutes, and then Lucas stopped and pointed at the dark outline of a pair of horses.

"The big one's Tango. The mare's Nugget."

"We're there?"

"Finally."

Lucas approached the tree where Sierra was perched in the branches, watching the factory through his binoculars, and called up to her in a stage whisper.

"Sierra? I've got Tim here."

The leaves rustled and Sierra's legs appeared. Lucas grabbed her waist and helped her down, and then she was running to Tim, tears coursing down her cheeks, softly saying his name over and over.

Tim sobbed right along with his mother, both of them whispering, "I love you," repeatedly, her arms enveloping him in a tight embrace.

Tim pulled away slightly and murmured to his mother, "I knew you'd be back."

"Of course, baby, of course. Nothing can keep us apart." She hesitated. "I'm so sorry for everything you've gone through."

Tim choked back more tears, his face growing serious, but for a brief moment he looked like a frightened young boy rather than a hardened field slave who'd suffered daily at the hands of brutal masters.

Lucas stood aside, giving Sierra some privacy, and moved to Nugget and lifted one of the saddlebag flaps to feel inside. He extracted their other night vision monocle and donned it while Sierra and Tim hugged each other, and switched it on to verify it was working. After a long moment he turned it off and searched Tango's bag for his M4. He withdrew four full magazines along with the rifle, taking his time as he filled his flak jacket with ammo, and then gave Tango's nose a rub, whispering a quiet word to the horse.

He waited half a minute before he swung up into the saddle and activated the M4's night vision scope. Lucas raised it to his eye and gazed at the buildings through its high-magnification lens for any sign of pursuit, and when he saw nothing, thumbed off the power and rested the stock against the saddle horn.

He glanced at his watch and spoke to Sierra. "Get Tim into the saddle with you. We need to move. They'll be after us soon enough, and they might have dogs."

Sierra brushed away her tears and straightened as she released Tim and drew near Tango's side. "Lucas, I can never repay you…"

"Save it for once we're in the clear, Sierra. Mount up. It's going to be touch and go."

"How did you—"

He cut her off. "I had some help. I'll explain later. Now get into the saddle, or this will all have been in vain."

Sierra didn't need to be told again. She boosted Tim onto Nugget and hoisted herself up, the boy seated in front of her. Lucas took a final look around and then snapped the reins and guided Tango deeper into the brush, keenly aware that now every second of lead they had might be the one that bought them their lives.

Chapter 44

Zach stared at his handheld radio like it had bitten him. The report from the rum plant emanated from its speaker at whisper volume, the cane field around him muting the extent to which sound carried. He'd left instructions that nobody was to use the special frequency the handhelds had been tuned to unless it was an emergency, but what he was hearing qualified.

When the Crew guard finished with his report, Zach was already in motion, raising the radio to his lips as he ran. "I'll be right there. I'm on my way. Over."

Five Crew gunmen had been sent into the warehouse when it became obvious to Zach that something had gone wrong. And now Whitely's gamble was unraveling with each second, and Zach had to pick up the pieces or face Snake's wrath for allowing it. Even though Zach didn't report to the Crew leader, he recognized the drug-fueled rage with which the man acted out, and he didn't want to be a target.

Zach arrived at the loading dock door and flipped up his night vision goggles before shouldering through to where the five Crew gunmen had their LED flashlights trained on a prone Whitely.

"What the hell happened?" Zach demanded, each syllable dripping fury.

"I...he...he knocked me...out," Whitely stammered.

Zach studied the gash on the side of Whitely's head and the blood that had dried down the side of his face, and nodded. "I can see that. How, exactly, and why?"

"I was showing him to the door, and the next thing, everything went black. I...I'm guessing he didn't want to take the chance it might have been a setup. I don't know. That's the only thing that makes sense."

"You have no idea where he went?"

"I told you. I was unconscious until just a few moments ago." Whitely touched the swelling on the side of his skull and his fingers came away smeared with crimson. "How much blood did I lose? How long have I been out?"

"Not enough to kill you, obviously. As to how long, ten minutes or so."

"Then he can't have gotten far. He's saddled with the kid."

Zach looked at the gunmen. "I want you to search the exterior of the plant. He must have left a trail. The ground's mush." The men stared at him like he was speaking Swedish, and Zach glowered at them. "Did you hear me? Move. They're getting away."

The Crew thugs sprang into action and made for the row of doors. Whitely struggled to his feet and swayed unsteadily. Zach shook his head in disgust and barked into his radio, "Get back to the factory. They're gone. Over."

"We should mobilize everything we've got," Whitely said.

"We do that, and they're sure to hear us coming, which defeats the purpose."

"What about bloodhounds? We can round some up."

"Again, they'll give us away. Right now they have a slim lead. If we can find their tracks, we won't be far behind. We put fifty men on this or get baying dogs into the mix, and we can kiss our chances to hell."

"I'd say our chances are blown at this point. We should throw everything at them," Whitely insisted, and then grabbed at the stack of crates for support, overtaken by a bout of sudden dizziness.

"You need to get stitched up," Zach said, and then his radio chirped. He raised it to his lips. "What is it?" he snapped.

"We found footprints. By the west door. Over."

"I'll be there in a second. Over."

Whitely shuffled toward the sleeping quarters. "I'll catch up with you. I can have the medic sew me up. Shouldn't take too long."

Zach was already running across the warehouse floor, unconcerned whether Whitely lived or died, much less made it into the field. The Illuminati mercenary had his work cut out for him, and a wounded fool was the last thing he needed slowing him down.

"Whatever. Do what you have to do," Zach said, and pushed open the door at the other end of the warehouse before disappearing into the night.

Whitely wiped his bloody fingers clean on his pants, thankful that the dull ache in his head and the pain lancing from the wound with every move made it easy to stifle the smile that threatened to play across his face.

Now Lucas and his companions were in a footrace, but Zach didn't know that Lucas understood what he was up against. Whitely saw the man's face in his mind's eye and nodded to himself, wincing at the unwise move.

He was glad he wasn't the one who would have to take on Lucas.

Because judging by his demeanor, many had tried; and even though Zach was a verifiable badass, Lucas radiated menace like few Whitely had ever met.

A Crew guard appeared at the door connecting the warehouse to the factory, and Whitely eyed him with a sour expression. "Get the medic out of bed. Got a job for him. And be quick about it," he ordered, and the man spun to comply. Whitely was high in the Crew's hierarchy, and as such to be obeyed unconditionally. At least until word of Lucas and the boy's escape reached Snake, he reasoned. Then all bets were off.

~ ~ ~

Lucas paused and checked behind him on the trail, where Tango's and Nugget's hoofprints stood in stark contrast to the muddy soil around them. He shook his head in frustration and wiped dried blood from his face.

"What is it?" Sierra whispered.

"This isn't going to work. A toddler could follow this trail."

"Right, but you said once it rains…"

"You see any rain?"

She shook her head. "No."

"In the meantime, they can ride their horses as hard as they want, but we can't. Ours need to make it for weeks – theirs for minutes."

"So what do we do?"

He indicated an area ahead. "We go into the swamp."

Tim spoke up. "That's a bad idea. Quicksand, alligators, snakes…"

"Not sure we have any choice. We stay on the trail, they'll catch us. Simple."

"Then what – we ride into the bayou and get stuck in quicksand? Or eaten by an alligator?" Sierra blurted, her voice growing in volume as she spoke.

Lucas shushed her. "Follow me, and keep your voice down. No more talking."

He pulled on the reins and urged Tango toward the swampland, which crystalized into view as they neared. To Lucas's relief what he'd thought was marsh appeared to be dry land blanketed with grass and needles from the thousands of bald cypress trees that stretched as far as he could see, bisected by a brook that trailed off into nothingness.

"Let's try following the creek a ways," Lucas suggested. "Won't leave any tracks in the water."

"What about the alligators?" Sierra asked warily.

"What's bearing down on us makes alligators the least of our problems, Sierra. Now no more talking. Please," he said, and spurred Tango forward, the trees rising straight up into the night. Tim raised his head to look at the cloudy sky overhead and then whispered to his mother, his voice so low she could barely hear him.

"Whatever happens, I love you, Mom."

She swallowed a baseball-sized lump in her throat and hugged him closer. "It'll be okay. You'll see. We didn't come this far to fail."

Tim nodded in the darkness, not because he believed her, but because it seemed important to her that he did, his life experience during his short stay on the planet having taught him that few things turned out okay, and fewer still that involved the Crew. Every so often one of the boys had tried to escape, and the Crew had delighted in catching them and making a spectacle of their punishment, the abuses so foul just the memory made him squirm.

He sat forward and repeated the only prayer he remembered over and over in his head, hoping that someone was listening and would save them, because sure as sin the Crew was coming for them, and nobody escaped them for long.

Chapter 45

Zach cocked his head and held up a hand to warn his men to remain still, the night quiet around them, the air heavy with approaching rain. His horse shifted beneath him and he patted its neck to settle it and then motioned at where the hoofprints veered from the trail toward the cypress swamp.

"They're smarter than I thought. The grass will cover their tracks, but they can't be far."

Zach led the five Crew fighters off the trail. The surroundings glowed in their night vision goggles, the trees thrusting into the sky like totem poles. He cocked his head again as they approached the forest and whispered to the lead gunman beside him, "Hear that?"

The man shook his head. "No."

"Splashing. They're following the creek."

Zach pointed his horse toward the stream and urged it forward, sure that the riders were just ahead. The Crew gunmen followed, and then he stopped again and listened intently before shaking his head.

"What is it?" the gunman whispered.

"I don't hear them anymore."

"Maybe they're back on dry ground."

"Maybe," Zach agreed, his tone betraying his doubt.

Zach spurred the horse on, and as they reached a bend in the creek, the leaves around them began popping, slowly at first and then faster as a cloudburst pelted them with rain. Zach cursed under his breath and then spotted movement ahead – no more than a hundred yards away. He increased his pace, ignoring the sheets of rain as visibility faded, intent on not losing his quarry now that he was close.

The men rode through the trees as the downpour intensified, weapons at the ready, and Zach was at the creek when gunshots stuttered from ahead and the rider beside him jerked in the saddle with a spray of blood and tumbled to the ground.

Shots barked again and Zach's horse went out from under him. He threw himself to the side as more reports reached him, and then his men were taking evasive action, dismounting and using the narrow trunks for what cover they could.

Zach hit the ground and rolled, his left arm instantly numb from the impact, and then he was returning fire at the shooter he could barely make out with his goggles. Answering fire shredded the leaves around him and he rolled again, taking cover behind a felled tree and using it to stabilize his aim until his arm recovered. He blasted off two bursts at the shooter, and then the rain masked the man for several moments as a curtain of water obstructed his field of view.

When the rain lessened, there was no trace of the gunman. Zach waited, secure that eventually the shooter would have to move, and when he did, Zach would have him in his sights. The men behind him, combat veterans from countless Crew skirmishes, sensed his strategy and held their fire.

Seconds ticked by and nothing happened. Nothing could be heard other than the tattoo of the rain. Zach forced himself to be patient, there being no place to go, the confrontation all the evidence he needed that Lucas understood he'd reached the end. Nobody would take on a party of gunmen if they had a choice, which meant he didn't.

"Unless," Zach whispered.

Unless he was sacrificing himself to buy Sierra and the boy time to get away.

In which case Zach was playing right into his hands.

Zach was tensing to force himself to his feet when he spotted the movement he'd been waiting for and opened up at the spot, the AK rattling in his hands. His men fired as well, spraying the area with lead, and when no fire answered their volley, Zach leapt up and signaled to his men to advance.

They crept toward the creek, staying low, and were nearly at the water's edge when a single shot popped from Zach's left and the man beside him crumpled, half his skull gone. Zach opened fire at the shooter along with the others, the hail of bullets a wall of death that nobody would survive.

When his magazine emptied, Zach jettisoned the spent one and slapped a fresh one into place, and then gestured to his left and zigzagged away, his intent to flank the gunman while he was pinned down by the Crew. No further shots followed Zach's progress, raising his hope that Lucas had at least been hit, if not killed, by the last barrage.

He adjusted his goggles and searched the trees, and then an AK on full auto chattered behind him, shattering the silence. Zach shook his head at the amateur move – one of his men had lost his nerve and was shooting at ghosts, wasting precious ammo and potentially giving away his location.

Zach couldn't allow the distraction to diminish his focus, and he continued creeping through the trees, now nearly to where he'd last seen Lucas. He paused behind a trunk, slowing his breathing, and then some primitive part of his brain caught movement to his right and he twisted toward it, gun in hand.

"Drop it," Whitely called out, his AK pointed at Zach.

Zach grinned and dropped to the ground as though the earth had opened beneath him, firing as he went. Bullets thumped into the cypresses around Whitely, and the older man loosed a volley as he ducked behind a tree, but the shots went high and missed Zach.

Zach continued shooting as he pressed his advantage, and then a familiar voice called out from behind him.

"You heard the man. Drop it," Lucas said.

Zach twisted with his rifle, and Lucas fired a burst. Zach jerked like he'd touched a high-voltage line and Lucas fired again, liquefying his skull at the close range.

The forest quieted again, and Whitely called out from behind the tree, "Is that it?"

"You can come out."

"I took care of the others. I figured you could use a hand," Whitely said, stepping from his hiding place.

"I had them." Lucas gestured at Whitely with his gun. "No offense, but I'd feel better if you tossed your AK aside."

Whitely nodded and did as Lucas instructed.

Lucas eyed him. "Pistol, too."

"Oh, come on," Whitely protested.

"Humor me."

Whitely slid his handgun from its hip holster, dropped it by the rifle, and then held his hands out. "Satisfied?"

Lucas nodded and called out over his shoulder, "Sierra? It's over."

The rain lessened as a pair of figures approached through the haze, leading two horses – the boy and a slim woman carrying a rifle.

Sierra stopped dead when she saw Whitely, and the blood drained from her face. "You," she said, and raised her rifle, a look of hatred twisting her features.

Chapter 46

Lucas held out his hand to stop Sierra from gunning Whitely down. "No," he said. "He's not with them."

"The hell he isn't. Don't you know who he is?"

Lucas hadn't told her about his encounter with Whitely, figuring he could recount the story during the weeks they'd be on the trail.

"Sierra...he's the one who helped me back at the factory. Lower your gun. Now," Lucas ordered, his voice hard as flint.

She slowly obeyed, her eyes puzzled. "*He* helped you?"

"He's not what he seems, Sierra. He was Jacob's inside man."

"I...I don't understand. He's in charge of security in Lubbock, as well as the vaccine development. He's not our friend."

Whitely nodded. "It's true I was in charge of security and the vaccine – that's one of the reasons you were able to escape, and why the effort to develop an effective vaccine's gone nowhere so far. Jacob and I agreed early on that the best way to stop Magnus was to work from the inside."

"You killed him, didn't you?" she spat.

"No. Magnus's men did."

"You let it happen."

"I had no choice, Sierra. It was either sacrifice Jacob, or the entire resistance would have lost any ability to stop the vaccine. That couldn't happen."

"So you say. You're alive; he isn't."

"I just saved your son, Sierra. And got you out of deep weeds here. You're still breathing because of me." Whitely let his words sink in.

"Why? Doesn't this jeopardize your standing with the Crew?" Lucas asked.

"I'm afraid so. But it doesn't matter now that the vaccine's in the field and being distributed."

Lucas indicated Zach's corpse. "Who was he really?"

"Illuminati. Or rather, he worked for them. They've been directing the Crew's efforts against you."

"What? I thought they didn't exist."

"Oh, unfortunately evil like theirs has always existed and always will in one form or another."

"He fed me some cock-and-bull story about Elliot being a megalomaniac, wanting to rule the world."

"Nonsense, of course. If you've spent any time with Elliot, you'd know that's a lie. He's one of the most benevolent and caring men on earth."

"I didn't believe him."

"Nor should you. But remember that's how these creatures work – they control through duplicity, through misdirection, by twisting the truth and mixing it with lies so artfully crafted you can't tell the difference. They've had a lot of practice at it, and they don't care who loses as long as they win."

"You sound like you're well versed on their tactics."

"Oh, both Elliot and I know them well."

Sierra spoke up. "I don't trust him, Lucas. He says the Illuminati lie to fool people, but it seems to me they're not the only ones. I've seen him in action."

"Sierra, I know you hate me, and I can't say I blame you, but think for a moment," Whitely said. "You waltzed out of Lubbock and got away clean. Do you really in your gut believe that was an accident? Or do you think it might be possible that I ran cover for you and directed the security forces down blind alleys so you had time to get away?"

Sierra's anger seemed less sure. "Which could all be lies."

"You're standing here with your boy, in one piece, and you think I did this to…to trick you in some way?"

"It could be. Maybe you want to find out where Shangri-La is so you can sell us out."

"Sierra, I have no interest in where Elliot's holed up. I just hope he's done a good job and can stay hidden, because my experience with the Crew and men like this one is they don't quit."

"So what now?" Lucas asked. "What are you going to do?"

Whitely managed a tired smile. "That's none of your concern. I've accomplished what I needed to do. Now I fade into the background, and you go on with your lives."

"You can't go back to the Crew," Lucas countered.

Whitely gave a snort. "No kidding."

"So that's it? You just walk away?" Lucas asked.

"My role in this little chapter is over. Yours is just beginning. Don't worry about me. Take care of your own. I'll be fine." Whitely eyed Sierra. "Now, if you don't mind, my head's splitting, and I'd like to get out of this soup at some point."

"Stay there until we're gone, Whitely," Lucas warned. "I don't want to have to shoot you."

"I'll stand here like a statue, Lucas. I've come this far without being gunned down. I'd like to extend my winning streak a little longer."

"And don't try to follow us," Sierra growled.

"Sierra, if I'd wanted to kill you, you'd be dead. Get out of here before the Crew follows the gunshots and this all becomes a moot point."

Lucas headed over to Sierra and the animals. "It's time. Mount up."

"You're just going to let him go?" Sierra asked.

Lucas studied Whitely for a long beat before angling his face toward Sierra, his eyes never drifting from the older man. "Seems like you may have that one backwards."

Whitely smiled, and Lucas nodded to him as he climbed onto Tango's back and spun the horse around, twisting as he did so.

Whitely remained motionless, his hands raised at chest level until Lucas and Sierra vanished into the drizzle, the rain washing away the blood from his face, his expression unreadable.

Chapter 47

Elliot, Michael, and Arnold watched as Craig wiped the sweat from his forehead while he labored to retrofit the pump they'd retrieved from the mothballed plant. There had been some differences in capacities, and he'd had to modify the piping into the pump, this one being slightly smaller than the one that had failed, but he'd calculated that operating at fifty percent capacity, the generator wouldn't overstrain the parts and could function indefinitely – or at least as long as it would take to get the machine shop up to speed to manufacture suitable spare parts, and source more gasket material for the seals.

"How much longer?" Michael asked.

"Don't know. Maybe an hour or so. Don't want to rush this and blow it," Craig answered.

"No, that wouldn't do at all," Elliot said. " I guess we'll leave you to it, then."

"You'll know when I flip the switch."

"Good man."

They left the geothermal site and walked down the main street toward the community center. A dusting of snow still covered the road and the homes that lined it, and the surrounding mountains were a dazzling white in the high-altitude sun. The trip back had taken a day longer than the one to reach the mothballed facility, due to the speed at which the young girls had been able to goad their horses along.

"Did you get any sense from Duke about his interest in setting up a trading post?" Elliot asked Arnold as they passed the darkened remains of a strip mall.

"No. But I know Aaron's death hit him hard."

"Were they…?" Michael asked, leaving the end of the question off.

Arnold shook his head. "No, nothing like that. They'd just been through a lot together. You see that in combat. You grow close – there's a special kind of bond that's hard to explain."

"Who's our second choice if Duke decides not to do it?" Michael asked.

"We don't really have one, although Luis indicated he'd be game."

"I still don't trust him," Arnold said.

"He's given you no reason not to."

"Once a criminal, always one."

"Well, in actuality, no," Elliot said. "There are plentiful examples of sinners who came to find religion late and went on to lead productive lives. Might have been that circumstance drove him into the life. Judge not, and all that."

"Spoken like a bleeding heart liberal," Arnold grumbled.

"A distinction that has no meaning these days, my good man."

"I like Sal and the girls," Michael said, changing the subject. "They're good additions."

Elliot nodded. "Agreed. It's becoming obvious that if we're to thrive, we need more like them. Sal's strong as an ox and resourceful, and the sisters are capable, if somewhat scarred from their experience."

"I wish it was possible to shoot those shitrats all over again a dozen times. Sal filled us in on what went down. A despicable bunch," Arnold said.

"All the more reason to value our way of life. Which can't continue unless we grow," Elliot said. "You go back to the lab; I'll be there shortly. I'm going to pay a call on our trader friend and see how he's doing."

"I've got some things that need doing," Arnold said, his

enthusiasm for Michael's company clear.

"Yeah, me too," Michael said. "I'll stop in later."

They went their separate ways, and Elliot trundled to Duke's house, nodding at passing residents on the way, the general mood optimistic and their smiles sunny in spite of the chill. When he reached the trader's small clapboard house, Duke was sitting on his porch at a small table, playing cards with Luis and John. They looked up as Elliot mounted the steps, and Duke nodded to him.

"Pull up a chair. We're just killing time," Duke said, indicating a rickety wooden stool by the door.

Elliot smiled at the men. "Gentlemen." He glanced at Duke. "Need to have a word with you about the matter we discussed," Elliot said.

Duke raised an eyebrow. "I was wondering when you'd circle back about that."

"We need to establish a presence so we can vet and recruit people. That's now the top priority for us, aside from the vaccine."

"Right. That's *your* top priority. I understand that," Duke said.

"I'm asking for your help. If you don't want to run the place, I understand. But at least set it up so someone else can take it over. Nobody in our group has operated a trading post but you."

"Funny, because Luis and John here were just discussing that. We were talking about what to do next now that everything's calmed down and now that at least two of us are rich." Duke sighed. "Always thought being rich would feel different, but apparently it's just like being poor. At least after the end of the world." Duke smirked at Luis. "Which kind of sucks. We got robbed."

"Always the bridesmaid," Luis agreed.

"You don't want your gold, I'll take it," John quipped.

Duke chuckled. "It would just ruin you, young man."

"I'm ready for ruin."

Elliot smiled good-naturedly, but his eyes stayed on Duke. "And what did you decide?"

Duke laid his cards facedown on the table. "Well, I figured you wouldn't give up till I said yes, so we decided I'd help these boys set it up and run it for a while, and when I get bored with it, or they get sick of me ordering them around, I'll let them run it into the ground and come back here to enjoy my retirement."

Elliot beamed at them. "Why, that's wonderful news! Let me know what you need and when you plan to leave."

"Never hurts to have a bunch of stuff to trade, for starters. And animals to carry it."

"Consider it done."

"We're going to ride out tomorrow and scope out a location while we've got a break in the weather. Seeing as there's no power, there's no point in hanging around here," Duke said.

"That should be resolved shortly, actually. Craig's wrenching away as we speak."

"Still. Don't fancy riding in a blizzard, and our window's closing."

Elliot nodded agreement. "Just give me a list of your requirements, and I'll see to them."

"Send lawyers, guns, and money," Luis said.

"Or in this case, a radio, guns and ammo, and meds. Those will be the most valuable out of the gate. I can handle the gold part," Duke offered.

"And keep all the profit to yourself," Luis grumbled. "Not a chance. Fifty-fifty."

Elliot left them to their bickering, his step lighter now that his errand was successfully concluded. He had faith that the trader would pick a good spot and have a thriving enterprise in no time, even though the weather would slow any traffic until spring. But as long as they had a hub to qualify and recruit promising candidates, they would prosper.

Female laughter reached his ears as he continued toward the lab, and he returned a wave from Cody, Sal's middle sister, who was playing with her siblings while Sal worked on the roof of the abandoned house they'd selected. The young man stopped hammering and offered a salute, and then went back to patching holes as Elliot continued on.

"We'll be just fine," he said under his breath, and he offered silent thanks as he gazed up at the sky's brilliant blue, the afternoon idyllic in the way only late autumn in the mountains could be. "Indeed we will," he finished, and continued on to the community center, where hopefully soon the lights would come back on and he'd be able to continue the job of saving the world from itself.

Chapter 48

Houston, Texas

Lassiter's unblinking stare bored holes through Snake as the Crew warlord reported on his organization's progress; or rather, the lack of it, since Zach had been found dead outside Alexandria. Snake had returned to his home base in Texas once New Orleans stabilized, and reasserted his role as the master of ceremonies at the evening executions that placated the public and punished those who challenged him. The big navy vessel had reappeared at the port that morning, and Snake had dreaded the meeting he knew was inevitable.

"So, in the end, my man's dead, and your trusted security chief has disappeared," Lassiter summarized, after Snake's rambling narrative.

Snake thought about the abrupt summary and decided not to challenge the lack of nuance. "That's right."

"And you've lost the man you had in custody, as well as the boy, who was the only leverage you had to ensnare the woman." Lassiter paused. "And you have no idea where any of them are now and no coherent plan to find them. Did I cover everything?"

"We've put out a huge reward. It's just a matter of time until someone spots them and turns them in."

"Assuming they're careless enough to allow themselves to be seen. Have they seemed especially careless to you so far?"

"Nobody can stay hidden forever," Snake assured him with a confidence he didn't feel.

"To say we're disappointed in this performance is an understatement."

"Look, from what we can piece together, it was your guy who was calling the shots. So if you're unhappy with the way things turned out, blame Zach, not me."

"I'm not looking to assign blame. I need this problem solved." Lassiter studied Snake's face like he was examining an insect under a magnifying glass. "Perhaps our faith in the Crew's ability to perform was misguided."

"Like my faith that you'd fix the refinery," Snake fired back. "Still waiting for that to happen. Maybe if we had fuel, we could search for the woman more effectively."

Lassiter motioned impatiently with his hand. "You don't just wave a wand and fix a refinery that's been down for five years. We've discussed this."

"So you say. All I know is I hear promises, but no delivery." Snake caught the warning glance from the Illuminati functionary and hurried to backpedal. "What I meant is that it's hard to perform with one hand tied behind my back. And relying on horses to move men around isn't doing either of us any favors."

Lassiter's eyes narrowed. "I know what you meant."

"I didn't mean to offend you or your group. I'm just frustrated. We all are."

"Noted. But that's not getting us anywhere."

"We're doing everything we can think of. If you have any suggestions, I'm all ears," Snake grumbled.

Lassiter rose and stood with his hands on his hips, facing Snake, who shrank a little in his chair at the man's quiet presence. Lassiter took a step toward him and spoke softly. "Here's what we're going to do. I'm going to assign a new advisor to you. He'll be here before the week is out. He's a more senior man than Zach. Perhaps we overestimated Zach's abilities – I'm willing to concede that much. You are to treat him as if it were me advising you, and I'd strongly suggest you do whatever he says. There's a limit to how long we'll tolerate failure, and I can share with you that we're near that limit. If you can't execute, we'll have to find someone who can."

"If you're so powerful and smart, why do you need me?" Snake blurted, and instantly regretted it.

"That's a good question. For your sake, you better hope the answer isn't that we don't."

"I don't like being threatened," Snake warned.

"I don't threaten. I offer counsel. And here's my counsel to you: if I want, I can flatten Houston with my big guns in under an hour and wipe you from the earth like a bunch of tattooed cockroaches. We've allowed you to operate your territory as you like, but you're either an asset or a liability – and right now you're tilting to the liability side of the equation." Lassiter let that sink in. "And Snake, trust me: you don't want to be a liability."

Snake watched as Lassiter stalked to the door and opened it, the guards outside withdrawing deferentially as he brushed past them. Snake's head throbbed and his stomach twisted in fury at being addressed like a servant. He was the head of the Southwest's most powerful cartel. He had the power of life and death over thousands and more territory than anyone else in the land. That this effete pencil pusher in a suit dared to read him the riot act was unthinkable.

Snake imagined Lassiter spread-eagled at tonight's executions, being dismembered slowly by starving rats for the amusement of the crowd, and smiled at the mental picture. Of course, he couldn't do it, but the image calmed him as his mind savored the Illuminati man's agonized screams.

Snake got to his feet and gulped two pills, washing them down with the last of the home-brewed ale from lunch. He needed to calm down and think clearly, not entertain impossibilities, and he couldn't do that if his nerves were too close to the surface.

The truth was he didn't much care if they ever found the woman or Shangri-La's new location or any of the rest of it. That was Lassiter's fixation, not his. But Snake would play along for now, until the refinery was operational, and put in a best effort while appearing to hang on the new advisor's every word.

And then when he'd gotten what he needed from them, the

advisor would disappear or suffer a horrendous accident or choke on a chicken bone – it didn't much matter.

But now wasn't the time to challenge his sponsor.

That would come later.

Chapter 49

John called out to Duke from his position at the gate of the new trading post located on a secondary highway near an intersection of the interstate that stretched from east to west, a bit more than two days' ride east of Pagosa Springs. "Rider. About a hundred yards out."

Duke was sitting by the entrance of the office he'd set up as his showroom. "Only one?"

"Yup."

They'd been in business for a week and had been surprised by the number of migrants on the road. They'd found an ideal location and taken it over: a motel with a perimeter wall. The main structure was two stories tall and had been built from cinderblock and rebar sometime in the forties, before the construction technique had changed to sheetrock and studs. Duke had always favored more durable structures because of their ability to withstand Mother Nature's destructive moods, as well as stop bullets when things got nasty. But what had decided it for him was a steel windmill that provided juice for the well pump and, with some modification, sufficient power to operate the radio.

"See what he wants."

The rider neared, and John eyed his tattooed face with a somber stare. "Looks like Crew, Duke," he warned.

Duke rose, AR-15 gripped by his side, and moved to the sandbagged guard post at the side of the gate. "Good thing Luis isn't here. Might get a little difficult if they saw each other," Duke murmured.

Luis had ridden into the hills several hours earlier to try his luck fishing for brook trout, and they didn't expect him back until dusk. The ex-Loco boss's ink might have raised uncomfortable questions in a member of the Crew, if that was, in fact, what the rider was.

Any doubts Duke had about the new arrival's affiliation evaporated when he spied the eye of Providence on the man's forehead as he slowed to a stop at the gate. Duke looked the rider over, noting the powerful arms connected to a torso that resembled a fireplug, and nodded a greeting.

"Howdy. What can we do you for?" Duke asked.

"Looking to trade for some supplies."

"What do you need?"

"Provisions."

"What do you have to barter?"

"Ammo."

Duke and John exchanged a glance. That was their business, so they couldn't refuse to let him in. Duke nodded again, and John shouldered his rifle strap and sauntered to the steel barrier to slide it open. The rider guided his horse through and directed the stallion to a hitching post Duke had rigged near a fifty-gallon barrel they'd cut in half and filled with water each day.

"Mind if I water my horse?" the rider asked.

"That's what it's there for. Cost you a round."

"That's fair. Don't suppose you have any feed, do you?"

Duke grunted. "Sure. Cost you two more."

"A bargain."

"Given the location, a steal."

The rider swung from the saddle and dropped to the ground. John approached after closing the gate, his gun in hand. "Rule is no weapons inside the wall," he said.

The rider nodded and shrugged off the strap of his AK, held it out to John, barrel down, and then did the same with his pistol. When the man was unarmed, Duke motioned to the office. "Come on in and take a gander. We're a little thin on some things, but got plenty of cured meat and some dried provisions that might get the job done."

"Don't suppose you have any citrus or vitamins, do you?"

"Got some expired vitamin C. Should still be good. Only two years past the date."

"That'll work."

Duke mounted the steps, followed by the rider. Inside, they got down to business, and Duke negotiated a more than fair exchange for what the newcomer wanted. When they were done, the rider leaned against the reception counter and rubbed his stubbly chin with a dirty hand.

"You just open up?" he asked.

"Yeah, maybe a week or two ago. Figured we'd try our luck at it."

"How's business?"

"Can't complain, although it could always be better."

"See a lot of travelers?"

Duke nodded. "Enough to keep me in sin." He hesitated. "Where you headed?"

"Just riding. You know how that is. No particular destination – they're all the same these days."

"I'll take your word for it."

"You seen any big parties?"

"Nope. Onesies and twosies, mostly."

"Huh. Any communities around here to trade with?"

Duke's tone remained flat, his face a mask. "I wish. Make my life a lot easier if there was. More traffic."

"I heard there might be one around here. Maybe new, too."

"If you find one, stop back in and tell me where it is. Because nobody who's come by to trade has seen anything but scrub and rock for hundreds of miles in all directions."

The man nodded agreeably. "You hear anything about the big fight south of here?"

Duke nodded. "Heard from a family headed north there are a bunch of abandoned trucks and the like. Long ways south, though, isn't it? New Mexico or Texas?"

The man's placid expression didn't change. "Down by Los Alamos is what I heard."

"Don't that beat all."

The rider collected his purchases and moved to the door. At the threshold, he looked back at the hand-lettered sign over the reception desk. "Duke's Trading, huh? Like John Wayne?"

"My daddy didn't have a big imagination."

"Nice to meet you. Name's Dale. Might see you again if I swing back this way."

"Open sunup to sundown."

"Good to know. Didn't think there was anything out here."

"Casino and dancing girls go in next week."

Duke and John watched Dale ride slowly away, and Duke narrowly resisted the urge to put a bullet in the back of his head. John scratched his head. "He's looking for them, isn't he?"

"Damn right he is."

"Better get on the radio and warn them."

"Tonight. But if he's out here, he has no idea where they are."

"Think he'll give up eventually?"

"If he does, another will take his place. That's just the way it works."

"You could have sent him east. Told him fifty riders came by when you were opening up the place."

"He'd have been back when he figured out I'm the only one who ever saw 'em, and we'd have tipped our hand."

"You think he suspects anything?"

Duke watched the Crew scout disappear down the road and spit in the dirt by his boot. "Hope not."

Chapter 50

Ground fog hung over the town and its bare trees, the morning a cold one. A few of the residents were pushing carts along the main street, their faces wrapped against the frigid breeze, their progress slowed by the slush on the pavement from melting snow.

Arnold sat inside his house, watching the flames dance in the fireplace as he sipped a warm cup of instant coffee – one of the few staples they still had, which, like rice, never went bad. His two-way radio crackled on the table, and the voice of Loren, on guard duty at the eastern end of town, emanated from the tinny speaker.

"Got three riders approaching. Over."

Arnold leapt to his feet and moved to the device. "How close? Over."

"Couple hundred yards. Over."

Arnold swore. There had been no incidents or encounters yet. The town was so far off any path that travelers didn't realize it was there; the signs at the highway intersection had been taken down by Arnold's security detail and the road leading into town removed with picks and crowbars and replaced by felled trees and sod. He'd thought that with the snow and the subterfuge, they might remain hidden indefinitely, but he'd just been proved wrong and would have to deal with it.

"I'm on my way. Over."

He scooped up the radio and pulled on a heavy jacket, a size too big but stuffed with down, and made for the door. He was halfway to the checkpoint when the radio crackled again.

"I recognize them. Over."

Arnold paused. "Who is it? Over."

"Lucas. Over."

Arnold picked up his pace at the news and rounded the corner and made for the Humvee that blocked the road. Lucas, Sierra, and a small boy on a chestnut mare were ambling down the street and stopped when they saw Arnold. Arnold put out a call to Elliot as he approached them, alerting him that Lucas had arrived safely. Lucas gave Arnold a wave with a gloved hand and Arnold mirrored the gesture.

"The prodigal returns," Arnold announced as he neared.

"Better late than never, right?" Lucas said.

"Suppose so." Arnold peered at Tim. "Is this who I think it is?"

Sierra beamed at him. "Arnold, meet Tim, my son."

Tim smiled shyly, and Arnold held out his hand. "Nice to meet you, Tim."

Tim took it after a slight hesitation and mumbled a greeting, and Lucas adjusted the hat he'd acquired outside of Shreveport, along with Tim's horse. "See you made it back in one piece," Lucas said.

"Yeah. But it looks like St. Louis got taken down, so we might as well have stayed home."

Lucas's brow furrowed. "You sure?"

"Haven't heard a peep out of them since a few days after we gave their guy the goods."

"What does that do to the distribution plan?"

"It's not positive, but we'll manage. Just means we need to find someone else in the Midwest who can help. But nobody's going anywhere until spring, so we have time."

"Anything change around here? Did the other groups make it back?"

"They did. No casualties." Arnold's face clouded for a moment. "Except for Aaron, Duke's friend."

Sierra's hand flew to her mouth. "Aaron? How?"

Arnold recounted the story of their trip and finished by telling them about Duke's trading post. When he was done, Lucas nodded. "Always figured he'd go back to that. Man loves to dicker."

"But why Luis as a partner?" Sierra asked.

"Maybe because I wasn't around," Lucas said. "He made me an offer earlier; then I got...sidetracked."

She smiled and looked over to Tim, his face serious as he listened to the adults. "Well, I for one am glad you got sidetracked."

Elliot rounded the corner with Ruby and Eve in tow, the older woman's long gray hair billowing in the breeze and her body swaddled in layers. They dismounted and Ruby hugged each in turn, and Sierra introduced Tim, who looked increasingly uncomfortable with each new arrival. Eve approached him and smiled, her eyes blazing blue, mirroring the cobalt sky. "Is he my new brother?" she asked Sierra.

"Yes," Sierra managed between laughing and blushing. "Yes, he is. So be nice to him."

The two children sized each other up. Eve looked at Lucas. "He's awful skinny," she said. "But you kept your promise. You're back, and everyone's safe. I knew you would – I knew it."

Lucas suggested they get out of the cold and paused before speaking to Elliot in a low voice. "Need to talk to you and Arnold. Got some stuff to fill you in on."

Elliot looked confused, but amenable. "Certainly. You know where I hang my hat."

"Be by once we get settled."

"Of course. Take your time."

They walked the horses the rest of the way and found the house exactly as they'd left it.

"I've been stopping by every week to dust and make sure nobody's squatting or anything," Ruby said.

"Where's Terry?" Sierra asked.

"Oh, that man spends every spare minute at the airport, fussing with one of the planes."

"Has he gotten one running?"

"Not yet."

"He does enjoy flying," Sierra observed.

"He enjoys trying to fly almost as much."

"You're getting along?"

"Oh my, yes," Ruby said, color flushing her cheeks. "He's a fine man. Just a little quirky." She took a deep breath. "But at my age, quirky's just what the doctor ordered."

"Thank you for taking care of Eve."

"She's an angel. You're very lucky."

"I know."

"And you got your boy back! You must be walking on air."

"I am. It's like a dream come true. Or the end of a nightmare."

"All's well, right?"

Sierra looked through the back doorway at where Lucas was standing beside Tango, removing his saddle as the big horse nuzzled Eve, to her delight, with Ellie the pig a few feet behind her, just out of range of the stallion's hooves. "It couldn't be better. I just took the long way around."

Sierra stepped from the house, walked to Lucas, and planted a kiss on his lips, taking him by surprise.

"What's that for?" he asked.

"Just 'cause." She smiled at Eve and Tim. "I'm just really, really happy to be home, to have my family together…to be safe."

Lucas hoisted the saddle and made for the back porch. "Can't ask for much more."

Sierra watched him disappear into the house and shook her head slowly. "No, I really can't."

Lucas showered off the road dust in icy water as they waited for the electric water heater to warm some and, after a meal of eggs Ruby had procured for them, made for Elliot's on foot. When he arrived, Arnold, Michael, and Elliot were waiting inside, the room warm and inviting after weeks on the trail.

"Have a seat, Lucas," Elliot said.

Lucas pulled up a chair and Elliot gave him a welcoming smile. "So, tell us all about your adventure."

Lucas adjusted his hat and started his account at the rum factory, giving them an abridged report until he arrived at his encounter with Zach. He detailed the story Zach had told him, watching Elliot for any reaction. He didn't have to wait long. Elliot half rose out of his chair, his face red. "That's preposterous! The man was lying about everything."

Lucas swallowed his doubts and continued. "I didn't believe him. I just thought you'd want to know what you're up against."

"These scoundrels are absolutely diabolical. They'll stop at nothing," Elliot proclaimed.

Lucas eyed him. "No, I don't expect they will." He hesitated. "Which brings me to Whitely."

Elliot's ruddy complexion blanched. "Whitely!"

Lucas nodded. "That's right. He was there. The new head of the Crew sent him. He helped us escape, but he compromised himself in the process."

"He must have had good reason. They must know the vaccine's made it into distribution, so he doesn't need to stay on site any longer."

"Could be. But I got the impression that this is all bigger than the vaccine. Zach's group is playing for keeps, and they're in the big league. I don't know what the real agenda is, but that part of the story rang true." Lucas told them about Zach's claim that the Illuminati had at least one enclave that had survived the collapse.

Arnold's face tightened with a frown. "Doesn't surprise me. We've all heard the rumors. Figures the scum that ran the world into a ditch would look out for themselves first." He sat forward. "Duke radioed in a few days ago. Said a rider with Crew markings was nosing around. So they haven't given up."

Michael shook his head. "But the real question is, what's the Illuminati's end game? What's their objective? Any ideas?"

Lucas shook his head. "World domination? The return of the antichrist? Who knows?"

It was Elliot's turn to frown. "You're not far off. Perhaps all of the above. Those people are the epitome of evil, make no mistake."

Lucas's eyes narrowed. "You seem to know a lot about them."

Elliot's demeanor changed back to his jovial self. "Oh, it used to be an area of interest of mine back before the lights went out. I collected conspiracy theories like boys collect baseball cards. Many had the same theme – a secret group that engineered outcomes to achieve their goals and ran the governments of the world from the shadows. There's some truth to it, that I can tell – all the world's central banks, with only a few exceptions, were owned by the same people, and so were the media companies and the arms manufacturers and drug companies. I used to say that if it was a conspiracy, it was one hidden in plain sight." He eyed Lucas thoughtfully. "Their aim was always to create a one world government they controlled, where the world's population were their serfs. It's not that odd that at least some of them survived with their megalomania intact."

Lucas finished his account with the story of their trip back. When he was done, Michael looked puzzled.

"Back to Whitely. The last you saw of him was in the forest?" he asked.

"That's right. He told me not to worry about him – to mind my own business, basically."

"That sounds like Whitely," Elliot agreed.

Lucas was going to ask how Elliot knew him, but Arnold interrupted his train of thought. "All of this underscores the importance of finding another hub, though. The sooner the vaccine's in widespread national distribution, the sooner nobody's going to much care about where we got to."

Michael nodded. "I never thought I'd say this, but I completely agree."

The meeting broke up, and Lucas returned to the house to find Tim and Eve helping Sierra make it livable again, both children smudged with dirt and Eve holding a plastic dustpan, a look of distaste on her face. When she heard him come in, Sierra looked up from the kitchen sink and pushed a lock of hair out of her eyes.

"There's spiders everywhere," Eve announced.

Sierra smiled and raised an eyebrow at Lucas. He considered the tableau, and for a moment a memory of his wife flitted through his mind, nodding as though everything would be fine. He blinked the mirage away and then removed his hat and closed the door behind him before coming over to them with his fiercest scowl in place.

"Spiders, huh? We'll just see about that."

About the Author

Featured in *The Wall Street Journal*, *The Times*, and *The Chicago Tribune*, Russell Blake is *The NY Times* and *USA Today* bestselling author of over forty novels, including *Fatal Exchange*, *Fatal Deception*, *The Geronimo Breach*, *Zero Sum*, *King of Swords*, *Night of the Assassin*, *Revenge of the Assassin*, *Return of the Assassin*, *Blood of the Assassin*, *Requiem for the Assassin*, *Rage of the Assassin* *The Delphi Chronicle* trilogy, *The Voynich Cypher*, *Silver Justice*, *JET*, *JET – Ops Files*, *JET – Ops Files: Terror Alert*, *JET II – Betrayal*, *JET III – Vengeance*, *JET IV – Reckoning*, *JET V – Legacy*, *JET VI – Justice*, *JET VII – Sanctuary*, *JET VIII – Survival*, *JET IX – Escape*, *JET X – Incarceration*, *Upon a Pale Horse*, *BLACK*, *BLACK is Back*, *BLACK is The New Black*, *BLACK to Reality*, *BLACK in the Box*, *Deadly Calm*, *Ramsey's Gold*, *Emerald Buddha*, *The Goddess Legacy*, *The Day After Never – Blood Honor*, *The Day After Never – Purgatory Road*, *The Day After Never – Covenant*, *The Day After Never – Retribution*, and *The Goddess Legacy*.

Non-fiction includes the international bestseller *An Angel With Fur* (animal biography) and *How To Sell A Gazillion eBooks In No Time* (even if drunk, high or incarcerated), a parody of all things writing-related.

Blake is co-author of *The Eye of Heaven* and *The Solomon Curse*, with legendary author Clive Cussler. Blake's novel *King of Swords* has been translated into German by Amazon Crossing, *The Voynich Cypher* into Bulgarian, and his JET novels into Spanish, German, and Czech.

Blake writes under the moniker R.E. Blake in the NA/YA/Contemporary Romance genres. Novels include *Less Than Nothing*, *More Than Anything*, and *Best Of Everything*.

Having resided in Mexico for a dozen years, Blake enjoys his dogs, fishing, boating, tequila and writing, while battling world domination by clowns. His thoughts, such as they are, can be found at his blog: RussellBlake.com

Books by Russell Blake

Co-authored with Clive Cussler

THE EYE OF HEAVEN
THE SOLOMON CURSE

Thrillers

FATAL EXCHANGE
FATAL DECEPTION
THE GERONIMO BREACH
ZERO SUM
THE DELPHI CHRONICLE TRILOGY
THE VOYNICH CYPHER
SILVER JUSTICE
UPON A PALE HORSE
DEADLY CALM
RAMSEY'S GOLD
EMERALD BUDDHA
THE GODDESS LEGACY

The Assassin Series

KING OF SWORDS
NIGHT OF THE ASSASSIN
RETURN OF THE ASSASSIN
REVENGE OF THE ASSASSIN
BLOOD OF THE ASSASSIN
REQUIEM FOR THE ASSASSIN
RAGE OF THE ASSASSIN

Made in the USA
Lexington, KY
14 April 2017